Golden Lads
and Girls

A novel about a clandestine affair between a professional young
women and a married Member of Parliament

by

Mavis Frost MBE

Grosvenor House
Publishing Limited

This book is published by
Grosvenor House Publishing Ltd
Link House
140 The Broadway, Tolworth, Surrey, KT6 7HT.
www.grosvenorhousepublishing.co.uk

This book is a work of fiction. Any resemblance to
people or events, past or present, is purely coincidental.

A CIP record for this book
is available from the British Library

ISBN 978-1-78623-231-1

CONTENTS

FOREWORD

Mavis Frost, my late wife and author of this book, died before she could promote publishing her work. Therefore in her memory I am self-publishing her novel.

Mavis draws from her experience as a personal secretary to Members of Parliament and working in Number 10 Downing Street during Harold Wilson's time as prime minister.

This book is written in the first person involving a clandestine affair between a professional single girl and a married M.P., and a murder that overwhelms this relationship.

Although obviously biased, I found Mavis's script compulsive reading and demonstrated a talent of which I am proud. I know that you will enjoy reading this book.

Mavis was a lovely person and wonderful wife. Her memory lives on in all those that knew her and this book adds to her testimony.

Donald Frost

PREFACE

Let me tell you about my affair.

We never went out, he and I. Not even for intimate dinners, tucked away in a hidden corner of a discreet restaurant. As a rising young Member of Parliament, he had too much at stake to risk his reputation over potential scandal.

And it was easy for him. From the House of Commons he could walk down to the Embankment Station and take the Underground to Baker Street. My flat was less than five minutes' walk from that busy intersection. If he met any of his cronies, he could tell them he was going to Selfridges to shop for shirts or socks or underpants. For his convenience our encounters always took place in the late afternoon. Thursday afternoon.

He was careful. And so was I. I told nobody about my lover. But, don't worry! There is action in my story. Too much philosophy jades the spirits.

CHAPTER ONE

It had been another frenetic Monday. There was always build-up material over the weekend. When women were called secretaries, it was understood they were at everyone's beck and call. Now we are Personal Assistants, with our degrees and diplomas and cockiness, nothing has changed, except that we are held responsible for management decisions as well.

When I unlocked the front door at 19a Nottingham Place at seven o'clock that evening, all that was on my mind was a hot bath, a cold drink and a message from Michael on the answering machine.

Mrs Margoloys was hovering in the entrance hall, a long passage that ran straight from the front to the back of the house. On my left was the staircase that led to the two upper storeys. Halfway along on the other side were the stairs leading down to the basement flat. Mrs Margoloys occupied the small room at the back on the ground floor. She frequently wandered about the hall, drooping and shuffling, hugging a thick, colourless cardigan against her scrawny body.

'Hello, Mrs Margoloys! How are you?' My voice sounded brightly false. I was terrified of becoming like her in thirty or forty years' time.

'Had a good day, dear?'

'Oh! So-so, you know!' I tried not to look at her broken-backed slippers and the uneven hem of her skirt. She had wrapped her arms around herself, pressing the disgusting cardigan against her body. She must be so lonely!

I turned to go, putting my foot on the bottom step. I was desperate to reach my flat. Just once, just this once, Michael may have left a message for me.

'How are you, Mrs Margoloys?' I asked again, over my shoulder. She stood there, her mouth dropped open, a hurt bewilderment in her eyes. I paused. 'Have you been out today at all?'

'Oh, yes!' She was always eager to share her joys. 'I have such an easy life compared to all you stressed young people.' She did sometimes meander around the surrounding streets and perhaps have a cup of tea in a small snack bar. Not for the first time I wondered if she had seen Michael sneaking in on Thursday afternoons. She had never mentioned him. Perhaps she thought he was visiting the high-class prostitute who occupied the rooms on the first floor, the largest apartment in the building. But I knew Francesca was a 'lady of the night' and her clients did not arrive before eight p.m. She spent most of her days sleeping and was seldom seen.

'How nice! Where did you go?' A tantalizing image of a winking red light on my answering machine bobbed before me.

'Just round the block, dear. As far as Baker Street. And I had a cup of tea at Sainsbury's.'

Of course! She could sit there in the warm cafeteria, opposite Fruit and Veg. and ten kinds of orange juice, people-watching for hours. I continued up the stairs. 'Glad you enjoyed yourself.' She had probably talked to the distracted mother with her two boisterous toddlers or the introverted young man who wanted to be left alone. Mrs Margoloys put out a detaining hand. She obviously wanted to tell me about her encounters.

'Sorry, Mrs Margoloys! I have some work to do.'

Archie from the basement flat came bounding up the stairs. As an out-of-work actor, his movements were unpredictable. According to his latest project, his progress varied between snail-slow advance and cheetah-like bursts of speed. Mrs Margoloys turned her attention to him. He was a better prospect for diversion than me. If he were in the mood, he would talk for hours, amusing her with his nonsense, asking if she were practising for the Marathon and when she was next taking tea at Buckingham Palace.

'Archie!' exclaimed Mrs Margoloys, beaming at him. I reached the first floor landing.

'Can't stop now, Mrs M. Got an interview. Very hush-hush.' He tried to tap his nose at the same time as he wrenched impatiently at the heavy front door. He saw me hovering halfway up the stairs and winked at me. 'All right, darlin'?'

'Sure,' I called to his receding back as he eventually negotiated the doorway. 'Good luck! See you!'

As I turned the corner past Francesca's apartment and started up the short flight of stairs towards my own door, I glanced down the stairwell and saw Mrs Margoloys still standing on the chequered tiles, perhaps bewildered by the sudden change from noise to silence. Then she turned and shuffled off down the passage to her own small room.

My flat felt cool, remote. These days I kept it tidy, even though my inclination was for a glorious muddle of books and belongings, with my rooms stuffed as full as a rebellious flower border. But I knew Michael would be appalled by such lack of order. So one painful Saturday afternoon when I knew Michael was enjoying quality time with his family at Alton Towers I ruthlessly culled my belongings. I bought a stack of black plastic bags and purged my possessions of everything I might need, rather than what I actually did need. As the bags filled with reminders of my past life I pounded Michael's oh-so-lucky wife and his little children into smithereens in the pestle and mortar that went into the first bag.

Archie helped me drag the bin-liners down the stairs and to the dustbin area at the back of the house.

'Being a bit thorough, aren't you?' he remarked, as he sweated under the weight of my discards. 'Sure you won't regret this?'

'Perhaps we should burn the lot', I said.

'No!' Archie raised his hands in mock protest. 'Count me out. Somebody is bound to call the fire brigade.'

He was right. We lived in a built-up area. Many of the houses had been divided up into flats. A fire quickly could get out of control. So, reluctantly, I chickened out, even though a big conflagration would have suited my mood just then. Instead, we went out for an Indian takeaway with Archie's flatmate, Jason, and got riotously drunk on cheap, red wine. I alternatively laughed and cried. The boys assumed I had just finished a relationship and were funny and kind and didn't press for information.

I woke up next morning minus shirt and trousers under the duvet in my own bed. My head thumped and my stomach lurched and I didn't enquire who had assisted me to undress. A washing-up bowl thoughtfully had been placed at my side. I hung over it, feeling like death. But after a wretched morning, I busied myself rearranging my sparse remaining possessions and tried to persuade myself that I liked the new, minimalist look. After all these months, it was still a shock to return to my stripped abode. Michael had grunted a little on first sight.

'Don't believe in clutter, do you?' he said. 'Good!' And that was it. I wondered what his own home was like. I imagined it in neutral tones of black and cream with straight-lined furniture and a few hugely expensive ornaments in abstract chunks of stone. I would never know. I contemplated my question: What is your house like, Michael? Like everybody else's, I suppose, he would reply with an irritated glare. No way would he let me in to the other part of his life. That was to be for me as the dark side of the moon.

Now, I switched on the central heating and went to the telephone. There were no messages. Sod him! Why the hell for once in his miserable, blood-sucking life couldn't he leave me a fucking message? The trouble with my secret life was that all my other friends were shunned or neglected. Just in case that any arrangements made with them clashed with my lover's requirements. And, so that he could not be embarrassed by inadvertent meetings. In any case, let's face it, I wasn't interested in anybody else. Five minutes with Michael were more important to me than six months with the rest of the world.

Why the hell couldn't he find time to make a short 'phone call? If I asked him the reason, he would say no privacy, walls have ears, no time, do you know all the million and one things a Member of Parliament is expected to do. And he would be annoyed that I had questioned him. Our relationship depended on the fact that I was to give him no grief. No demands. No recriminations. Ever.

But I knew he wasn't being strictly honest. Life for an M.P. was exactly what the Members themselves made it. They could slave away eighteen hours a day, seven days a week. On the other hand, they could dump their mail in the bin and pile work on their assistants while they went off on their own devices. Look at all the non-executive directorships they manage to hold! What was the phrase that eminent M.P. used to cover all eventualities? It was the least I could do! That covered condolences and congratulations very nicely, as well as his ignorance about the case.

I slipped off my jacket and hung it in the large, unwieldy closet that took up a great deal of space in the small bedroom. It was a pity I hadn't been able to purge the furniture in my rented flat, as well as my own belongings.

'That bloody wardrobe isn't going to fall on us, is it?' asked Michael, the first time we made love in my bed. Obviously he could envisage the tabloid headlines: Member Found Flat in Lover's Flat. Pancake Day Comes Early in W.1.

'I suppose it is a bit Chronicles of Narnia,' I had responded weakly, through my humiliation. I buried my head into his shoulder and resisted adding, 'I could think of worse ways to go.'

He didn't stay long after coitus. We had no long, lingering tactility. The job was done, as far as he was concerned. He got up, dressed and left.

I was devastated by his sudden departure. As deflated as he was. Tentatively I had hoped he would take me out for a quiet meal. Nothing elaborate. My area was relatively quiet on weekday evenings. Most people made the short journey to Leicester Square and Soho.

I didn't expect to see him again. I kicked the wardrobe savagely, bruising my toe, but the pain was nothing to that in my chest. I knew there was no way I could remedy the situation regarding my bedroom furniture. The owner of the house was invisible and the agents were dismissive when I rang them to suggest the wardrobe could be removed. They were Italian and their English became unintelligible if unwelcome propositions were put to them. I gave up. In any case, I needed that wardrobe to store the few possessions I had saved from the cull. Boxes of belongings were kept at the bottom of that closet. The top shelves were piled with the detritus of the life that hadn't gone into the black bags in the back yard.

As I said, I didn't expect to see Michael again. But the following week there was a message on my answering machine. I was light-headed when it came. I had spent the preceding nights sleeplessly pacing my rooms, drinking until I was sick but not drunk, smoking cigarette after cigarette, which was not my usual custom, before returning to my bed where I continued to toss and turn. After a few days of this, the top half of my head seemed to be missing and I expected nothing more of the machine than a message from a work colleague or a thoughtful and loving enquiry from my mother.

It was Michael! To be ponderously analytical, why do passionately desired events take place when hope has been abandoned, so that their realisation fails to bring the relief and ecstasy which should attend them? Not until later, anyway. Could I manage Thursday afternoon? He didn't promise, but he would try and come round to the flat on Thursday afternoon. Thursday afternoon! Convenient for him because that is when the House of Commons winds down for the weekend and Honourable Members make the journey back to their constituencies. The perpetual lump in my throat jumped agonizingly and burned itself down into my belly.

Two days! How could I wait two whole days? But it was long enough to pay some attention to the flat and myself. I would buy some colourful throws and cushions to brighten up the sitting room. We could lie on the floor rather than on the bed. And I would have my hair cut during my lunch hour tomorrow. Better not have it re-styled. He might not like it. He must have all those glamorous women fussing round him in the Commons: Members and assistants and officials. How many did he personally employ? I had no idea. Should I ask him? I began to be grateful for his marriage.

* * *

I filled the kettle and switched it on. I wormed my way on to the chair inconveniently placed beside the kitchen table. It was the only spot where it would fit into the small room. I took a cigarette from the packet on the table. It was long, white, menthol-flavoured. He didn't like the taint on my breath. It was a small gesture of rebellion in retaliation for the lack of communication. Why couldn't he bloody well ring? He almost never did, but that didn't stop my desperate hope that this time would be different. Now I would have another evening of anguish while I fretted that he was tired of me. You would have thought after the weekend he could have managed to breathe a few honeyed words into my ear. Was that too much to ask? Just check that Thursday was okay for me? It never occurred to him to consult my timetable. I once was foolish enough to mention that I had a job as well.

'Oh, grow up, Frances,' he had returned. 'You P.R. people work when you like. Come and go as you please. Invent an appointment! I shouldn't think that was beyond your ingenuity.'

He had this dry, caustic way of talking that, if I were honest, I found stimulating. So I bit my lip and shut up.

Anyway, if I argued or made difficulties for him, I had no doubt he would stride away without a backward glance. He had never said so to my face, but I am sure he felt he could always get another woman. No doubt they fell over themselves every day to simper at him beside the statues in the Central Lobby.

For about the millionth time, I felt totally excluded from his life, from the huge swathes of it that did not include me. What a bastard he was! And what a sad fool I was!

The kettle worked itself up to the boil and I poured hot water on to instant coffee grains. Michael did not like instant coffee but then, he seldom waited for coffee anyway. I conceptualised Michael's elegant wife pushing down her manicured fingernails on the plunger of the coffee percolator in their state of the art kitchen. No sugar for her, I imagined. Or for me, either. It wouldn't do to get fat. A woman on a diet would drive Michael crazy. Milk was permitted, though. I squeezed out from my chair and took a carton from the refrigerator. I would not drink black coffee so early in the evening.

How many months and years had I been sitting here like this? Two years, four months and nineteen days, to be precise. Not long in the context of a lifetime, but an eternity in my time.

I closed my eyes and took a deep draught of the scalding liquid. Many, many were the women who had sat and waited. Mariana in her moated grange. Penelope at her bloody boring perpetual weaving as she waited for Odysseus. So many had sat and waited, far longer than I had, for deliverance, for space with the beloved, for death. Waited for any crumb of comfort, waited to willingly subjugate their lives to some unworthy shit of a man.

The Houses of Parliament are notorious for their infamous liaisons. One special relationship ended after twenty years when the Member of Parliament joined the new Government and decided it was time to put his house in order. One mistress, for want of a better word, could not attend her lover's funeral because of his family's hostility. And one Member unfortunately died of a heart attack while in flagrante delicto in his secretary's arms across his office desk. God help us all!

I was under no illusions. I had no expectations from Michael. I was like a patient with terminal cancer. All I could do was hang on from day to day. I knew that if there were the faintest whiff of opprobrium attached to our connection, Michael would be off quicker than a bat out of hell. He would deny everything and expect me to do the same. I had to be constantly on my guard. His ambition was paramount. And it all made my life very wearisome.

I drew on my cigarette. This time of day, in contrast to the frantic bustle of my days, I spend in futile self-analysis. Was the short time I shared with Michael worth the loss of any other meaningful life? I always came up with the same answer to that question. Yes! Yes! Yes!

I should eat something, even though I was filled to the brim with pain and apprehension. I took a brown loaf from the freezer compartment of the refrigerator and spread two slices with low fat margarine. Then I grated some mature Cheddar on top, before adding a dash of Worcester sauce and putting the pan under the grill. I hadn't the patience to prepare proper Cheese Rarebit but I hoped my amateur effort would be sufficient to tempt my taste buds.

Had I grabbed any lunch that day? I couldn't remember. A client proposal was required urgently and I had stayed at my desk. I think Margot brought me a sandwich when she returned from her sortie down the street. I had taken a couple of bites and dropped it in the waste bin while she was out of the office. I really must buy some fruit, apples or something, to munch at my desk when I went to work tomorrow. Otherwise Margot would be giving me grief about my lack of eating habits. Anyway, Michael liked to bite into an apple while he dressed after lovemaking. I kept the cores until they were wizened and disgusting.

CHAPTER ONE

The cheese sizzled and browned. I removed the grill pan and slid the bread on to a plate. The smell of toasted cheese filled the flat. My stomach was rumbling as a small, insistent rodent gnawed my guts.

I sat down at the table and cut into the melted cheese. I looked at it. It hung in thin, gooey strips from the knife. I opened my mouth as the portion on my fork travelled upwards. The telephone rang. Damn! Blast! Fuck! Surely not Michael cancelling Thursday's appointment? And now the meal I don't really fancy will congeal and become inedible. I paused, tempted to let the answering machine do its work.

I squirmed my body around the chair and sped into the hall. I lifted the receiver. An unfamiliar voice with the unknown name of Debby enquired if I would be interested in giving to St. Anselm's Home for the Aged Distressed. I said I had other things on my mind at that moment. I put the telephone down on its cradle. Perhaps she thought I was in the middle of a gluttonous dinner party as she pursued her thankless task of trying to raise money for the needy. Why was life so full of petty irritations?

I was emptying my half-eaten supper into the trash bin when there was a rap on my door. Now what? I didn't want to be disturbed. I couldn't be bothered with anything these days. Surely it wasn't Mrs Margoloys! She never climbed the stairs. I opened the door. Archie stood there with his outdoor jacket draped over his shoulders.

'You're back quickly,' I greeted him, expecting him to say his appointment hadn't materialized and his expectations had been dashed – just like mine.

'Darling! Great news!' He came in and sniffed appreciatively. 'Something smells good.' His eyes took in my empty plate.

'Sorry, Archie! I've just finished.' I really didn't feel inclined to make more toast for him. 'Would you like a coffee?'

'Not just now, darling.' We moved into the sitting room and he sprawled on my sofa, his legs akimbo.

'How did the interview go?'

'Brilliant! D.S wants to see a portfolio. He suggested I get some fresh pictures taken quickly.'

'Well, that's great! Congratulations!' I moved towards the door. 'Archie, I'm just clearing up. I won't be a minute. Keep talking to me.'

I went to the sink and began to scour the grill pan. I should have covered it with silver foil before I started. Too late now!

Archie came and stood in the kitchen doorway. 'I've rung my photographer buddy. He's coming round pronto to take some photos down the road at the church.'

There was an impressive neo-Gothic church on the Marylebone Road just around the corner from Nottingham Place. Flights of steps led to a large portico high above the busy London artery.

'What a great idea! Just the right background! Good work!' Sometimes my P.R. speak got on my own nerves. I wondered why Archie had climbed the stairs to tell me about his assignment, rather than walking down the road to meet the photographer.

'Come with me! I'm meeting Gus at the church.' (Gus! What kind of a name was that?) 'You can be an impartial observer and give us the benefit of your advice.'

'Oh, yes? I'm sure your buddy will be ecstatic if I start questioning his professional judgement.'

'Oh, he's not professional. It's just a hobby with him. But he's bloody good. Couldn't afford a professional's fees at this stage.'

I was surprised. I had imagined that Archie and Jason gave all for their art. Archie had on his pleading, little boy look. He was a handsome fellow, with his sleeked black hair and chiselled profile.

'Come with me! Honestly, I want you there, Fran.'

What was this? Was Archie more uncertain than I gave him credit for? He needed an ally in his dealings with the photographer. He was going on, 'You have an expert eye.

You will be a definite asset. Gus won't mind at all. He might offer to take your picture for free. You're quite presentable.'

'Well, thanks!' I wiped the grill pan and put it away. Why didn't I go? Sometimes I felt too jaded to bestir myself at all. But this evening I was restless and upset. Too much adrenalin was pumping. Anything would be better than sitting staring at my own four walls.

'Okay, then. But I don't want to be down there all night.'

Archie bounded over and gave me a hug. 'No! Certainly not! I don't want to be down there all night, either. You can come back any time you like.' He picked up my jacket and twirled around with it in parody of a macho bullfighter. 'You're an angel, Fran!'

I picked up my keys and opened the door. 'Come on, you idiot!' We ran down the stairs but slowed and quietened as we reached the hall. For the first time I realised that we all tried to avoid Mrs Margoloys if we could.

'Mustn't disturb Mrs Margoloys,' Archie hissed in my ear as we tiptoed down the hall. We were silent as mice until we were through the front door and down the four steps to the pavement and the railings above Archie and Jason's flat.

'Didn't Jason want to come?'

'Not in, darling. He's gone to see his little boys.' He began to act about, limping and dragging one foot behind him, then jumping from the pavement to the gutter.

'Archie! Be your age!' I took a deep breath. Time suspended. I looked up at the sky, noticed the dark shapes of trees stencilled against pale evening cloud. Normality, everyday life was just an air breath away.

'We didn't wait for Gus,' I said. Archie was good for me. He took me into his fantasy world as though I had joined him in one of his projected plays, whether it were one of Shakespeare's multiple disguises or a hilarious Feydeau farce.

'Meetin' 'im at t' church, me darlin',' he said. He now had his arms in the air and was pretending to be an aeroplane.

'You should have gone with Jason to amuse his sons'.

Vehicle lights, sharp as strobes, meeting, mixing and receding, shone before us as we turned the corner into Marylebone Road.

'Ah! There he is!' We saw a lanky figure, whose white tee shirt glowed in the dusk, standing at the top of the church steps. He was leaning on the near balustrade and looking in our direction. Archie sped towards him. I slipped on my jacket as the first evening chill crept up my arms. The rear light of a receding taxi reminded me of my lonely answering machine. Was Michael even now dialling my number?

Archie waved impatiently from the top of the steps. 'C'mon, darling! You're dragging. Gus's time is money.'

As I climbed the steps towards the massy bulk of the church, the emaciated young man unwound himself from the pillar against which he was leaning.

'Hi!' he said, without moving his lips. An expensive-looking camera was hung round his neck. 'What kept you?'

'Well, here we are now,' said Archie, impatiently. 'Is the light all right?'

'So long as we get on with it.' Gus took the half-smoked cigarette from the corner of his mouth and put it on the balustrade. 'Together, is it?'

'Just me, mate. Portfolio, you know.'

Gus sniffed. I warmed to him. Straightforward. No pretensions. Not much time for this acting, woofter lark.

'Frances is here to give us the benefit of her expertise in the Public Relations field.' Archie was reacting to that sniff.

'No, really,' I protested. 'Archie's joking. I'm only along for the ride.'

'Usual rates,' said Gus. 'All right?'

'I knew your usual generous terms would apply.'

'Let's get on with it, then.'

I walked a short way from them and sat on the balustrade to watch the proceedings. Michael came with me and spoke in my ear. Good background, he whispered. Good thinking. (Now I know that if Michael is too much in evidence, he will get on your nerves, as he does on mine. But he did walk with us down the street and I didn't mention him.)

Archie was posing with the confidence of much practice and the two men had cut the crap and were working together with dedicated professionalism. Gus was arranging his shots with meticulous attention to detail. I wondered if he spent all his time on cut-price pictures for struggling actors and aspiring models or if he had a different, daytime occupation. He obviously took this one seriously. Archie was displayed framed by the arches, leaping across the pale skyline and leaning against the heavy stonework that admirably accentuated his athletic slimness.

Twilight was deepening. In the dim shadows of the portico, the flash gleamed again and again.

'Backdrop of the street?' queried Gus. 'The traffic lights will look good. Sit on the balustrade. Yes! Good.'

Archie was a good subject. He knew the exact angle at which to turn his head to show off his Grecian profile. His straight nose and sprung back hair were the stuff of film idols from the silent era. Rudolf Valentino reborn. And how many women worshipped him?

An acrobat began to perform a vigorous routine in my head. I felt trembly and desolate. Lack of food did have this effect on me. I kept remembering the long strips of gooey cheese and wanted to heave.

How arbitrary life was! Some put in so much effort for so little reward. Some were rewarded without merit. Some were punished without cause. Would all the boys' efforts this evening result in a boost for Archie's career?

'One film, was it? One left. How about one sitting on the steps with the church doors behind? You never know. You could be going in one day.' Gus guffawed.

It was finished. Archie unwound his long legs and rose gracefully to his feet. His future success could depend on these very images. Perhaps in ten years' time I would see one of these photographs displayed on billboards all over London.

(Michael is always having his picture taken. Every time he makes a constituency visit, a local reporter will be present to gather information for the Women's Institute or the Children Play Group. Then there is his election pamphlet. And that one will have his wife and children in tow. All the propaganda about happy families. I have never, ever, had a photograph taken with him.) I pressed my hands to my eyes. You would think, after two years, the anguish would subside. If anything, it became more acute.

Archie glanced in my direction. 'Shan't be long now, darling. Nearly through.'

I had thought they were. The temperature had dropped. I shivered and pulled my thin jacket close around my body.

'That's the end of the film. Want any more?'

Archie shook his head. Obviously cost was on his mind. The two men stood together at the end of the terrace, talking terms or whatever. They could be planning to have a beer in the nearest pub. I should go home. I felt too weary to move.

Archie came towards me. 'Thanks, darling! You've been a great help.' I hadn't said a word during the whole of the session. 'I'll buy you a coffee for being so patient.'

'No, Archie. I'll only come if I pay.' I was conscious of the basement boys' chronic shortage of money. There were times when they couldn't find fifty pence for the electricity meter. Coffee was cheaper than beer. That was an unworthy thought! I pushed it away.

'Count me out,' said Gus. 'I'm going to get on with the developing.' He nodded to me and strode off in the direction of Regent's Park. I wondered where he was going. Certainly not to any of the great houses around Park Crescent.

'Brilliant photographer,' Archie informed me. 'He's planning to open a studio as soon as he has gathered the finance.' He pulled my hand through the crook of his arm and we turned in the opposite direction towards Madame Tussauds and the lights of Baker Street. My feet longed to walk of their own accord back to my small flat and my uncooperative answering machine. I felt I very well understood Marcel Proust and his need for cork protection around his bedroom walls.

'Wonder when we'll be in Madame Tussaud's,' said Archie.

* * *

He was coming on Thursday at four, exactly a week after our last encounter. Why does my every thought have a sexual connotation? Days and hours and minutes and seconds. How would I fill them, except with longings for my beloved? Behold thou art fair, my love!

In the early days of our relationship he had made it (see what I mean) on Fridays. I suppose he told his wife he had Commons business to attend to, but his Constituency Office began to put in appointments on Friday mornings and it was difficult for him to continually refuse them. When his wife noticed that neighbouring Members were home on Thursday evenings, he panicked and returned that night to the bosom of his loving family. My feelings he never troubled to consider. He informed me his only free time was late on Thursday afternoons, for at most an hour. Take it or leave it.

Who knew about my affair? Nobody. I told nobody. Baffled and bewildered by the strength of my feelings, I was hardly in a state to communicate with anyone, even with an intimate friend. And I had no intimate friend.

I assumed Michael was as discreet as I was. He had, after all, so much more to lose. His career could be badly dented if our annexation became public knowledge. God knows why, in this day and age! Behold thou art fair, my love!

* * *

Tuesday evening! I paced my narrow domain with a glass of whisky in my hand. Every so often I took great gulps of the fiery liquid. I hated the stuff normally, but it was the strongest drink I had in the cupboard. I was I in a state of fever and excitement. Another forty-four hours and he would be with me.

The telephone shrilled. God! He wasn't coming! There had been times, not many, but a few, when I had sat in a state of déshabillé through the interminable hours of Thursday up till twilight, while my furniture blurred in the dusk and my tears trickled, until it became obvious he wasn't going to show. My reward was nothing more than a perfunctory apology: you know how it is, Frances. Pressures from all sides. Don't know how we stand it. If you are going to give me a hard time, we will have to call it a day. My stomach had lurched and dropped at his dismissive words. A burning sensation travelled down my oesophagus towards my innards. 'No! Don't say that! I know how difficult it is for you. He had patted my hand. Good girl! It is best if we both understand the situation.

Oh, I understood the situation all right. There was nothing in this relationship for me, except the miracle of his company on an uncertain, curtailed basis. But without these frenzied, frantic afternoons, my life would not be worth living.

I picked up the receiver.

'Hi, Fran!' Relief gushed through me. It was Jason from downstairs. 'Archie's out, and I'm feeling very bored. Would you like to come down and we'll go through my lines for Love's Labour's Lost? I'm auditioning on Saturday morning.'

Not a brilliant invitation, but it would get me away from my telephone for a couple of hours.

'Okay! Are you ready now?'

I picked up the bottle of Whisky and made my way down the stairs. Music was blaring from Francesca's flat. She was singing along in a passable contralto and obviously preparing for her evening's employment. She had very high-class clients whom I sometimes met on the stairs: Arabs and Americans. I wondered vaguely how much she charged.

I skipped smartly across the hall – I didn't want an encounter with Mrs Margoloys just now – and down the basement stairs. Jason's door was open and he called out as I lifted my hand to rap. 'Come in, darling. And close the door behind you.'

He came into his tiny hall. He was wearing a dark blue towelling dressing gown. His straight fair hair was rumpled as though he had just emerged from the shower.

'Am I too soon?' I asked.

'No, darling!' He kissed me softly and sweetly on the mouth. His breath smelled minty, of toothpaste or chewing gum. 'Just woke up.' He ran his hand through his hair in a backward gesture and shook his head like Hairy McClary. 'Give me a minute and I'll be fine. Exhausted after yesterday.'

I tried not to look at the state of the flat. My idea of homely muddle was totally confounded here.

'How are the boys?' I remembered Archie remarking he was seeing his sons.

'Adorable! They are so beautiful. You've brought a bottle.' He kissed me again. 'I love you.'

He took two tumblers, wiped the rim of one on his dressing gown and poured out two generous portions. Michael had brought the Whisky on one of his visits to my flat and it gave me a vindictive pleasure to see another man tipping it down his throat.

'Coffee?'

'So so! Yeah!' I probably looked as if I needed it. 'Perhaps it would be a good idea.' Wake him up and sober me down. I remembered I had not eaten. 'Have you had supper yet, Jason?'

'I'll get a bite later.'

He took the Penguin Shakespeare from amid the muddle on the coffee table and put it into my hands. It fell open at Act IV, Scene III. Pencil markings festooned Berowne's speech.

'You're reading for Berowne? He's one of the main characters.'

'You know it?' Holding the kettle of boiling water poised above two mugs, he looked at me in admiration. 'Good on yer, darling!'

'I saw the film with Kenneth Branagh.'

I noted in a detached way his excessive good looks. He would make a good King of Navarre.

'You're a woman of many talents,' he said. 'As surprising as you are beautiful.' He handed me a steaming mug of coffee. A faint whiff of stale milk came from it.

'You see the speech?' he asked.

It was Berowne's treatise on love:
But love, first learned in a lady's eyes,
Lives not alone, immured in the brain,
But, with the motion of all elements,
Courses as swift as thought in every power,
And gives to every power a double power
Above their function and their offices.

He was almost word perfect and spoke the lines well. He was indeed a pleasure to look upon – tall, slim and fair. My mind wandered as my eyes automatically followed the words. Why did some achieve greatness while others did not? Take the glamorous professions, films, television, modelling, it seemed that the ones who made it seemingly had no more to offer than those who did not. Like love, really. Some grabbed at it, time after time, while others were left in the back row with their begging bowls empty. Determination, perhaps. Persistence. Push your way to the front. But did persistence always pay off? At some stage, didn't persistence turn into pathos? The aging second-rater, still striving against all the odds? God! What was going to happen to us all?

I became aware that Jason had stopped declaiming Berowne's philosophy and was talking to me in his own voice. 'Shit, darling,' he was saying, 'I don't know how much longer I can stand it.' I looked at him, surprised by this sudden transition from the Bard.

'What's the matter, Jason?' I knew he had financial problems and wondered if he was about to ask for a loan.

'I see my kids only about once a month.' He crashed his right fist into his left palm. 'Is that acceptable? Is that right?'

'Where did you take them last evening?' I asked to distract him from his distress.

'We went to Regent's Park. Ran around with a ball.'

'Well, I'm sure they enjoyed that,' I said lamely. 'Running around with Dad.'

I saw his problem. Children these days expected to be amused, entertained. Expensive toys. Computer games. Money had to be expended.

'How the fuck can I afford to take them anywhere?' He dropped into a chair and put his head in his hands. Then he looked up. 'But they're brilliant. Didn't ask for anything.' For a moment I thought he was going to cry. With his ruffled hair and trembling lip he seemed scarcely more than a child himself.

'We played football,' he repeated. Then he brightened up. 'You know what? Alex, the little one, he's only four, was really good in the goal. He was fantastic at catching the ball. He put his hands behind it like a pro. And Max, he's just seven, is in the Junior Football Team.'

'You must be very proud of them,' I said, gently.

I was getting a glimpse of another problem beyond my own. What were my problems compared to the ache of parents for absent children? Mine was just the selfish anguish of a jealous lover.

'What a fucking mess!'

I said nothing. Something priggish such as he should consider living for his art was inappropriate at this juncture. Anyway, who was I to proffer advice in view of my fractured, pitiful existence?

'Oh, to hell with it!' He appeared to shake off his melancholy as easily as though he was indeed Berowne playing his stage role.

I looked down at the Penguin Shakespeare, which was still on my lap. 'You're word perfect, Jason.'

He took the book from me and threw it across the room. 'I know. And so are all the other buggers.' He tossed his head back as though he were shaking off water. 'Enough! I fancy diversion. Let's go to the flicks and watch Bonjour Tristesse. They've got a revival going.'

The cinema was nearly empty. I tried to buy the tickets, but Jason was adamant. 'Collected the old Lloyd George today,' he said.

We sat in the cheap seats at the front while the huge figures of the doomed lovers hung over us. My attention wandered as my stomach rumbled. We'll have a burger on the way back, I promised myself.

The story about a daughter's fury over her father's affair and her ultimate destruction of it was not a whole barrel of laughs, but it suited my present mood of maudlin sadness. All I wished to do, really, was to wallow in my misery. Here, cocooned in the warm, safe dark, I could think about Michael, the way his eyes crinkled at the corners and his mouth set obstinately when he was annoyed. I could relive our lovemaking, luxuriate in every touch, kiss and fondle.

After the film finished and we left the cinema arm in arm, I was desperate to be alone to continue my dream world. I yawned ostentatiously as we waited at the burger bar.

'Sorry, Jason! I've a busy day tomorrow. And I'm whacked! I'll have to get back.' The stink of onions in this vicinity was making me feel sick, anyhow. Whisky on an empty stomach was taking its toll. I pressed a five-pound note into Jason's hand. He tried to give it back. Oh, the pride of the poor! 'I don't want it.'

'Yes, you must take it. You bought the cinema tickets. Fair's fair.'

He submitted graciously. 'Shall I bring you one back?'

'No! I'm not hungry,' I lied. 'I'm just going to fall into bed.'

I turned for home. It was not far. Just a short walk down Marylebone High Street to Nottingham Place. I was desperate to be solitary with only my desires and dreams for company. Michael and I in a handsome cottage, cradled in the arms of the South Downs, where pools of daffodils danced in the Spring sunshine beneath quivering willow trees. The glint of water below a rustic bridge and old woodlands a short walk away. God! What a deluded fool I was! Then into this vision Michael came striding from the rose-covered doorway and climbed into his waiting Aston Martin and drove away.

CHAPTER TWO

On Thursday morning I casually mentioned to Margot, my office colleague that I had a potential client to check out. Afterwards I would work in my flat. Margot raised her eyebrows but made no comment, which told me more eloquently than any innuendo that she suspected a man in the case. She had only worked alongside me for six months and we had gelled very well, but now I had to come up with plausible excuses for my regular absences on Thursday afternoons.

Fortunately we had begun to share an office just after Christmas when Michael was away on the parliamentary break until well into January. I had made sure I was at work at all hours, so she became imbued with the idea of my conscientiousness. Just perhaps as she was noticing that my out-of-office work tended to occur on Thursday afternoons, Easter was upon us and the pattern was broken. And in the summer, of course, the House rises for almost three months.

Also, Michael could be unreliable; so when Margot could have become curious about my absences, he had some Commons business to attend to, and had to be present at Westminster. Consequently, there I was, conspicuous by my presence, beavering away at my desk. Maybe I should have suggested to Michael he stagger his visits to throw off suspicion. But that would have been inconvenient for him and no way did he relish being ordered around.

'For Heaven's sake, Frances,' he would have said, accompanying his words with an impatient glare, 'I thought you were your own boss at that place you work at. I didn't realise anybody was watching your comings and goings.' And

I would have shrugged it off. 'We'll leave it then, shall we?' In any event, the only meaningful time of my life was when he was with me.

As usual on Thursday mornings, I was on pins in case any urgent business materialized that would positively require my presence in the office that afternoon. The thought of Michael turning up at an empty flat was unendurable. I couldn't imagine him doing so on more than one occasion. In panic at the idea of him fruitlessly knocking at my door, I have given him keys to the outer and inner doors so he can slip in as speedily as possible. But the possibility of him arriving during my absence and finding the sitting room a veritable tip brings me out in a cold sweat.

Before Margot's arrival, nobody had observed my movements. If I met a colleague while on the way out, I had indicated I had an appointment outside the office. The senior staff came and went at will. But now it was inevitable that Margot and I knew a great deal about each other's movements. Manufacturing non-existent interviews over a lengthy period exercised all my ingenuity.

However, Margot was good-natured and accepted my vague explanations without question. To my advantage in this situation was the fact that Margot was sometimes absent herself without apparent cause. I began to imagine that she had a clandestine affair of her own. But Margot was no slouch at logic and must have put two and two together. However, for once, something worked in my favour.

Jason, God bless him, had called unexpectedly at the office to ask if I could let his little boys into his flat if he were late home, and keep an eye on them. After that, Margot was half convinced he was my boyfriend, if not my paramour and, in view of the divorce and the children, there were difficulties in the relationship. She attempted to catechize me after he left. 'He lives in your block, does he? Do you go out together sometimes?' 'Yes, Margot. We do go out together sometimes,' I answered truthfully.

Archie and Jason were like the brothers I never had. We had an easy, laughing camaraderie, but no way would I contemplate any escalation in the relationship with either of them. Jason was still fixated on his estranged wife and Archie was at least ten years younger than me. However, their habit of punctuating their conversation with endearments could give bystanders the wrong impression. I gave no further explanation to Margot. Any obfuscation would be of benefit in my irregular life-style.

At three o'clock I was walking along Marylebone High Street. Michael would not arrive for almost an hour, so I had time to tart up my flat a little. I would buy lilies and roses to fill my silver ice bucket. I loved the flower shop with its aluminium vases stuffed with milky blue delphiniums and the scent of tiger lilies perfuming the air. I inhaled deeply and bought a great armful. As an afterthought, I also chose a small bunch of cream freesias for the mantelpiece. Michael would see them if he lifted his eyes as his buttocks rose and fell with the symmetry and grace of the butterfly stroke. I gulped and ran my fingers over the smooth, perfect skin of his shoulder blades. I closed my eyes.

'Are you all right, Madam?' The salesgirl (or person, if you prefer) was holding out the change from my £10 note. She was looking at me in surprise.

'Yes! Thank you. Quite all right! Sorry! Came over a bit faint.'

I took the change and backed from the shop, clutching my flowers to my bosom.

'I would go home and have a cup of tea if I were you. Live round the corner, don't you?'

'Yes. Thanks. I'll do that.'

Damn! I wanted to buy cheese, crackers and fruit. Michael would sometimes nibble while he got dressed. It would have been more sensible to buy the food first.

I did as the girl suggested. Took the flowers home, arranged them, plumped up the cushions and swept a quick duster around the room. I would not put the sofa cushions on the floor until after Michael's arrival. Otherwise it all looked too contrived and obvious. I made a quick cup of tea and then slipped back to the mini market for the snacks. I added a pineapple to my purchases. It would look attractive and, being fresh, would not fill the flat with its overpowering aroma.

Michael never stayed for a meal. In his view, that would take up valuable fucking time. My prime importance in his mind was clear.

I sighed a little as I approached 19A for the second time. The advantage of returning this way was that it was nearer the corner, so there was less chance of being seen. In any event, I was safe from being noticed by the occupants of the flats with front windows overlooking the street. The music students who lived in the ground floor room with the big bay were always at their college at this time of day. No doubt Francesca was resting on her bed. Mrs Margoloys would certainly have been a danger, but her little window faced nothing more exciting than the back yard. Archie and Jason could have noticed my feet passing on the pavement above their heads, but neither of them was the type to be stargazing for long. They were usually dashing about on their own devices. I once met Archie and told him I was dropping some shopping back in my flat after a late lunch hour.

I had also on one occasion bumped into Mrs Margoloys in the hall. Didn't the bloody woman ever stop meandering about? She had the potential to be more troublesome, particularly as she tended to drop out snippets of acquired information about our lives to the other tenants. In a totally disingenuous way. Trying to prove she had some involvement with us, I suppose. Fortunately, the other tenants were too caught up in their own concerns to pay much attention to her ramblings. I told her I had come back to the flat to check something on my computer. As we stood in the hall, one of the music students, manhandling her cello, came through the front door. Mrs Margoloys immediately turned her attention to the new arrival. The old lady had reputedly performed in musical comedy in her youth. I suspected her veracity on this matter, but perhaps that made her feel at home with young musicians and aspiring actors. The music students were not often visible and Mrs Margoloys would not pass up on this opportunity for a chat.

After a couple of minutes I came downstairs again. The music student was now edging through her half open door and took advantage of the distraction of my appearance to slip inside. I walked round the block before going back. The hall was now empty. I closed the door quietly behind me. I knew every nuance of that door: the sharp slam that usually accompanied the departure of Archie or Jason; the slight creaking on Francesca's comings and goings; the careful dull bang if Mrs Margoloys was herself venturing out; the discreet click of closure adopted by Francesca's clients. For my part, I adapted all sounds to my own purposes.

Mrs Margoloys was slightly deaf and would think I had left the building to return to my office. On that occasion, I crept up the stairs, holding my breath and trying not to giggle. There was no danger from Francesca. She would not surface for another six hours.

But today I had no trouble, despite my two entrances. If I had met Mrs Margoloys, no doubt she would have said, 'Checking your computer again, dear?' I wondered how many of the other tenants had been informed by her that I had to return home to check my computer. However, today Jason was off auditioning for some play. Archie was God knows where.

I didn't mind this excessive caution entering my own front door. I felt it would give me an insight into what Michael must experience every Thursday afternoon. And how I wanted to share his experiences! Get inside his head. Did he enjoy the dangerous frisson? Would he find it exciting, part of my attraction? At least, he was too proud to wear a cap pulled low and a scarf over the bottom half of his face. But then, he was not one of the well-known faces in the Commons. Not yet!

Once inside, I did a quick check over the state of my flat. I moved the bucket with its burgeoning lilies to a more tasteful site. I put the freesias on the coffee table. I hoped Michael would not send them flying if his arm performed a too extravagant gesture. I dried the mugs and cereal bowl from the draining board in the kitchen. Michael might stand in the doorway with a pained look on his face as I made coffee. I wondered if his wife lived in a state of civilised sluttery during his weekday absences, and then had a cleaning woman do a blitz the day he returned home.

I arranged the grapes and pineapple in a cut-glass bowl. I put the cheese and crackers on a tray and covered it with cling foil. I switched on the electric fire and looked at the clock. Three forty six. In less than half an hour he would be with me. Had I time to take a shower before he arrived? Just. But that would forgo the pleasure of being undressed by him, unless I put my clothes on again. I would have to shower afterwards, anyway.

I went to the bathroom and cleaned my teeth, patted on some Ylang Ylang. I took off my dark business suit and put on a scarlet dressing gown. It occurred to me that if the house caught fire and I had to scramble down the fire escape on to the street, I would cut a most bizarre figure. Wouldn't Margot's eyes pop if she saw me on the ten o'clock news?

I looked at my watch again. Was this the week he wouldn't come? I felt sick. Wanted a cigarette, but he would smell it on my breath. Feeling foolish in the red gown, I went back into the bedroom and put on a grey tracksuit. Had I taken a pill? I couldn't remember. I ought to check. I heard the soft scrape of a key in the lock. He was here!

'Oh, Frances! I wish you wouldn't!' were his words of greeting. 'How often have I told you I detest that dirty habit?'

I looked down. A half-smoked cigarette was burning in my fingers. I had no recollection of lighting it. Hurriedly I moved to the kitchen and dropped the stub down the sink.

When I returned to the sitting room he had removed his jacket and was already unbuttoning his shirt. I helped him, running my hand down his lightly haired chest. The hair was darker than that on his head. How well I knew his body!

'If you were ready,' he said, 'it wouldn't take so long.'

After all my anticipation and preparation! Tears stung my eyelids. I turned my head so he wouldn't see them. I threw the sofa cushions on the floor and my clothes after them. A thick skim of bile formed in my throat.

He was already disposed on my floor in his naked magnificence, in eye line with the uncomprehending, beautiful lilies. I went to his arms and he began to nibble my ear. I found this habit irritating and wanted to shake my head as he had shaken off my eager hands.

It is difficult to write about sex, describe the sexual act. After all, what is there to say about the insertion, consolidation and withdrawal of a piece of erectile muscle? After all the stroking, caressing and repeated explorations of the known terrain, the clichés and metaphors and fantasy, it may be, at best, boring and, at worst, risible. Exploding fireworks and crashing waves! They have been done to death.

It is nothing of the mind and all of the body. I came, without seeing or conquering! As two sweat-soaked bodies, glued together by their own secretions, peel apart with an audible squelch, what is there to say except that the pleasure is soon over and yearned for again and again. Love is of the mind. Lust is of the body. The mind has little place in this scenario. We were mismatched! I had known that from the beginning. The pure intensity of my love was no adversary for the cruel lust of his loins.

'Haven't much time,' he said. 'I shall have to dash off. Got an appointment in the Whips' Office at half past five.'

* * *

Something was brewing. There was a smell in the air and it wasn't just my coffee bubbling away in the percolator in the kitchen. There was trouble in the Commons. Michael occasionally made laconic remarks about political shenanigans but he certainly didn't discuss parliamentary business with me.

I had become a news addict since the beginning of our liaison. I wanted to know why he had become a politician, what causes he espoused, how he spent every minute of his day. I knew the names of the Standing Committees he attended, the groups and bodies to which he belonged, in case he gave attendance at these functions as excuses for his absence.

So I had to garner my information from television and radio discussions. I read analytical articles in prestigious periodicals. And over time I gained a fair insight into the workings of the Mother of Parliaments. I had gathered the impression that Members – with a few honourable exceptions – were, by and large, able, ambitious, unscrupulous, professionally charming and plausible, with skins thick as rhinoceroses and consciences to match. Michael, of course, was different.

I avidly devoured my study material, which demonstrated how biased was much of the Press reporting. I got to know the prevalent slant of the leading journalists. I read about the same event in three different newspapers and realised you could be forgiven for thinking they were not reporting the same story. However, I kept my opinions to myself. Michael did not visit my flat to take part in a political philosophy lesson.

I knew enough by this stage in our relationship to be aware that Michael's attendance at the Whips' Office was not unusual. The Whips were shadowy figures, wielding power in closet ways. Apart from the Chief Whip, they were unknown to the general public. They could be tough and ruthless as they pressurized recalcitrant Members to stay in line. There had been a time when they were largely drawn from Northern constituencies, ex-blue collar working men, coalminers and plumbers, all Trade Unionists. They understood that their purpose was to persuade, cajole and threaten. They had to get the Members through the lobbies to vote the Government's way and uphold its fragile majority.

But that was long ago, before Michael's time. The Whips now used subtler instruments of persuasion, such as the possibility of a step up the parliamentary ladder. Of course, all M.Ps. understood the score. Vote against your Government once too often and you are never going to be part of it. Rebels are troublesome enough on the Back Benches. They have no place within the machinery of power.

I had no fear about Michael's insurrection. He had too much sense of self-interest to jeopardize his prospects. But was he in for a reprimand of some kind? Was there any hint of my part in his life? We had been so careful, but walls have ears. Spies are everywhere. Journalists surface from the woodwork. Could it be that my flat was under surveillance? Michael must have been jumpy about the forthcoming interview. That would explain his irritability. He had also failed to make it. Not that that is relevant.

I dropped my scarlet silk kimono on the floor and stood under the shower. In ten minutes Michael would know his fate. Sometimes I wanted his smell on me, the dark, pungent smell of male excitement. But today I only wished to be sweet, to wash away the unsatisfactory lovemaking. To be ready for us to begin again!

I soaped between my legs, rinsed and soaped again. Michael would be walking through the corridors leading to the Members' Lobby where Churchill's massive statue regarded all comings and goings with benign indifference. I prayed there had been no delay on the Underground or he would never come to my flat again.

I was anxious, my movements clumsy. I dropped the soap and scrabbled for it on slippery tiles. My heart was thumping. I was desperate to dry myself and put on fresh underwear. Michael's anxiety had become my own. Was I beginning to find these encounters more trouble than they were worth? Why did I spend my life in feverish expectation, only to suffer the deflation of disappointment so soon afterwards?

I stepped out of the shower and into my pants. Why didn't I show the bastard the door? The thought horrified me. I grasped the towel rail for support. What would my life be without the prospect, the possibility of Michael's presence? I was shaking. But the bathroom was chilly, even after the steam from the shower had fuzzed over the mirrors. Good thing Michael didn't spend long in here!

Were the Whips about to question him regarding his private life? Was there another lover whose company he sought on Monday mornings? Or was it something innocuous, such as next week's Government business? Heavy black lines on the Order Paper. Just make sure, Michael, you are in the Chamber on Wednesday, or Tuesday, or Thursday afternoon, for the three line Whip. A gentle reminder of future priorities. What bills were in the pipeline? I had better buy the Times tomorrow and check pending legislation.

If only Michael weren't so uncommunicative! I pulled on black trousers and a light cashmere sweater. I wandered around. Tenderly stroked the cushion that still bore the imprint of his head. I lit another cigarette. To hell with it! I was giving way to nervous debility. I was being shit stupid. Why should anyone have knowledge of our secret trysts? I liked that word. Tryst! It sounded Mediaeval, chivalric. Romaunt of the Rose stuff.

The front door banged. I could barely hear it in my flat. One of the boys, or possibly the music students, I would expect. I looked at my watch. Five twenty six. If Michael hadn't had to rush back to the House of Commons he could have been leaving now and met on his way out whoever had just arrived. How many times had we been similarly lucky?

I felt ravenously hungry. I didn't fancy any of the tempting snacks I had arranged with such loving care earlier that afternoon. Instead I looked in the 'fridge. Eggs, bacon, bread, milk. Not quite convenience! Fuck! Let's get fat! It occurred to me I had an organised mind where food was concerned. Don't forget the basics! Drink milk, my mother told me, if you haven't time to eat.

I wasn't a fan of fad diets. I didn't much like pitta bread and I didn't drink bottled water. I was naturally thin, anyway. My perpetual anxiety prevented the build-up of additional pounds. The constant bombardment of slimming aids bored me. Why worry about weight gain when it wasn't an issue as far as I was concerned? Nothing like misery to keep you thin! Not true, I knew that. Some traumatized souls binged all the time.

I shut the refrigerator door and took a couple of large potatoes from my vegetable rack. To hell with everything! I would have a good fry up of eggs, bacon, chips and baked beans. What a pity I hadn't bought sausages and mushrooms as well! I imagined Michael and me sitting squashed together at my kitchen table, squeezing tomato ketchup on to oven ready chips before popping them into each other's mouths.

Should I slip out for the additional items? I felt restless and reckless, glad I had dressed rather than lounged for another hour beside the sofa, uselessly dozing and dreaming. Reliving our encounter.

No! No! No! Far too dangerous! Someone was in downstairs and if I were seen it would be obvious that I had been in my flat all the time. I could say I hadn't felt well and had come home. Then there would be solicitous enquiries, attempts to cheer me up. Besides if my delicious cooking smells were sniffed, that story wouldn't wash. If it were one of the boys, I would feel obliged to cook for him as well. No! I could not leave my flat. I would make do with the food I had.

More than an hour later, with stomach distended by fries and baked beans; I sat down in the living room, kicked the floor cushions away into the corner and switched on the television. Time for the Channel Four News!

I closed my eyes momentarily as his fingers caressed my neck. I saw the contour map of his body: the ripple of his shoulder muscles, the deep valley of his waist and the swell of his buttocks above the long lean thighs and shapely calves. Tanned and exquisite in the dim light. He put his arms around me and I curved myself against his perfection. We fitted together like a jigsaw puzzle. By this time he had relaxed following his cautious entry into my apartment.

I remembered him once asking, 'Why don't you try for a flat on the ground floor, Frances?' 'Well, none of the ground floor flats here are the right size for me,' I had replied. 'Anyway, if you are worried about being seen, the stairs are nearer the front door than any of the flats.' He had frowned, registering my argument. 'And once you turn the bend in the stairs, there is only Francesca between us; and she never ventures out before evening. She is a night bird.' He absently stroked my breasts as I spoke. I went on, 'If there is someone in the hall, they will see you. But, apart from Mrs Margoloys, none of the others are much interested in anything but their own concerns.' He said nothing as I repeated, 'Francesca never leaves her apartment before seven. Even if she met you, she would think I was taking a leaf out of her book.' As I spoke I realised I was not so far from the truth, except I dealt with one rather than with many, and I didn't get paid. I giggled a little. Sometimes my lifestyle made me hysterical. Michael had glared at me. 'I wish you wouldn't be so flippant, Frances! Our relationship is really important to me.'

Oh, it was important to me, as well! I would go scarlet at the sight of him, as my breathing changed to quick, short pants. And I am not talking about the post coital flush of red splotches, German measles fashion, which spreads between neck and navel. No, this was a blushing of my face as I became hotter and hotter and felt my blood would boil in my veins. My body took over in his presence. There was nothing my mind could do about it. Thank God I didn't lose control of my bladder! I hadn't noticed that other people were similarly afflicted by their lovers. I must be a strange, weird woman. Nevertheless, my heart swelled at his words. Compliments from Michael were few on the ground.

'I'm so glad,' I replied simply, as I ran my hands through his thick, dark hair. Then I suppose he rolled and entered.

A determined stud, was Michael! Nothing put him off. And soon I was moaning like a deranged hyena. Hyena? Why are my similes so peculiar? Thoughts of Michael affect my brain as well as my thighs. I wanted so much to be inside his head. I was inadequate, inside my own.

Bangs and noise aroused me. Damn! I had missed the beginning of the News while I was away in my secret paradise.

Tanks and soldiers on the small screen. Another Israeli Palestinian confrontation! Perhaps this was the lead story. If there was a political happening, it hadn't yet been reported. I watched the screen assiduously for the next ten minutes, but there was nothing overtly political. No rumour of an impending Cabinet reshuffle, no disgraced Member shown, head down, scuttling down his garden path.

I was sitting on the floor. I stretched my legs before me but mastered my desire to roll around like a bitch on heat. Michael! Michael! Michael! What had happened in the Whips' office? Why don't you tell me something, anything, about your life?

His hand snaked down my body until it came to rest on the smooth protuberance of my belly. Stroking, stroking the curve, resting his little finger in my navel. I was emitting little groans, squirming with anticipation. I knew, even though my eyes were closed, that he was watching my face. He moved his hand, slowly, between my legs and began to work on the clitoris. I tossed my head from side to side on the black suede cushion.

There was a tap at the door. Fuck it! Who the hell was that? I had a mental picture of John Richardson, the podgy Chief Whip, standing on the landing with two uniformed officers beside him. Thank God I had put my clothes back on!

The tap came again, more insistently. 'Fran! Are you in?' It was a woman's voice: Emily, the violin-player from the front bay.

'Yes! Hold on a minute!' I deposited my greasy plate in the kitchen and opened the door.

The music students did tend to look like Little Orphan Annies. I had difficulty distinguishing between them. Emily was much addicted to grey, shapeless sweaters and tight, longish skirts. Occasionally the skirts were exchanged for battered jeans.

'Sorry! Are you eating?' She was a pale, rather timorous girl. Her thin hair was in need of a wash.

'No! Just finished.' I smiled at her, wondering if she was transformed with a violin in her hands.

'Smells good.'

'Come in.'

'I won't. Lots of practice to do.' She had something in her hand and held it out to me. 'I've got these two tickets for the Wigmore Hall tomorrow night. We get them every so often – complimentary, you know.' She trailed off.

'How nice!' Did she want me to go with her?

'I can't go because I've promised Mummy to go home this weekend.' She spoke quickly, as though she had rehearsed her lines before coming to my door. She held out the envelope in her hands. 'Can you use them?'

'Well ... um!'

'Doesn't matter if you can't! Give them to a friend, or drop them off at the box office. I haven't time to try anybody else.'

I took the envelope. 'Well, thanks! Thanks very much. I'll probably use them myself. It's ages since I went to a concert.'

She smiled with relief and was already moving towards the stairs. 'Wouldn't one of the boys like ...' I trailed off. No! I couldn't see either Jason or Archie at the Wigmore Hall.

I carried the envelope back into the living room and put it on the coffee table. The perpetual lump in my throat swelled to painful proportions.

Why, oh why, just once, couldn't I say to my lover, casually, offhand, 'Oh, I've been given two tickets for this recital. Would you like to go? Very up and coming young pianist, I believe. A rising star! Might be rather fun to be there, don't you think?'

He would call for me at my door with a taxi, and we would mingle in the foyer with all the established twosomes and then go to the bar at the interval for a glass of sparkling wine. Nothing ostentatious! Just an ordinary couple, enjoying an evening out! What had I done, that none of the sweets of romance were available for me? Was I so wicked? Was I being punished for the sins of my forefathers?

I picked up the tickets. No, it wasn't a young pianist who was performing on Friday night. It was a well-known quartet of elderly players.

I dropped the tickets with a sigh. I should be grateful that Emily had climbed the stairs to offer them to me. I couldn't decide now whether to use them or not. I might. I might not. I would think about it again tomorrow.

* * *

After Thursday afternoons my life stretched into a week of trivialities and meaningless time until it was Thursday afternoon again. Michael was by my side every moment of every day.

Weekends were torture. Then, I would imagine Michael at home with his family. Friday he would give over to constituency business - perhaps a visit to a school or an Old People's Home. The staff would fuss over him, giving him fresh baked cakes and coffee. He would be jolly and hearty with old ladies, quizzing and teasing them, meeting their uncomprehending stares with Nice to see you; treating you well, are they? He would chat sensibly and seriously with relatives who happened to be present, lapping up the applause and thanks he was accorded.

Did his wife accompany him on these little excursions? I could envisage her sitting at home, dressed in blonde wool and pearls, painting her nails as she gave orders to the gardener: My man, that border is full of weeds! I didn't even know if she were a working wife. I had pored over her photograph on

Michael's election leaflet, taking in every detail of the dark, thin-faced, handsome woman. No doubt she had money and family connections to recommend her. Michael wouldn't discuss his home life. Once I had made the mistake of enquiring about his children. He quickly shushed me. They are lovely kids. I don't want to talk about them now, he said. I did know they were attending some exclusive, private school. That's Labour Party double standards for you.

Michael had totally compartmentalized his life and he didn't want me sniffing around his private patch. If I pushed too hard at the gate, he would come out with both barrels blazing. I had no doubt of it and I couldn't take the risk.

But I still couldn't help my wretched inquisitiveness, my desire to understand, to know all there was to know. An intense, constant, painful pricking of my skin.

So I went about it in devious ways. He was, after all, a public figure, accountable to Parliament and his constituents. I wrote to Labour Party Headquarters, explaining I was thinking of moving into his constituency and enquiring who would be my parliamentary representative. I asked for a copy of his publicity material. The information arrived quickly and it was from this leaflet that I had my first view of his wife's photograph. I read the short resume of his career. Degree in politics and economics from a redbrick university. No surprise there. Worked in family law business. Why hadn't he joined the Tory Party? He thought there were more opportunities to rise in the Labour ranks, no doubt. Married Jane, etc. Two children, boy and girl, eight and ten years of age when I read the pamphlet. Couple of years older now. Leisure pursuits, cricket and archaeology.

I crushed the paper between my hands and went to throw up in the lavatory bowl. My chagrin and anguish were extreme, even by my standards. Who was he but an ordinary man with nothing extraordinary about him? But the extent of the sunny uplands of his life of which I had no knowledge appalled me. Cricket! He played cricket. And went on archaeological digs. Never a word had he spoken about these pleasant pursuits.

As I gasped and wiped my face with a towel, I admitted to myself that I didn't really like him. In fact, I rather disliked him. We had nothing in common: no shared history, no future plans, no mutual relatives, no children. But my passion and his lust had nothing to do with liking. It was sheer need, utter animal instinct to come together and fuck, and fuck, and fuck.

I felt besmirched by my behaviour, disgraced by my helplessness. As a rational, educated, professional woman, I should have more sense. But he was as necessary for my survival as food or drink, as the air I breathed. No other man would do. I put my head in my hands and tried to breathe slowly and deeply. I knew no one else could feel as I did, suffer like I did, or they couldn't go on living. How could two people live together and cope with all the demands of communal life if they inhabited the supercharged state in which I operated? Indeed, often they sought artificial aids for stimulation: drink, drugs, adultery. How I managed to survive, in a constant state of anticipation, apprehension, regret or sheer bloody misery, was a mystery to me.

My mind told me I was being incredibly foolish. Life was passing me by. But my brain suffered from white-out. I was as lost as if struggling through a blinding snow storm. Nothing in my life was relevant except my obsession with my love.

My weekends had become interminable because there was little political news. Westminster wound down. Certainly Michael wouldn't feature unless he did something drastic, like getting himself killed! Not for the first time I wondered if there were other mistresses, perhaps with irate husbands in tow. My breath came short and shallow. The world blackened around me for an instance. Jealousy was a powerful monster. I must extricate myself from its clasp. I came back to myself clutching hold of the back of a chair and staring at the reflection of my pale, agonized face in the mirror above the fireplace.

* * *

Friday passed in a dream. I stood apart and watched myself operating with the smooth efficiency of an automaton. But evening came. I left the office at 6 p.m. Most of the staff had packed up half an hour earlier. Friday night was an exception to the late hours' rule.

'We're meeting in the Rising Sun at seven. Do come, Fran!'

'Thanks. I'll think about it.' But they were youngsters from the ground floor and I didn't know them well. Margot had a family christening to attend and she had rushed off at four to Paddington Station, carrying her smart suit in a travel bag, and for once she had not admonished me on my lackadaisical attitude towards my social life. Pity! I could have impressed her with my ticket for the Wigmore Hall, but she was willing the dilatory printer to hurry up as she pulled a cover over her computer and rushed into her jacket.

'Don't worry about it,' I said. 'You go or you'll miss your train. I'll finish it for you.'

'You're a brick, Fran. The Underground might be dicey.'

She checked her handbag. 'Ticket? Yes. I bought it this morning.' She made for the door. 'Oh, I haven't ...'

I took her shoulders and steered her out. 'Go! Don't worry! I'll check over for you. Off you go! And have a good time.'

'Thanks! You're a brick,' she said again. She did use archaic expressions sometimes: jolly hockey sticks and Enid Blyton-isms. 'I'll do the same for you one day.'

'I'll make sure you do!' I laughed. 'Enjoy yourself.'

The click of her high heels sounded along the corridor; then receded down the stairs. She wasn't waiting for the lift.

Silence. The office seemed very empty without her. Sometimes I went in over the weekend when the building had sunk into an unnatural calm. The shrouded machines, deserted rooms and open spaces felt ghostly and threatening. A place for violence, sex and murder behind the photocopier! This weekend I wasn't planning such an incursion.

I finished my own report, saved it, stretched and decided to print it on Monday morning. For once, there was no urgency.

Monday would come eventually. I switched off Margot's printer, placed the sheets in a folder and then into her top drawer, which I locked before putting the keys into a flower pot on the filing cabinet. Our office was a mixture of old and new equipment, which seemed to suit us very well. Transition hadn't quite completed its process here.

I sauntered to the cloakroom to check my make-up before leaving. I don't know why I bothered. But it would take up a little time before I faced my lonely flat.

Doors were banging downstairs. Shouts of farewell and laughter floated up the stairs as workers left for the weekend. Two of their colleagues were in the cloakroom and again invited me to join them for an evening drink. I imagined their previous conversation. 'Shall we ask her? She seems quite nice. Why not?' 'She won't come. Bit standoffish. She probably has a live-in lover.' 'Well, let's see if we can find out. She might let her hair down with a drink inside her.'

But the invitation was probably spur of the moment. No thought or discussion. Why not? Join the party. The more the merrier! Just like those in the Soho bar the night the bomb went off. Death! Disablement! Shattered lives! Come with us, Fran. All welcome!

No, I wouldn't go. I wanted to think about Michael. I just wanted to go home and sit quietly by myself and think about Michael. If I went to the pub, I would be fielding questions or sitting solitary in the crowd, listening to their silly chatter.

'Well, that would have been nice,' I answered them now. 'But I'm going to a concert at the Wigmore Hall.'

One of the girls pulled a bit of a face. 'Classical, is that?' she asked and they both giggled.

'I was given the tickets,' I said. 'I may as well use them.'

* * *

Emily's two pink tickets lay on the coffee table where I had dropped them the previous evening. I picked them up. The concert began at seven thirty. I had really had no intention of going. But Wigmore Hall wasn't far from my flat. What the hell! Why not? The music would be calming. It was an excuse to be alone in the midst of a crowd. And I would be able to hand in the spare ticket at the box office.

I changed my dark trouser suit for a cream one with a terracotta silk shirt, banged my door behind me and went down the stairs. I met nobody in the hall, but Archie was meandering down the street with his arm around the shoulders of a girl I hadn't seen before.

'Hi!' I said as I passed them.

'Oh, Fran!' Archie managed to convey the impression that he was struggling to remember who I was. 'Going somewhere nice?' His eyes ranged over my dressed up attire.

'Mm!' I replied, in a non-committal way.

We walked on without pausing. He turned, squeezing the girl against his side. 'Enjoy yourself.'

CHAPTER THREE

The foyer at the Wigmore was crowded. Why had I imagined it would be half empty? I left the ticket at the box office and bought a programme from a young girl near the entrance to the concert hall. Not yet twenty past seven! How interminable these minutes seemed to one wandering around alone! Did I want a drink before the performance? Yes! But there would be no doubt a horrendous queue for the loo during the interval. I would wait until then for my drink. It would give me something to do with my hands and fill in the time.

I moved into the hall and found my seat. Not too bad. Four rows back. Of course they would want the front rows occupied. People were beginning to filter in and sit in splattered groups amongst the seats. Surprising, how many were alone! By accident or design? Probably some significant others had discovered urgent errands at the last minute. Wigmore concerts could be a bit heavy. Perhaps I should have gone to the pub with my office colleagues.

I opened the programme. Schubert and Beethoven. I read the notes from beginning to end. Wasn't it half past seven yet? I wondered if Archie and his girl friend were already in bed. And if I would have been happier at the Rising Sun, squeezed between breasts and bellies and sitting at a beer-slopped table, giggling with the juniors.

I glanced over my shoulder into the auditorium to check if all the seats were taken. I was conscious of the empty place beside me. People would think my date had failed to show up. I looked down at my programme again to ascertain the first item as a shuffling on the stage marked the arrival of the

Cecilia Trio. There was a commotion to my right as a late-comer excused himself past the occupied places, muttering and tripping over feet as he pushed his way to the seat beside me. He had an old-looking, young face and wore unfashionable spectacles with heavy frames. His haste seemed to have unravelled him – flapping scarf, loose anorak, grubby handkerchief hanging from his trouser pocket. He gave me a rabbit-like smile as he slid into his seat.

'Didn't think I'd make it,' he mouthed.

I looked at the stage where the musicians were settling and joined in the applause.

'Can I borrow your programme? Didn't have time ...'

I handed it over without looking at him. He held the programme before his eyes and pushed his glasses higher up his nose. He was obviously extremely short sighted. My heart heaved unreasonably at the indignity of having this youth sitting beside me. I hoped people wouldn't think we were together.

Michael! Michael! Michael! Where are you? What are you doing at this moment of time? You should be here with me, touching my hand, giving me a conspiratorial glance as the performance begins. Don't go much on this, but we are together. That is all that matters.

I tried to empty my mind and listen. Just listen to the music. Rippling. Intricate. Patterned. Returning. I closed my eyes. Michael and I were dancing, moving together in a large, secluded ballroom. The vision changed and we were white water rafting down a sheer drop until we floated on the quiet pool beneath.

My neighbour was tapping his finger against my programme. I held out my hand for it and turned slightly away from him. Why were other people such a damned nuisance? Good thing I hadn't paid for the ticket! I noticed his foot was flexing up and down. His mouth was taking on little grimaces as he appeared to have entered a state of trance. Trust me to have fetched up beside a bloody lunatic! I wondered if he were one of Emily's musical acquaintances.

The Schubert Piano Trio in E Flat Major came to a conclusion amid enthusiastic applause. The musicians left the stage. There was coughing and shuffling of feet. I looked at my watch. Just gone eight. The interval was timed for 8.40, after the Beethoven Archduke Trio. Then more Beethoven to complete the performance.

Specs, as I had christened him, fished deep into his anorak pocket. Why didn't he take it off? He must be hot, especially after his scramble to arrive on time. I would not have been surprised if he had produced a doorstop sandwich, but after much fidgeting around, he brought forth a half packet of Polo mints. With care, he extricated the upper mint; then, apparently as an after-thought, offered the truncated tube to me. I shook my head, as the musicians returned to the stage and re-tuned their instruments.

This time I had been brought sufficiently into the present by Specs' antics to observe their movements. He was still grimacing and tapping. Poor lad, I thought. He is going to have a rough ride through life. He has probably approached half a dozen girls for a date this evening and been turned down by all of them.

As the clapping prior to the interval died down, I made sure I was quickly out of the row in the opposite direction from my irritating neighbour. Thankful for the crowds of spectators, I moved deftly between them. If I wanted a drink before the bell, I would have to hurry or I would spend the whole of the twenty minutes at the bar. Everyone else had the same idea but, unhampered by a companion, I did well enough, pushing my way through the crowd to the counter. Not too many waiting yet. People milled behind me, their loud voices adding to the general hubbub.

Michael would have hated this scrum. He was more for using his money to buy convenience. See to it, my good fellow, he would instruct, before he went to stand in the doorway in the fresh air.

I began to study the programme again as I waited. This recital was high quality. I began to wonder why I had never patronised the Wigmore Hall on previous occasions. I had been to the South Bank and the Albert Hall a few times, but I decided I liked the intimate atmosphere of the Wigmore. Concert-goers around me were meeting up with friends, embracing, chatting animatedly. Why was I by myself? It wasn't fair! My throat lump became more pronounced and my eyes began to prick behind my lowered lids.

'Hi!' Specs materialized at my side. Hell's bells! He was panting noisily as he had been on his first arrival. Perhaps he was asthmatic. I smiled frostily and turned my back on him, brandishing a five pound note in the direction of the bartender. Damn and blast! His short-sighted eyes hadn't saved me from his attentions. Shouldn't have worn the cream suit. Vanity of vanities, sayeth the Preacher.

'Let me buy you a drink,' he said, beginning to fumble again in his deep pockets.

'No, thank you,' I said, trying to turn away from him and almost knocking a cup of coffee from the hands of an elderly woman beside me.

'I want to,' he said.

The man behind the bar had moved away during our little exchange. Now I desperately waved my note in his direction and he came over. 'Yes, madam?'

'Glass of red wine, please.'

Swiftly it was put before me.

'Four pounds, ninety five.'

Politeness was trying to insist that I offered a drink to Specs, who was still at my elbow. I ignored it.

'Of course,' he said, 'I don't drink myself. Don't go in for either drink or drugs.' He tittered in a stupid fashion.

'Good for you!' I tried to edge away from him amongst the convivial groups. He followed me. I found a space and stood, sipping the wine.

'Do you come here often?' he asked, unaware of the banality of the question.

'No!' I replied honestly. 'It's my first time. I was given a ticket.'

I gave up trying to move away from him. It was too exhausting to push through the crowded foyer. The interval was nearly over and he couldn't talk during the recital. It occurred to me that I could finish my drink and go home. Excuse myself by saying I was going to the Ladies. I could truthfully tell Emily I had used her ticket. In any event, I was sure that she wouldn't enquire.

'I come quite a lot,' said Specs, gazing intently into my face. He shuffled his feet and twitched his shoulders. Every ten seconds he hitched his glasses up his face. He was a restless young man. I gazed over his shoulder, not listening to what he was saying. However much I tried to back away from him, he always seemed a hair's breadth away.

'Perhaps we could come together.'

I stared at him, before registering what he had said.

'I'm sorry! I have a boyfriend. He couldn't make it this evening.' It sounded glib and untruthful, even to my ears.

At that moment, the warning bell sounded. I swallowed the remainder of my wine, replaced my glass on the counter and moved in the direction of the auditorium. He was still at my shoulder, bumbling away. People glanced at us. They would assume we were together. Look at that attractive girl and that odd-looking fellow! No accounting for taste! But it was noisy enough for me to ignore him as I made my way to my seat as speedily as possible.

The musicians were back. Was I pleased to see them! Sporadic applause died down as latecomers pushed into their rows. Then we were into the sublime experience of the Archduke Trio.

Specs was again away in a world of his own, his head bobbing with the rhythm. I would have to try and dodge him on the way out. If I went to the loo, he would no doubt wait outside. Perhaps there would be a convenient window I could climb through. The music flowed and swirled, melody pursuing and chasing itself.

I must get my life sorted out. Had I spoken aloud? I glanced round guiltily. Specs was still away in his own little world. If I had uttered the words, they had been covered by the crescendo of the strings. Nobody was staring at me. Specs had his eyes closed behind the thick lenses. Pity I wasn't at the end of the row. In the centre, I was helplessly trapped by dawdling crowds. Could I leave early on the pretext that I had come over faint? Too much commotion! And he would be sure to follow me out. That would be the worst possible scenario! And why should I miss any of this divine music for the sake of a silly boy?

'Would you like a coffee on the way home?' he was hissing in my ear, under cover of the applause.

'No, thank you.'

'Oh, come on! It's still early.'

'I have another appointment, thank you.'

Jesus! What was the matter with him? He must be at least ten years' younger than me. I dodged away from him as soon as the crowds began to move. He walked behind me.

'Or, if you would like to come back with me, I can make some coffee.'

'Good for you,' I said. 'But count me out.'

At last we were on the pavement. Should I wait for a bus, or walk? My state of mind made the decision for me. I set off down the road at a good pace, thankful for the crowds standing outside the hall, saying farewells and waiting for taxis. It made conversation difficult. Even if he followed me all the way home, the streets were well lit and he appeared weedy enough to pose no threat. But I didn't want him to know where I lived. I imagined him lingering outside my building, gazing up at the windows. Jason and Archie would find it hilarious. I turned to him.

'Look! Please don't follow me. I told you I have a boyfriend.'

He looked at me. 'You don't really, do you? Anyway,' he hitched his glasses again. 'You're not with him now. Why don't you come with me?'

My temper snapped. 'For Christ's sake, fuck off!' I screamed. Several passers-by stared at us and then quickly looked away. 'Stop bothering me, you stupid idiot, before I call the police.'

He backed off slightly, a hurt, bewildered expression spreading across his face. He appeared genuinely shocked by my words. People hurried by. We were now stationary on the pavement.

'There is no need to be like that,' he said, huffily. Then, to the passing pedestrians, 'I was only asking her to go for a drink.'

Nobody took any notice of him. Fortuitously, we had halted by a bus stop and a bus was approaching. I stuck my hand out. It stopped and I jumped on board. It would take me down the road.

'Don't give us much time, do you?' asked the driver, as I put some coins into his hand.

'Just two stops down,' I said.

Specs stood on the pavement as the bus pulled away. His scarf flapped in the light breeze. I sank into the front seat and was born away from him. I did not succumb to the temptation to wave. Gradually, the thumping of my heart slowed. I couldn't wait to get back to Nottingham Place and inside my flat. Home!

Contrary to my expectations of a relaxing lie-in, my eyes shot open at 7.40 on Saturday morning. I tossed and turned, pummelling the pillow, but the image of Specs, flapping and dishevelled, would not leave me. His bewildered expression as I leapt on to the 'bus stuck behind my eyelids and I had the guilty sensation I had done something wrong. Or, at least, unwise.

I got up and padded into the kitchen in my sloppy slippers, which I would have died rather than let Michael see. I put the kettle on. The weekend stretched before me, empty, meaningless. Thank God I had given Specs the slip. I felt outraged that I could not attend a concert in peace without being pestered by some uncouth youth. He had no way of tracing me, I concluded. Even if he waited for another 'bus of the same number, he would not know where I had alighted. And I would not be going to Wigmore Hall again. Definitely not alone on a Friday night.

Why was I so upset? He was just a pathetic, aggravating, lonely fellow creature. Sod him! My problem was I wanted to be with Michael and nobody else would do! I considered the difference in their situations, their stations in life. Michael was almost always surrounded by clever, attractive, admiring men and woman, even if they were constituents requiring attention, or business acquaintances requesting some favour. He was foreseen as able to manipulate, pull strings, make an impact on their lives. Whereas poor old Specs, no doubt, noticed people turning aside to avoid him. His company was an insult to my intelligence. He didn't even have a friend to go out with on a Friday night; whereas Michael had his loving, supportive family and at least one mistress on the side. Perhaps I was mistaken about Specs. Appearances were sometimes deceptive. He was only trying to be friendly. The poor bugger couldn't be expected to know my state of mind.

I sipped the scalding tea and contemplated my kitchen walls. The weekend with all its hours was mine to do with as I wished: shop, meet a friend, see a film, take in a gallery, read a book. London's possibilities were endless. Everything and nothing.

I opened my wallet to check how much money I had. I wasn't hard-up, but theatre tickets could be expensive if I decided on a show. A piece of paper fluttered to the floor. I picked it up. It was the advertisement I had clipped from Thursday's Times, requesting applications for the position of Assistant to a Member of Parliament. I considered it.

I had become an expert on political practice since my liaison with Michael. In the early days I devoured every political treatise I could get my hands on: Hansards, Statutory Instruments, Standing Orders, pink, white and green papers, anything which would help me to understand parliamentary activities. I became an avid watcher of news programmes – BBB1, ITV, News Night, Channel 4 News, 24 Hours, Question Time, News Night, to name the obvious. I read the Spectator, the New Statesman, Prospect, the Financial Times, any newspaper I could beg, borrow or steal. Anything that would help me comprehend Michael's preoccupations, his thinking, his way of life. He, of course, never read half of them. I read biographies of Tony Blair, Gordon Brown, Betty Boothroyd and Mo Mowlam. I assessed and analysed the problems in the Middle East and Africa and fell asleep over the arguments concerning the Euro.

I knew it was all a waste of time. Michael did not wish to discuss politics and would have been horrified at the state of my involvement. Besides, what the general public find fascinating is the tittle-tattle, the gossip, the scandal, the corruption, the sleazy deals, the rivalry between departments and individuals. The rest is the stuff of university theses. However, it now occurred to me that perhaps I had the qualifications required for the position of an M.P.s' assistant.

Before I dressed, not thinking too much, I switched on the computer and sent an e-mail to the number given on the advertisement. I gave bare information, just my name, address, age, academic qualifications and present employment. No doubt the Honourable Member, whoever he was, would be inundated with replies from nubile young women, gagging at the idea of working in close proximity to the centre of power. I would not, in all probability, receive an acknowledgement of my application.

Feeling somewhat wicked and recovered from the nasty taste left in my mouth from the encounter with Specs, I pulled on black, tailored trousers and a pink sweater and prepared to hit the town. By my kitchen clock, it was just two minutes past ten. So, a walk down Oxford Street as far as Marks and Spencer. There I would visit their Food Department and buy duck pate, crusty rolls and a mixed salad. I would follow that with a sortie into Liberty to look at the fabrics – their fabric hall is an Aladdin's Cave of Delights. Then perhaps Dickins and Jones to check the latest fashions. If I were tired by that time, I would have a light snack before spending the afternoon sauntering around the Royal Academy or the National Gallery, provided the queues weren't too long.

As I reached the bottom of the stairs, Mrs Margoloys was closing the back door. She had an empty plate in her hand.

'Just giving our feathered friends their breakfast,' she said. 'How nice you look, dear!'

'Thank you.' I nodded and smiled. I didn't want to stop. The fact that I had time to spare made my reluctance more insistent.

'Off somewhere nice?'

'Oh, just down to the shops, you know.' Politeness forced me to add, 'Can I bring you anything back?'

'Oh, no, dear! I wouldn't impose. I have plenty of time to do my own shopping.'

And not too much money to do it with, the thought popped into my head.

'Not like you young things,' she went on. 'Always rushing around with so much to do.'

'I suppose it does seem like that,' I said.

An unknown young man came out of the front flat. He was bare-chested, wearing scruffy jeans. He ignored us and went into the ground floor lavatory. Emily's flatmate was making the most of her absence.

'Hello, dear!' said Mrs Margoloys to his retreating back.

Good thing Mrs Margoloys takes everything in her stride, I thought. If she came across Michael, she would just say, hello, dear.

'Well, I'd better get on,' I said. 'I thought I may have a look at the Vermeer Exhibition later.'

'How nice!' said Mrs Margoloys. She obviously didn't know what I was talking about. Poor old soul! Why didn't I ask her to go with me? But I left her standing in the hall, and she turned back towards the half open door of her own room.

I was outside, down the steps into the cool morning air. I took deep breaths as I strode down the deserted street. People were not early risers in this area. I recalled how I had scurried back last evening and felt ashamed of my frustration over the antics of a harmless young man. I made my way towards Baker Street Underground. If I were planning to be on my feet for most of the day, I had better start off with a ride.

In spite of my renewed confidence, I still found myself peering around the corner down Marylebone Road before I walked towards the tube station. An old woman with a dog, an elderly man and a young girl were nearby, but no earnest, bespectacled youth was in sight. He was probably pestering somebody in Tufnell Park or Ponders End, or chatting up the landlady's daughter. Why had he decided to go to the concert at the last minute and called in at the box office on the off chance of a returned ticket? Was it his usual Friday night activity? Was he a music student, like Emily and her flatmate? In that case, why hadn't he been given a complimentary ticket? No! More likely he was a solitary menial worker of some kind, with no friends or colleagues for company. Just like me!

Busy with these thoughts, overlaid on the perpetual back-drop of Michael's beloved face beneath his thick, dark hair, I almost knocked into a stocky, florid man climbing the steps towards me.

'Watch it!' Then his face split into a grin and he put on a mock Australian accent. 'How ya doin'? Fair dinkum!' It was Sam, who rented the small back room in my building, which he seldom used.

'Hi, Sam!' I said, pleased to see him. He always seemed reassuringly normal, compared to the other occupants of 19A Nottingham Place. 'I didn't notice you.'

'Miles away,' he said. 'Must have been a good night.' He winked as he turned into Marylebone Road.

Not half as good as yours, I thought. He must be going home to collect clothes or belongings. He looked too cheerful for his girlfriend to have thrown him out. I wondered if she was married, with a long distance lorry driver husband and a love life as complicated as mine.

Other people's lives! Other people's problems! It was probably a perfectly straightforward relationship. My mind was becoming as sleazy as my behaviour.

Oh, to hell with everything! The sun was shining. Today, for once, I would try to relax and enjoy myself.

I seemed to bump into my flatmates all the time. How had Michael managed to come and go with impunity for more than two years? He must have seen some of them, sometimes. My fellow tenants were a surprisingly incurious lot. No doubt timing was all. Even taking into account erratic lifestyles, there wasn't much chance they would be lurking about in the hall in the middle of a weekday afternoon. With the exception of Mrs Margoloys, of course! And I suspected she had a little nap after lunch. Also, she did watch the afternoon television programmes.

Emily and flatmate, Vanessa, were at college; Sam would be working; there was no danger from Francesca as the other members of the household did not impinge on her consciousness. Archie and Jason were all over the place, but unlikely to be wandering around in the middle of the afternoon. They worked intermittently, were in rehearsal or fraternizing with friends from Finchley or Potters Bar.

I should have been consumed by anxiety, but I wasn't. My main concern was not the threat to Michael's prospects if he were noticed, but the certain knowledge that he would finish our affair if he were. He would lie and cheat to preserve his reputation and I would never betray him.

For my part, my life had become largely unreal. We were like divers, in deep water, swimming together in a dim, blurred seascape, far from the real world with its duties and obligations. Sharks snapped around us, but we were inviolate, weren't we? I moved in and out of this unnatural environment, occasionally to rejoin humanity, while the slurred edges of our couplings were a perpetual backdrop to my life. The fact that those around me had disjointed, surreal lives, seemed entirely appropriate. I lived for the moment, my upbringing and early life the prop on which I hung my behaviour. I wasn't manic or mad. In view of my chronic misery, I should have been.

I came up the stairs and around the corner into Oxford Street. A city smell of dust and diesel fumes smote my nostrils. Shoppers and sightseers milled about. Everything was messy and frenetic. People queued at the street stall near the station to buy oranges and bananas. Garbage had accumulated around the base as feet shod in sturdy white trainers tramped by. Red buses and black taxis crawled down the road, jerking and stopping as the masses poured across the street. The scene was as concentrated and agitated as a painting by Breugel.

There had been a time when you could walk the street's length in reasonable comfort. But no longer. I fell in behind a large, slow couple and was partly sheltered from the seething horde approaching from the opposite direction. They were clutching each other's hands and many plastic bags. They walked with splayed feet and wore identical denims and short, black leather jackets. I continued to follow them protected by their bulk, and watched four fat buttocks wobble and bounce before me, until they stopped at a fast food shop.

I passed them and dodged into Marks and Spencer. Classic suits and jackets in dark colours hung near the door, close to racks of summer dresses and sleeveless tees. It was betwixt and between time. Better, I thought. Those suits look really nice. They are beginning to get their act together at last, after all the problems of the lean years. But I didn't pause to look at the clothes, in spite of their pristine variety. I was here for the food.

As I rode the escalator to the basement, it occurred to me that I should be carrying my purchases all day and it would have been more sensible to do my shopping later. Should I just look around now, and then return after my tour of the Royal Academy? Or should I buy now and go back to the flat to drop off the bags? I did have a travel card so it would not cost any extra. Fuck it! Why hadn't I started in Knightsbridge, spent a couple of hours pottering around Harrods and Harvey Nichols and taken in Regent Street on the way back? Why hadn't I planned things properly before I set out? Typical of my disorganisation these days.

I paused at the bottom of the stairs, then wandered indecisively round the displays of sandwiches and fruit. People reached across me as I gazed unseeingly at convenience foods. My day was going to go badly, I knew it! You were never so inconclusive, prior Michael, I moaned to myself. I gave my head a shake. Don't be so fucking stupid! Buy while you are here. If the bags feel too heavy, take them back to the flat. It is only two stops up the line. The worst hazard is negotiating Oxford Street. Why the hell did you come here? Otherwise, take them with you. Less than what everyone else is carrying.

As I rounded the racks of bread and rolls, I saw him. There was no mistaking the slight stoop of his stocky frame and the heavy-rimmed spectacles that even now he was lifting his hand to push up his pale face. He was wearing the same fraying, dark blue anorak he had refused to shed the previous evening.

Bloody hell! I drew back behind the bread rolls, breathing deeply the fresh baked smell. What a rotten coincidence! The bloody man was haunting me! He had his head hanging over the yoghurt counter and was picking up cartons to peer at the labels. He was some way off. I had only seen him as a sudden gap opened between purchasers, only to quickly close again. Without making a conscious decision, I found myself on the staircase, mingling with the crowds climbing away from the basement towards the ground floor.

I put my head down and walked rapidly the length of the store to the outer door. Had he seen me? Was he even now charging through the throng behind me, and in another second would put a detaining hand on my arm? I was still taking deep breaths, trying to control my panic. It was unlikely he had noticed me. I doubted if he could see more than ten yards into the distance through those thick spectacles. He couldn't be chasing me. He had to stop at the till to pay for his yoghurt. But he hadn't been carrying a wire basket. He was probably just snooping about. Like me!

I turned right and made as much progress as I could towards Tottenham Court Road Underground. When I first came to London, my friends and I called it Totty Road, but given my present situation, I was rather more sensitive about the term.

Should I go and browse the bookshops on Charing Cross Road? Too risky! Too close to the sighting! I would imagine him behind every tier of shelves, lurking beside every Lonely Planet.

I turned into the station and inserted my ticket into the automatic entry machine. Rubbish blew around the open foyer.

Well, Harrods, here we come! The unexpected appearance of the obnoxious young man had clinched my mind. A saunter amongst the rich and famous was perhaps more my style. Ten thousand pounds for a dining room suite, five thousand for an evening dress would keep my mind off the sordid realities of existence. I might even buy a packet of crunchy ginger biscuits if I felt in an expansive mood. And I wouldn't be carrying an M. and S. bag and enduring the snooty stares of ignorant dowagers. Specs had inadvertently done me a favour.

Six hours later, I was back in my flat. The joy of having a base! I had seen the homeless in shop doorways on the Strand and could think of nothing worse than not having a door to shut to keep the world at bay. Michael would have shrunk to a gleam in my eye, unless we had been prepared to lie amongst the rotting litter on some derelict wasteland site. The incongruity of the thought made me snigger. Specs would be lying in his black bag beside us, debating the efficacy of the wind-shielding properties of the Times and Daily Mirror. How easy to slip into a lifestyle so very difficult to ameliorate. No home, no job, no money; no kitchen, no bathroom, no bed.

I kicked my shoes off and found my execrable slippers. If I had a little dog to chew them, he would be in heaven. I noticed dust under the settee. Had Michael seen it when we were lying on the floor? I must have a session with the Hoover before next Thursday.

I plugged in the kettle. A cup of tea first, before I sorted out my food. After the debacle of Specs in M. and S., I had succumbed to temptation and purchased fresh pate, mature cheese and crusty bread from Harrods Food Hall, as well as biscuits and a packet of dark, minty chocolates. I bought apples and a couple of bananas from a fruit stall. (Make sure you wash them, insisted my mother's insistent voice inside my head).

I had walked amongst Harrods' intricate displays until I was ready to drop, before stopping for a coffee and sandwich and making my way to Piccadilly. I ignored the queue for the Vermeer Exhibition. Instead I took a ticket for the display of photographs of the First World War. Not a cheerful choice, but I was disinclined to spend time waiting in the other queue.

I dawdled round the walls and centre stands, marvelling at the bravery of the infantry as they charged towards enemy guns. All the horrors of trench warfare were depicted: mud, and blood, and guts, but, most poignant of all, were the fresh, youthful faces as they smiled into the camera before leaving for the Front. The pity of it all! But you know that, don't you?

At four o'clock, I decided to call it a day and go home. Disappointingly, there were no e-mails or messages on my answer 'phone. Well, what did I expect? Michael certainly wouldn't call on a Saturday. I registered the familiar shaft of pain as I unpacked my green Harrods bag. He was playing tennis with his son, wasn't he? Or Monopoly with his daughter. Or was he fucking his wife? I sighed. More likely he had retired to his study to write a piece for the local Press. The sad face of Specs appeared in my mind's eye. I wondered what he had done with his day. Perhaps he was still peering at the yoghurt labels.

The kettle came to the boil with a hiss and a scream. At the same time the telephone shrilled. Now who the hell was that? I didn't want to be disturbed.

'Hello!' Silence from the other end.

'Hello!' Nothing. 'Hello!' My voice had risen with irritation. As if I hadn't enough to cope with without unknown ringers playing silly buggers on other people's telephones! I remembered the time I had rung Michael's home for the chance of hearing his wife's voice. It was low, husky and pleasant. I put the receiver down without speaking.

I replaced the mouthpiece. Was someone checking the occupancy of the flats? Or was a child playing with the dial? Perhaps it was just another of the innumerable, unsolicited calls that plague our lives with requests for money.

I set the kitchen table with a single place and switched on my small, portable television. The early evening news should be coming up any time now. As I ran water over the green salad, the football results were unravelling. I drained the salad and arranged it in a glass bowl and put it in the centre of the table. I turned the pate into a dish, sniffing its rich odour with appreciation. I added condiments and found a bottle of French dressing in the 'fridge. Then I opened a bottle of red wine and poured myself a generous glassful.

I had bought an Evening Standard on the way home. Now I collected it from the hall table and turned the pages to check the television timings. A small item at the bottom of an inside page caught my eye: Tricksters are bluffing their way into houses and flats in Central London. Householders are asked to be on their guard against bogus callers. So, what's new? At least, I am protected by two heavy doors and a number of hefty young men, not to mention Francesca's clients. I believe she entertains them in multiples at the weekend.

I was still scanning trivialities when the television News began. I squeezed into the chair beside the kitchen table and sipped my wine as I watched the screen. It reported the usual litany of death and disaster. Nine American soldiers killed in the Eastern mountains of Afghanistan; a suicide bomber in Israel; people in an overturned coach in Germany killed and injured. I was beginning to yawn and lose interest when an item of political news, rare on a Saturday, appeared on the set. Was it a follow-up to an earlier piece?

The Chief Whip had announced his resignation. He was shown in the garden of his desirable house in Surrey, saying he was leaving the Government to 'spend more time with his family.' I barely had time to register his words before the Sports News began to roll. I gawped at the screen, still seeing the unfamiliar features of the Rt.Hon. David Parry. Chief Whips were largely unknown to the general public. Reporters had shouted for more information, but the ex Government Member merely smiled, thanked them, went inside his house and closed his substantial front door.

So, what the hell was going on? Was some scandal about to break? Michael had an appointment in the Whips' Office on Thursday afternoon. So he said. I had suspected he might have been making an excuse to leave me early. And now, this resignation out of the blue. Had Michael been offered a Government job? Had he been promoted? Not to the position of Chief Whip, certainly. That would go to an experienced minister. But there would be a vacancy. Was he a Whip by now?

There were no more details. A cheerful chappie was announcing gales and rain approaching the North West, while it would remain dry and sunny in the South. I used the remote control and switched off.

My mind skittered over possibilities, considered what possible effects this information could have on Michael and me. If he had been promoted to the Government, would it change our position? The Whips' Office! The irony of the situation did not escape me. The watchdog of the Commons! The department that had the task of ensuring M.Ps. toed the line, voted with their Party and watched their behaviour. The function of the Whips was to keep noses to the grindstone and peccadilloes out of the Press. What price John Major and Edwina Currie?

What a strange way to announce a reshuffle! Well, it wasn't, of course. Just a resignation, in the middle of Saturday afternoon when Members were away at their constituencies. The reporters must have been summoned to the country. Selected ones, of course. Too few were present for the news to have been anticipated. There could have been an earlier news flash, whilst I was looking at war photographs in the Royal Academy.

The telephone rang again. I jumped convulsively. Michael! Or the other silent idiot? Had Michael managed to slip away from his ravening family to ring me, for once?

'Hello!' My voice came high and strangulated.

'Fran? You sound odd! Are you okay?' It was Jason's modulated tones.

'Jason! Yes, I'm all right.'

'Did I call at a bad time? Are you decent? Sorry!' He chuckled.

'Don't be stupid! I was just watching the News.'

'Try to avoid it myself. It is all so terrible.' He gave a theatrical sigh. 'Anyway, why I was ringing, darling, was to ask, if you are free tonight, whether you would like to come down for an hour or two and share a bottle. At a bit of a loose end tonight.'

'Oh!' Did I want to go down? 'Is Archie out?'

'Yeah! Found himself this new girl he's rather smitten with. And everyone else is tied up.'

'Oh!' I said again. I obviously wasn't his first choice. But tonight I had to think. Was I looking at the end of my relationship? I felt too agitated for bonhomie with Jason.

'Well, thanks, Jason. That's a nice thought.' I considered inventing an appointment to get him off my back. He would be insistent if he suspected I was moping alone upstairs. 'I'll see. I've been on my feet all day and feel a bit tired.'

'No problem! I feel bushed, myself.'

I couldn't be bothered to argue. 'Well, I'll come down for half an hour a bit later on. But I warn you, I'll be rotten company.'

'Me too, darling. We'll be rotten company together.'

I put the 'phone down. I hadn't the least intention of spending the evening with Jason. I would tell him I had fallen asleep. Anyway, he was quite capable of standing me up if one of his own acquaintances arrived. I would tell him something unexpected had come up. It certainly had on the television news. I would let him know when I had concocted a suitable story. I don't think any of us in that building expected absolute honesty from each other.

I refilled my wine glass. I had no idea what fate was going to throw at me next. My life was becoming too complicated for me to manage.

I awoke with a start. The wine had done its work and knocked me out for a couple of hours. It was twenty three minutes to eight by the kitchen clock. The green salad was drooping in its bowl and the pate had developed a shiny patina. A good thing I didn't cut the bread.

I was stiff and headachy. I moved into the sitting room and flopped on to the sofa. I closed my eyes. God! I felt awful.

Was Michael having dinner? En famille? Or was there a constituency function? If I were his secretary I would know what he was doing every minute of the day. No wonder M.Ps. had affairs with their secretaries! They had nothing to hide. I remembered my response to the job application. Would anything come of it? Was I mad to think it might?

I ached for some confidence. Why couldn't Michael tell me about his activities – his meals with financiers, bankers, insurers, businessmen, the Mayor and Corporation who no longer existed. Why didn't he complain about X bending his ear over the National Health Service or Y bothering him about planning permission. I would like to know what their discussions revealed, what jokes they told; I would like to be privy to all the machinations of his existence. All the dark corners of his public life. I would like to give him constant help, succour and advice. Let's face it, I would like to be inside his head with him, as he was inside mine.

If I went to work at the House of Commons, that sort of thing would be the substance of my daily life. I would feed on rumour and innuendo, I would feast on gossip and scandal. Nod, nod, wink, wink in the corridors and bars. How unbelievably exciting!

Give us this day our daily bread! Was his wife a good cook? Or had the au pair prepared supper? Did they have an au pair? Or a woman who came in twice a week to take care of the cleaning and the chores? I had no idea of his domestic arrangements. Perhaps they were having a Chinese takeaway and the children were stuffing sweet and sour down their pretty little throats before returning to their rooms and their video games. Was he an indulgent father? No doubt he was. Those most irascible in their daily lives were soft to the point of imbecility with their own children. Spoilt rotten, most of them, poor little sods! So much pressure on them, with their privileged backgrounds. No wonder they grew up to be drunkards and druggies.

You're getting very bitter in your old age, Miss Bonnington. Leave the children of the great and the good out of the equation. They should do well enough. They have money and influence on their side.

There was a soft tap on my door.

Bugger! I'd forgotten Jason and his invitation.

'Go away, Jason,' I called feebly. 'I've got a bad headache and I'm in bed.'

No answer! I would have expected, 'No problem, darlin'. I'll join you.'

The knock was repeated, more insistently. What the hell was the matter with him? Had he got wax in his ears? Couldn't I be left in peace in my own private domain?

I went to the door and jerked it back. My mouth was open to inform Jason in decisive tones to get lost. The words died on my lips.

Specs, still wearing his ratty anorak, which he had now crowned with a round, woolly hat, stood on the tiny landing outside my door. His hand was doubled into a fist shoulder high, as he prepared to knock for a third time.

I was extremely angry. Furious, in fact. I was gasping with rage and something approaching panic. For a moment I couldn't speak. He also stood silently, his eyes behind the thick spectacles boring into mine.

I found my voice and became voluble. 'What the hell are you doing here? Have you been following me? How the hell did you find me?'

Was Jason still in the basement? Would he hear my cries if Specs threatened to attack me? He ran his tongue over his lips, shifting his weight from one foot to the other. He still didn't speak.

'What the hell do you think you are doing, following me around? Who let you in? How the fuck did you find me? Don't you understand plain English when I tell you to piss off?'

My voice had risen with hysteria. I became aware that a stocky, middle-aged man of Middle Eastern appearance, wearing a brown overcoat with an astrakhan collar, was ascending the lower flight of stairs and was staring upwards in our direction. Shades of the Maltese Falcon! Francesca's door opened to admit him. I heard, 'Who's that fishwife up...?' before the door closed, cutting off his sentence.

I took a deep breath and swallowed. My voice was now a hiss, lower in volume, but with more venom in it than I would have believed possible of my mild tempered self.

'Get out! Just bugger off and leave me alone.'

He stood his ground. Men who looked like him had to be obstinate. His expression became aggrieved.

'There is no need to be nasty,' he said. 'I thought, seeing we are both alone, we could spend ..'

I came out of my doorway and gave him a shove towards the stairs.

'Piss off, or I'll call the police.'

He shrugged away from me. 'All right! All right!' He pushed his glasses higher up his nose and took three steps down the stairs. Then he stopped and turned back towards me. 'You haven't got a boyfriend,' he accused. 'If you have, why were you by yourself last night?'

Fleetingly, I wondered if he made a habit of lurking near box offices waiting for a lone female to return a ticket, before approaching the window and requesting that ticket for himself.

I retreated to my hall to watch him leave. Now I was at a higher level than him, I felt more confident. I ignored his question and gestured with my hand as though sweeping him away. 'Bugger off! And don't come back.'

Fear swept over me that he would stalk the building and be forever outside on the pavement, gazing at the windows and observing the movements of the tenants. He would be always hovering around the corner, ready to pop up at my shoulder as I made my way to work.

I realised I could have been alone in the building. I was profoundly grateful for Francesca's visitor. Would be have tried to force his way in, if that man hadn't appeared on the stairs? I was glad about Jason's 'phone call, and even about Mrs Margoloys' presence downstairs. How had he got inside? Had Jason left the building and he had slipped in while the door was open? The boys were careless about security. But even Jason could not have mistaken Specs for one of Francesca's clients.

He had now reached the lower landing and hesitated outside Francesca's door. For a crazy moment I thought he was about to knock on it and announce he had come to join the party. I leaned over the banister and flapped my hands in his direction. 'Go on! Get going!'

He continued down the stairs. I must watch him leave the premises. Nothing in the hall to steal except an umbrella stand full of old walking sticks. But since he had ostensibly called to see me, it was my responsibility to make sure he left. I crept down the stairs to the lower landing, from where I could see the front door. He was now in the hall. Again he turned, looking at me with a hurt, whipped dog expression. I repeated my flapping gesture, feeling foolish and compromised. He opened his mouth, as though he had another reason or excuse for his behaviour. He thought better of it and shambled to the outer door. It banged behind him.

I stood trembling outside Francesca's flat and listened to the agitated bumping of my heart. That was just what I needed, wasn't it? A callow youth adding complication to my life! I ought to go down and make sure he was not waiting outside the front door, ready to slide in again at the first opportunity.

I stood there for perhaps five minutes. I felt frozen, unable to climb the few stairs back to my own rooms. I could hear muted conversation from behind Francesca's door. No doubt drinks were being taken. Francesca would be an attentive hostess. What deduction would her guest have made regarding the sordid scene at the top of the stairs?

All was quiet! Shaking still, I stumbled back up the steps to my apartment. I closed my door and leaned against it. I couldn't stop my quivering. My haven had lost its tranquillity. Specs' appearance at my door had besmirched its neutrality evermore.

I grabbed a bottle of Beaujolais from the wine rack, found my keys and went out on to the landing. I made sure I double-locked the door. If Specs managed to get in again, I would clout him on the head with the bottle.

The hall was empty and silent. Pray God Jason hadn't gone out! I descended the steps to the basement and knocked on his door.

'Jason, it's me! I changed my mind. Can I come in?'

I heard voices. Damn! Jason had a visitor.

After a moment, the door opened. Jason flung his arms around me. Inside, Archie and the unknown girl were sitting wound against each other in the only armchair.

'Another bottle! You're an angel.'

I sat down and prepared to be gregarious. I had intended telling Jason about my unwelcome caller. However, perhaps it would not be wise to do so. After my reception of him, Specs would be unlikely to return. The only person who had seen him was Francesca's guest, who surely would not talk about his Saturday night entertainment at Nottingham Place.

I am ashamed to say we had an orgy. Or, rather I should admit I was not ashamed at all. Anyway, it is a fact. It happened. After Specs, I felt light-headed. I considered I deserved it.

So what? We were four young, healthy adults and three of that number were extremely attractive individuals. The girl's breasts were amazing. Perhaps she'd had a boob job. Mine paled beside them, but at least they were upstanding rather than soft and droopy.

You've never experienced an orgy? You should! It's fun. Especially with enough alcohol inside you to make you insouciant. We rolled together on the floor. Jason was kissing my mouth while Archie and his girl friend attended to the nether regions. I was aware my clitoris was being licked with an insistent tongue while a little finger was inserted up my ass. I clutched Jason and responded to sensation. Pictures of temple carvings at Khahajuro passed before my eyes, a multiplicity of erotic sculptures twisted intricately together, their plump arms, legs and apertures everlastingly conjoined. A stone testament to love in all its carnal intensity.

At one point I became aware that Jason and Archie were donning condoms and in my woozy state was touched by their display of public-spiritedness. Michael never wore a condom. Typical of his arrogance that he expected me to do all the spade work.

We seemed to have swapped partners. Archie folded me beneath him, while Jason paid attention to the girl's stupendous breasts. I was laughing, laughing uncontrollably. Shush! Shush! urged Archie who was approaching his climax. In my mind's eye, I saw Michael and Specs, both staring disapprovingly above us. I don't think that's very nice, said Specs. I couldn't decide whether Michael would say, Really, Frances! I didn't expect this of you, before he threw off his clothes and joined us.

It occurred to me that it was fortunate we were in the basement, or someone's ceiling would be witness to extraordinary goings-on. If we were performing in my flat, Francesca and client would be in no doubt about the cavorting over their heads. But here, there was sweat and stink and joyousness. The boys may not be overly successful in their working lives but, brother, could they fuck!

After a time, we were all in a heap in the middle of the floor. Jason had his arm resting lightly on my right breast. Archie had pillowed his head in the girl's crotch. It occurred to me that her body was now more familiar than her face. If I met her in the street tomorrow, I probably would not recognize her.

The perpetual soreness between my throat and gut had eased. But as we rested, panting, still twined together, it was back. Michael's pain. It took more than an orgy to remove it. But this was my secret from him. I would never, ever, admit to what had taken place in the basement flat tonight.

After a time, I gathered my clothes, wrapped them around me as well as I could, and sped up the lower steps, away from the inert bodies in the centre of the floor. I peered round the corner from the basement stairs to make sure the hall was empty, before making a dash across it. If I met Mrs Margoloys, she would probably say, Hello, dear! Had a nice time? I had to chance Francesca's gentleman caller, but it was unlikely he would be leaving yet. It was barely eleven o'clock and after what he must be paying for sex, he would doubtless expect his money's worth.

Clasping my shirt around my waist, and with my trousers round my neck, I tiptoed past her door, trying to contain my hysteria at the thought of Francesca's scandalized face if she should emerge on the arm of her wealthy client.

God! What a day!

I reached my flat and securely locked my door. I dropped my clothes in a heap on the bathroom floor, donned a white towelling robe and turned on the bath taps. I added a liberal dose of perfumed essence to the steaming water, before I wandered into the kitchen to prepare strong coffee. I needed it. But I felt invigorated, defiant. My life had been too drab and unadventurous for too long. No wonder Specs had latched on to me. He obviously thought he had found a fellow creature. The incongruity of the men in my life caused me to snigger again. Each of them would be horrified if they knew of the existence of the others.

I took my coffee with me and soaked in the bath for a long time, before jerking myself back into consciousness just as I was slipping into oblivion. I quickly patted myself dry, put on a clean nightdress and fell into bed. I slept dreamlessly for ten hours, and awoke with no hangover to a bright, Spring-like London morning.

After my long sleep, I had an easy day. Just after noon I put on jeans, black sweater and dark glasses and went to Baker Street Underground to buy a selection of newspapers. Instead of going straight home, I took a walk through Queen Mary's Rose Garden in Regent's Park to refresh my lungs and mind. Early roses nodded in tidy beds, families were strolling, while children chased balls and the smell of freshly cut grass hung in the air. Home again, I settled down for a lazy Sunday. I had found enough stimulation already to satisfy me for the remainder of the weekend.

I rustled through the newspapers and turned to the article about the resignation of the Chief Whip. I skipped over his previous career. He had been a junior minister before he was pumped up to that powerful, although largely anonymous, position. There was much speculation concerning the reason for his decision. Nobody believed the old chestnut about his wishing to spend more time with his family. Was he suffering from ill health? Was some scandal about to break? No firm information was forthcoming at present.

I sighed and turned the page. The departure of the Chief Whip was a story of little interest to the vast majority of readers. My own concern would have been minimal, apart from Michael's input and his recent appointment in the Whip's Office. How had he been affected? There was no announcement of the Chief Whip's successor. The news must have taken the Prime Minister by surprise, in spite of the tight rein held by the Spin Doctors in Downing Street. The P.M. was at Chequers, and all I gathered from the early evening news was that an announcement was intended on Monday afternoon.

It seemed to me that they had been caught unawares by the resignation. Was there some crumbling skeleton in the cupboard of which Number Ten were not aware? Had Alastair Campbell lost his grip for once? No doubt consultations and reproaches would follow. The office of Chief Whip involved a lot of work without credit or publicity. A poisoned chalice! Right for somebody of a Machiavellian turn of mind! No doubt some Members would relish the entry into Bluebeard's Castle. I shook my head to clear it. My metaphors were becoming lurid. Could it be that Michael had been asked to take over as Chief Whip? No! He hadn't enough experience.

I felt exhausted, even though I had only been awake for five hours. I lay on the sofa and watched Talk of the Town. I determined to ignore the 'phone or knocks on my door. Michael certainly would not ring on a Sunday, and I wasn't answerable to anyone else. So when the telephone trilled in the middle of the afternoon I stayed where I was for long moments, before losing my resolve and tottering to the hall just as the ringing stopped. No message was left. It may have been my mother, my sister in America or an urgent query from the office. I couldn't be bothered. I worked hard enough all week, for

God's sake! Why should I be available on a Sunday afternoon? If it were so important, the unknown caller would try
again.

However, all was quiet for the rest of the day: no noise from
downstairs. I felt resentful. Somebody could have checked to
see if I was okay. Perhaps Jason was meeting his boys.

Well into twilight, I switched on the lamps and drew the
curtains. I poached a couple of eggs and made some toast –
my first food of the day. After eating, I goggled senselessly at
the television screen for a couple of hours, before I roused
myself. I sorted out clothes and belongings for next day and
fell into bed.

Roll on Monday morning! Some time tomorrow, I would
find out what had happened in the Whips' Office. Until then,
patience was required. My last thought before I fell asleep
was how slowly and yet how quickly the weekend had passed.

CHAPTER FOUR

A young policeman stood on the landing. For a mad moment I thought Michael had sent
Someone to lock me up so I would not be an embarrassment to him.

'Could I have a word, Madam?'

I became aware of unfamiliar voices in the hall. The light air current told me the front door was open.

'What's going on?' This was the last thing I needed in my agitated state.

'Can I come in?'

I held the door open for him. At any rate, it didn't mean anything had happened to Michael. In that eventuality, I would be the last person to be informed.

I pointed the young man to my sitting room and he indicated that I should sit down. I was glad to sink into the old sofa. My legs felt rubbery, unequal to holding my weight.

'What is it?' My mother, my sister? My voice sounded high and panicky. Get on with it, for Christ's sake!

'The old lady downstairs,' the young policeman said. 'Did you know her?'

'Mrs Margoloys?' I drew a deep breath, and became conscious that the pounding of my heart had slowed. If this was about Mrs Margoloys, it wasn't anything to do with Michael or me personally. She must have been taken ill. For the first time that day I remembered our odd conversation and her worry about a strange man in the house.

'Mrs Margoloys!' I repeated. 'Yes, I know her.' I was speaking slowly, trying to collect my thoughts. 'Not well! Just Good Morning and a few words as I came and went.'

I began to feel guilty. I should have shown more concern about her anxieties. Heaven knows she was no trouble, most of the time.

'My flat is self-contained.' I went on. 'On the ground floor they share facilities.'

The policeman looked around and nodded. Why didn't he tell me what had happened? Had the poor old woman had a heart attack and been rushed to hospital? Was he making enquiries about family and friends? She had never mentioned any family to me, which now struck me as odd. Family were most old people's oxygen, even if that family lived at the other side of the world.

But I had never really registered her as a separate entity. I was agitated and irritated by her wanderings in case she saw Michael in the course of his incursions to the top floor. Francesca's clients had been in some way a cover, although their timing was different. Even so, I wouldn't have wished the old lady to lie unconscious all day before she was found.

The officer was still silent.

'What's the matter?' I asked. 'Has something happened to her?'

'I am afraid so!' Now he was speaking briskly. 'She has been found in her room. She had been hit on the head a number of times.'

'Oh, no! Is she badly hurt?'

'I'm afraid she is dead.' He said this in an expressionless, laconic tone, but he looked at me closely as he said it.

'Oh, My God! How awful!' My hand flew to my mouth and I swallowed sour-tasting bile back down my throat.

The officer went out of the room to the kitchen, filled a glass with water and brought it to me. I gulped it down, spilling driblets on my shirt as I did so.

'God! How awful!' I repeated. 'She's dead?'

Had she fallen and banged her head? Why did they think she had been attacked?

'Oh, yes! Very dead.' He took the glass from my nerveless fingers and put it on the table. 'So, if you feel up to it, I will have to ask you a few questions.'

'Yes! Yes, of course!' I realised he was still standing and indicated the armchair opposite. 'Won't you sit down?'

My brain was whirling, tangled images tumbling through it like clothes in a washing machine. My first thought was Michael. Would he have to be dragged in to the enquiries? They would want to know about visitors to the house. Just as he had become a Whip! How devastating for him! He would be furious. My second concern was myself. In burgeoning panic, I looked into the icy void of the end of our relationship.

I dropped my head into my hands. What a hellish thing to happen! I didn't realise I had spoken aloud until the officer answered me. And was he regarding me curiously? Did he think I had anything to do with it?

'You understand we need statements from all the residents here?' I nodded. 'At present you seem to be the only one home. Apart from ...'. He paused. What did he mean? And who had found the old lady?

Where the hell was Francesca? She was usually in at this time. And both Jason and Archie must be missing.

I tried to pull myself together. 'What do you want to know?'

'If you could just run through who lives here for me.'

'Yes! Well!' I took a deep breath. Stay calm! Perhaps I could get away with it for now without mentioning Michael. The young officer may already be suspicious that my shock was excessive. Thank God people tended to be histrionic these days.

'Starting at the bottom, two young men live in the basement, aspiring actors.'

A fleeting expression of amusement passed over the officer's fresh features as he noted their names in his notebook.

'So, are they in or out, most of the time?'

'Both, really.' It sounded shifty. I realised that, in spite of their seeming artlessness, I knew little about their lives. It seemed to be an unwritten agreement that we didn't ask each other personal questions. But I had no wish to compromise either Jason or Archie. I liked them a lot. 'They come and go. Rehearsals, performances, odd jobs, you know.' (I had a mental picture of Jason, encased in a sandwich board, walking down Oxford Street. I had quickly ducked into a shop doorway, so as not to embarrass him.)

'Are they the only occupants on that floor?'

I nodded. Surely nobody in the house had battered Mrs M.! It must have been a casual intruder she had disturbed. She did open the back door to feed the birds. But the yard was enclosed. Access was only possible by climbing a high wall.

'Okay! What about the ground floor?'

'Mrs Margoloys is at the back.' I swallowed. Was, my mind mocked. But I couldn't say it. 'The front bay is used by two music students.'

'Girls or boys? Or one of each?'

'Girls. They are often away at their college.'

He was writing as I spoke. 'All right. Who else? There appear to be a number of doors.'

Another thought hit me. Had it happened after I returned home? My fists clenched and my knuckles whitened.

'Just Sammy.' Surprising how calm and reasonable I sounded! 'He has the small room opposite Mrs Margoloys. But he's not here very often. I think he stays with his girlfriend.'

'You don't know his surname?'

I shook my head.

'This is just preliminary, you understand. So we can get some sort of general picture. We will be talking to all these people just as soon as we can track them down.' He looked at his notes. 'Do you happen to know the girlfriend's address?'

'Sorry! No! Somewhere in Tufnell Park, I think. But I'm not sure about that.' I shivered and made a conscious effort to still the shaking of my limbs. He had not yet asked one question about my own movements. Was he softening me up? Was it calculated policy to make me drop my guard?

'The flat on the floor below. Must be a big one, that?'

'Francesca! Yes, I think it is. But I haven't been inside.'

'And does Francesca,' slight pause, 'work?'

I wondered if she was on police records. Was she supposed to have a licence? It was my turn to pause. I didn't want to drop Francesca, or indeed any of my fellow residents, in the shit. But I had to cover my own back, if I could do so.

'I think she has some gentlemen callers.' It sounded ludicrous, even to my ears.

The officer looked up, and again that fleeting, amused expression crossed his face. He raised his eyebrows. 'Lady of the night,' he stated. I knew he was taking the piss and my cheeks reddened.

'I really don't know much about her,' I replied stiffly.

'Or any of them?' suggested the officer. 'It's what we usually find in these multiple occupancy buildings.' He turned over the page in his notebook and looked at me. 'But at least you know their names and something of their activities.' He shifted to a more comfortable position in his chair.

'Now, let's talk about you. Professional lady?'

I told him my name and place of work.

'Professional lady,' he said again, obviously taken with the phrase. 'And you've been at your office all day?'

'Yes,' I said. No, I hadn't. I had been in Chelsea all afternoon, and in the Houses of Parliament early this morning. Michael's furious face was distracting me, together with a disturbing image of Mrs Margoloys, lying in a pool of dark, congealing blood. Her mouth was gaping in the rictus of death and her terrified, open eyes were staring fixedly at her comfortless little room.

It was no good. I had to throw up. I excused myself and rushed to the bathroom. For the first time since his appearance outside my door, I had a couple of minutes to myself to decide what I was going to say to the man. Unless he asked specifically about my visitors for the past months, I would endeavour to keep Michael's name out of it. It was a vain hope, I knew. How the tabloids would love it! Member of Parliament, newly appointed Whip, frequent caller at the house of murder. The Whip's job was certain to be a casualty, even if he managed to salvage his parliamentary career and his marriage. But if I could at least warn him before the shit hit the pan, he would have a little time to prepare a story.

I remembered Specs. For the first time, I felt grateful for his persistence. At least he would be a diversion.

I splashed water on my face and dabbed it dry. My throat felt raw. Should I suggest a cup of tea? But that would prolong the interview.

I returned to the sitting room and sat opposite the officer. He resumed without enquiring about my state of health. I told him about my morning's interview. That was a secret I couldn't hope to keep.

'You are thinking of a change?'

'Not really!' He looked up but said nothing. 'I just saw the advertisement and thought it might be interesting to find out what was on offer.'

'And was it interesting?'

'No, not really! I don't think it is for me.'

'Probably a wise choice.' He tapped his fingers on his notebook, closed it, leaned back in his chair and looked at me. 'Tell me about your friends who come here to see you,' he said. 'Good-looking, professional lady like yourself must never be short of companionship.'

Was he buttering me up, trying to get me off guard? Suddenly, I was sick of it. He seemed to have been with me for hours. I wanted him out of my flat, wanted to consider my dilemma with regard to Michael. Above all, I wanted a cigarette and a stiff drink.

I began to tell him about Specs. 'I had a bit of an unfortunate encounter on Friday evening,' I said. If I got Specs harassed by Mr. Plod, so be it. Serve him right! He shouldn't have stalked me back to my flat. I told the officer, as dispassionately as I could – I didn't want him to think I was an hysterical woman – the sequence of events during and after the concert at the Wigmore Hall. 'I don't know how he got in,' I said. 'I imagine he could have slipped inside when someone went out.'

I told him about my last conversation with Mrs Margoloys. 'Funny!' I said. 'She was usually so good-humoured and tolerant of everyone. She spent a lot of time wandering about the hall waiting for someone to talk to. Of course, those rooms on the ground floor are not self-contained. There is a shared bathroom and loo between Mrs Margoloys and the music students.'

The young policeman appeared animated by my revelation about Specs. He left shortly afterwards to confer with the other officers. Mustn't let the trail go cold, he may have been thinking. He had apparently forgotten to pursue his line of enquiry about my other visitors. However, I had no doubt he would be back.

After his departure, I peered over the banisters to observe the activities in the hall. Officers in yellow, fluorescent jackets were carrying out various packages wrapped in black dustbin liners. As I moved down to the first floor landing for a better view, one of the officers looked up and saw me. 'Would you mind going back to your room,' he ordered. 'I must ask you not to walk about the stairs and passages more than necessary. Someone will be up to fingerprint you shortly. And to dust the staircase for prints. Keep your door closed.'

Feeling like a reprimanded child, I retreated. From the kitchen window I could see three police cars parked outside the premises. Then a Press vehicle arrived. How the hell did they find out about it so quickly?

I recalled that I had not asked the officer who had found the old lady, or at what time. Had there been an anonymous 'phone call from the perpetrator, anxious she was more injured than intended? Unlikely!

I tried to remember if there had been anything strange or different about the hall when I arrived home. I had been too busy endeavouring to sneak in quietly, so that Mrs Margoloys didn't buttonhole me before I could reach my flat. Even then, the poor old soul must have been dead and beginning to stiffen. Perhaps the murderer was lurking in the downstairs lavatory, washing the gore from his hands. If I had encountered him in the hall, he would probably have battered my brains in as well. How ironic that the one day I hadn't worked late, all this mayhem was awaiting me!

My stomach felt hollow. I made a sandwich with brown bread and honey and forced a few mouthfuls down while I sat in front of the television, changing from one news channel to another. Was it important enough to make the national news? A quick flash came up on News 24. Just the bare bones of the matter. Old woman found beaten to death in her own home in West London. Then the next item came on immediately. Obviously not much was known yet.

Should I ring Michael? Was my telephone tapped? Had they been in my flat before my return? No! How could they? Where the hell was everybody else? I needed to talk to someone. Normally, at this time, somebody would be in, somewhere. Or was it just that it seemed that way, since Mrs Margoloys was ever present?

I went again to my kitchen window. By craning my neck, I could just see a police officer at the bottom of the steps by the front door. A blue and white tape stretched around our entrance, halfway across the street. As I watched, Archie and his girlfriend came loitering down the road. They saw the activity around our house and paused, before coming on again. The girlfriend seemed reluctant and pulled back on Archie's hand, arguing with him. He put his arm round her shoulders and urged her on. If anyone were watching them, her behaviour would suggest a guilty conscience. But not for the crime just committed! More like an unease at the presence of police officers.

God! Did we all have our unsavoury secrets? What is she into, drugs or possession?

I returned to the television and my stale sandwich. I picked it up and put it down again.

I ought to ring Michael. Someone, somewhere, must know of his clandestine assignations at 19A. It would all come out and he should be warned. The Press probably had a file on him and were saving it up for an appropriate time when they wished on one more occasion to discredit the Government.

I had never, ever, rung Michael at the House of Commons. I knew constituents did so all the time, as he frequently complained.

I picked up the telephone. For the second time in four days, I rang the number that reverberated in my head like a familiar refrain. Even if I had to endure a diatribe, I would have done my best for him. A man's voice answered. Not Michael! Were there men on the switchboard, then? 'I'll try him for you.'

The 'phone rang and rang. I imagined the sound echoing around an empty room. Computer covered, desk devoid of papers, light wood furnishings, tasteful green and white patterned curtains. The anonymous voice came back. 'He's not in his office. Could be anywhere at this time of day. Would you like me to page him for you?'

'No! Don't bother. I'll try again later.'

I certainly wouldn't have him called to the telephone in the bar or dining room: Perhaps from some jokey conversation with his colleagues, only to receive my shattering announcement down the line. Would he turn pale as plaster? Would his companions enquire if he had received bad news? More likely he would return to them not having turned a hair, but excuse himself very quickly to go away privately and rant and rave. Or would he ring me up for the first time ever? Would he plead with me to keep his name out of it, not caring that he was asking me to pervert the course of justice, to save his own skin at the expense of mine?

My telephone rang. I jumped so much the contents of my coffee mug splashed scalding on my hand. Trembling, I picked up the receiver.

'Hi!' said Archie. 'What a turn-up! Do you want to talk about it?'

'It's terrible! Awful!' I said. My heartbeat stopped its imitation of the Haydn Drum Symphony. 'Come up, if you like, Archie. Are you by yourself?'

'Yeah! Chloe wanted to go home. I put her in a taxi.'

'Are the police still in the hall?'

'I don't think so. Just one outside the front door.'

There was a slight pause. Then he said, 'Okay! I'll be up in a minute.'

Five minutes later he rat-tatted at my door and I heard his cheerful voice outside. I had already decided to say nothing to him about Michael. The one most likely to have seen him was Mrs Margoloys. And she wasn't going to do any talking. If anybody else had noticed him on the stairs or in the hall, they would no doubt tell the police and I would have to account to them. In the meantime, I would keep my mouth shut and thank God for Francesca's callers.

At least I could tell Archie about my last conversation with Mrs Margoloys. I opened the door to let him in. Archie's expression was uncharacteristically serious, but his eyes were sparkling. This was all a great adventure for him, I realised. He came into the kitchen with me while I made more coffee and told him about Mrs Margoloys' worries.

'Well, that's amazing! Almost as if she had a premonition! She never seemed to have a frightened bone in her body. A real doughty old woman! What do you make of it?'

'I don't know.' I knew how I felt. Choked! I poured boiling water over instant coffee, added milk and put the sugar basin on the tray. Archie carried it into the sitting room.

'Francesca?' he asked.

'I don't know,' I said again. 'Could have been one of her clients, I suppose.'

'She's not in,' said Archie. 'The police said there were only the two of us in the house.'

'She must be playing away from home this evening,' I said. 'Lucky for her!' I shuddered. 'God! What an appalling thing to happen!'

'Mmm!'

We both sat silent, busy with our own thoughts.

'Where's Jason?' I asked, eventually.

'Oh, didn't he tell you? He's got an evening job at a theatre bar. He won't be back for hours yet.'

I leaned my head against the sofa and closed my eyes.

'The Fuzz must think we are a difficult lot to pit down,' said Archie. 'Peripatetic! You are the only one with a regular job and an exemplary life-style.'

'I wouldn't say that,' I said, not knowing whether to feel annoyed or amused. 'That crazy stalker followed me from the concert.'

'Well, that wasn't your fault. Did you tell the police?'

'The young officer who came up just now? Yes.'

'Did he come back again today?'

'Specs? I don't know. Why should he? I was at work.'

It crossed my mind that Mrs Margoloys could have been alive when I returned.

I wouldn't have heard any struggle from my top floor flat. She was probably hit from behind, anyway. And she was too frail to struggle.

'Did they tell you who found her?'

'They said they had a 'phone call. A tip-off.'

'Bloody hell! Somebody bashed her head in and then rang the police, in panic she might die?'

'Seems that way. They thought it could be a hoax. But they checked in case it wasn't. No time to trace the call, except that it was from somewhere in this area. Telephone box down the road, I expect, or at the Tube. Daren't risk the mobile.'

The corners of my mouth turned down. I wasn't going to cry. No way! I closed my eyes and breathed deeply.

I heard Archie jump to his feet. 'What you need,' he said, 'is a stiff drink. Nasty shock for us. We all liked the old dear. Have you got anything in? We drank all the Whisky you brought down.'

I opened my eyes. Would the police come back again tonight if drink loosened my tongue? 'In the cupboard in the kitchen. Opposite the door.'

Archie disappeared; then came back with two glasses containing generous measures of Glenfiddich.

'In a good cause,' he said as he put one into my hand. 'Would you like me to stay with you tonight?'

I took the glass and poured some of its contents down my throat. I even managed a smile. 'No, Archie! No need for that. What would your girlfriend say?'

'Does it matter? I wouldn't tell her, anyway,' he said guilelessly. 'I know class when I see it.'

'No thanks, Archie! This will probably knock me out and I shall sleep until eight in the morning.' I yawned ostentatiously. I did indeed feel exhausted. It seemed a century since my interview that morning.

'Crippling, isn't it? All the bad news. Well, here's to Mrs M.'. He raised his glass. 'May she be as happy as shit, wherever she is.'

I raised my glass in parody of his. 'To Mrs Margoloys,' I said simply.

He left shortly afterwards. But his presence had been a comfort. I prepared for bed, brushing my teeth and getting undressed. Then I stood in front of the television with my hairbrush in my hand. I switched on the remote control. I was desperate for, and terrified in case there was, more information about the crime in our building: the crime committed beneath my feet.

But there was only the same short snippet as before. Either they genuinely had no more news or, at police behest, were keeping it low profile.

Should I try again to contact Michael? Did he know what had happened by now?

I climbed into bed and switched off the bedside lamp. I hugged the sheets under my chin. In the fractured darkness, lights from vehicles outside played across the ceiling. I closed my eyes. Tomorrow was another day!

We became high profile. Next morning the Press arrived in posses. I was surrounded immediately I stepped away from the sanctuary of the blue and white tape. Flash bulbs popped in my face as a microphone was thrust within an inch of my nose. I put my head down and attempted to ram raid my way through the pack of milling reporters.

I became aware of Press and television vans parked as far as Marylebone Road. Little groups of residents from the other houses had emerged hobbit-like from their dwellings, and now stood together complaining about the infiltration and speculating about its cause.

I tried to keep cool. I tried to merge with them. In my mind's eye I saw Michael's horrified face, watching my progress on his television screen as he knotted his tie.

'I'm so sorry,' I said to no one in particular as I forced my way through the throng. 'I have to go to work. I am rather late now.'

I was obviously the first resident to leave the building, and the Press were not going to let me go quietly. Questions were being bellowed in my ear: Who found the body? Did you know the old lady? Stabbing, was it? Two policemen looked on with amusement. They had no intention of coming to my rescue.

I resisted the temptation to kick out or flail around with my shoulder bag. I barged through the blockage; then strode down the street with as much dignity as I could muster. I was pursued all the way down to the main road, but as I turned out of Nottingham Place towards the Underground, they dropped back, perhaps fearful of missing the next unfortunate occupant to emerge from 19A.

They will be a lucky, I thought, with grim satisfaction. I don't think Sammy is around. If he watches the News, he will no doubt keep away for the time being. There is not much chance of Jason or Archie or the music students leaving before lunchtime, and Francesca won't go out at all.

However, Jason or Archie may put in an appearance for performance sake. A bit of free publicity for them: too good an opportunity to miss, in case Mr. Important Director is looking for a lead in his next production.

I sighed as I paused at the crossing. Red buses, black taxis and a gamut of variegated vehicles bucked slowly by, only to queue interminably when they reached the traffic lights. I could do without this sideshow, what with all the other complications in my life. At least Specs wasn't the only one staring at the building now. I wondered if he knew what had happened. Or would he come blundering into the middle of it? Not if he was in any way involved! Was he involved? Mrs Margoloys had been all right until he showed up. Poor Mrs Margoloys! I shivered. Had I been the inadvertent catalyst of her death?

'Are you okay?' Margot's first words as I entered the office. 'Caught a glimpse of you as I was swallowing my shredded wheat. It looked horrendous.'

'Yes! Thanks! Just about. You saw me on the News?'

'Mm! What a terrible thing to happen!'

Margot turned back to her screen. She wanted to know all about it but didn't like to probe and upset me. 'Nasty business,' she went on as her fingers travelled the keyboard. 'Be careful! Watch yourself in that house.'

'It's unbelievable!' I said, as I hung up my jacket. 'It has always been so sedate there.' I removed my computer cover. 'If it weren't for Jason and Archie, it would be silent as the grave.'

Margot looked up, gave a faint smile and made no comment on my Freudian slip. 'Would you like some coffee?'

I had slumped in my chair, but now jumped up. I was exhausted and adrenalin pumped-up at the same time. 'I'll make it.' I seized the kettle and moved to the tiny kitchen at the end of our corridor. I remembered Miss Bellamy proudly telling me that they had the use of a kitchen in the House of Lords. Two of the downstairs staff were in animated conversation on the corridor, but they barely registered my presence. Obviously they hadn't watched the News.

I pushed the kettle under the tap and momentarily closed my eyes. I was agitated and bewildered. How was I going to work all day with any degree of competence? The situation would have been bad enough without the Michael involvement. One thing was certain: I couldn't plead a migraine and go home since the Press pack was in attendance. I thought of my mother's tranquil existence on the Norfolk coast. I used to imagine I would go mad up there for longer than a week. Now it seemed a most desirable haven.

I longed for Michael's arms, if not his reassurance. Could I keep him out of this? Could I keep him, after this? I knew the answer was no, on both counts. The police would demand lists of all our visitors. Francesca and I were in the shit. Her wealthy businessmen wouldn't welcome the spotlight either.

And if I didn't mention Michael, our liaison would be disclosed by some enterprising hack. Michael must have dropped hints about my existence. He couldn't help self-aggrandizement. Or somebody had noticed his surreptitious visits to my area every Thursday afternoon. There were spies everywhere. Some little old woman across the road probably timed her tea and biscuits on his appearance. I knew if I admitted the relationship to the police, it would become public knowledge. But that would be better than it coming out in dribs and drabs, with queues forming to buy the Daily Mail every morning of the week.

God, what a mess! What a mess! I splashed cold water on my face and dabbed it away with a paper towel. I looked pasty and mottled. I felt decidedly sick. The ground seemed to be shifting around my feet. What was I to do? What had I done?

I turned off the tap. The kettle was too full and I poured half its contents down the sink. I had done nothing to hurt anybody, apart from Michael's family. And he had taken exaggerated pains at my expense to make sure they didn't suffer. I couldn't have been the first, or the only one. Maybe there were others now. I had only done what every other married woman in the country was doing all the time.

My gut wrenched. I put my hand on my stomach and stumbled into the nearest cubicle. How could I continue to endure such trauma?

After what seemed an age, but in reality was probably no more than five minutes, I pulled myself under control, picked up the kettle and returned to the office.

'All right?' asked Margot. She was obviously concerned on my behalf, but didn't want it to look as though she were fussing round me. After a first glance, she tactfully kept her eyes on her work. 'Horrible shock for you,' she said.

'Sure! I'm fine.' I busied myself with mugs and coffee jar.

'Thought you'd been buttonholed by somebody with a macabre taste in entertainment. Some nosey bugger,' she added.

'No! Nobody was there.'

I sat down at my desk and tried to work on the party in Chelsea. Normal people with normal lives! Letters and figures danced before my eyes. Every time the telephone rang I jumped uncontrollably, expecting the police summoning me back to Nottingham Place. Or Michael!

To my relief, Margot had an appointment in the middle of the morning, so I had the office to myself after ten thirty. Careless of callers, I put my head on my desk. It was aching in a dull, pounding fashion. I had to get myself together. The police would want to interview me again.

I let the 'phone ring several times before I picked it up to silence its stridency. An unfamiliar voice sounded in my ear. Michael's wife?

'I am the bearer of good tidings,' it announced.

'I'm sorry! Who is this?'

'Miss Bellamy! I have spoken to Mr. Jones and he is happy with your curriculum vitae and my report. Very happy, in fact!'

Her last words activated my sluggish brain. The woman in charge of the battery hens!

'He would like you to start as soon as possible, of course.' A faint sound of rustling paper travelled down the wires. 'I don't think I asked you how much notice you are required to give. I don't suppose you could manage next week? Mr. Jones is very anxious to have it settled.'

Over the telephone, her voice was higher than I remembered. A little strangulated. Cultured vowels. But the interview now seemed totally irrelevant in the light of what had happened since then. I pondered whether to turn her down outright, or to give myself more time to consider my position by pleading other interviews. But I was tired of it. I wondered if she had seen me on the news bulletins and had a morbid interest in finding out more about the murder at 19A Nottingham Place.

'Hello! Are you there?' From her end, she must be registering my marked lack of enthusiasm.

'Yes, Miss Bellamy! You have come back sooner than I expected.' My professionalism had kicked in and my voice was calm and unfazed. 'I am so sorry, but I have decided the situation isn't really for me.' Let's finish it. Get it off my back.

'Oh!' she flustered. 'Oh dear!' Then, rather more annoyed, 'I thought you were a serious candidate.' She would have to explain to an irate M.P. that I had chickened out. Should I repeat my apology? I kept quiet. The least said by me, the better!

'Oh dear!' she repeated. 'Mr. Jones won't be pleased. He was looking forward to working with you. He had you picked out. He doesn't like his time to be wasted.' I hadn't noticed it was his time that was being wasted.

'I am sorry,' I said again. I didn't add that if the salary were higher it might attract more suitable candidates. 'I thought I was a little over-qualified.' That wasn't necessary, I chided myself. I heard her swift intake of breath. 'Thank you for letting me know.' I replaced the receiver.

I straightened my back. The call had cheered me up. Life was full of opportunities, after all. Full of the likes of Miss Bellamy spending their days massaging the egos of self-important bosses. The fact that my university degree and work experience enabled me to escape the fate of the cubicle women was a source of satisfaction.

I clicked on the mouse and found I could now concentrate on my work. When Margot put her head in the door some time after one, I was well into it.

'Thought you might go straight to lunch,' I said, momentarily pausing in my rapid flight across the keyboard. I smiled at her. 'How did it go?'

'You look better.' She came inside. 'It went well. I just popped in to see how you were. I was worried about you this morning. You looked real ropey.'

'Well, thanks for those few kind words,' I laughed. 'I'm fine now, really. It was a nasty shock. I was fond of Mrs Margoloys,' I lied. 'Then the Press outside! It got to me.'

'Poor old soul! Terrible for you.' She slipped papers into her top drawer, her mind already turning to other matters. She looked up and repeated, 'Well, you certainly look better now. Nothing like a change of environment, even if it's here.' She turned back to the door. 'I'll get off. Looking for a christening present, of all things.' She gave a little grimace. 'You look well into it. Do you want me to bring you a sandwich back?'

'No, thanks! I'm going out myself in a minute.'

'Good idea! Get some fresh air into your lungs.'

'What, round here?' I laughed again.

After she had gone, I stretched extravagantly before rising from my chair. I had told Margot I was going out so she didn't return with a stack of food for me. But now I thought I would walk the streets. It was unlikely that anybody would recognize me. I could have a look into Selfridges and shelter amongst the racks of anonymous clothing. I might even buy something. For once, I would take my lunch hour.

* * *

Two policemen were on duty when I returned to Nottingham Place. Most of the Press had departed in pursuit of other prey. What was this, after all, but another unfortunate pensioner, fatally mugged for the sake of a few pounds?

One of the young bobbies checked my name on his list, then held up the tape so I could pass through to my front door. Feeling like a pariah, despite the absence of spectators, I found my bunch of keys and unlocked the door. Inside the hall, I paused, uncertain and uneasy.

'Hello!' I called, the first time I had done such a thing. 'Is anybody in?'

No response! The silence seemed to reverberate back towards me as I stood alone on the tiled floor and looked up the stairwell. The pulsing brass movement from the Rite of Spring drove relentlessly through my head. Either the house was empty or the inhabitants did not wish to declare themselves. I remained a moment longer, trying to analyse my anxiety. The two policemen were, after all, only half a dozen steps away on the other side of the outer door. But there was something that was not right, something missing. What was it?

It was Mrs Margoloys, pottering around, shuffling from her room, saying in her friendly manner, 'Hello, dear! Had a nice day?'

I ran up the stairs, my keys jangling in my hand, until I reached my own flat. Panting, I fumbled with the lock; then I was inside and had slammed the door behind me. I leaned against it and watched my chest rising and falling with the beating of my heart.

At that moment, I wished I had taken Margot up on her half-hearted offer, 'Come home with me if you like. But I do have to go out. I am meeting somebody.' Then she added, it seemed to me grudgingly, 'I suppose I could put it off.' It would obviously be inconvenient for her to have an unexpected guest. I could imagine my own reaction if things had happened the other way round on one of Michael's days.

'No Margot! Certainly not!' I had raised my hands in mock horror, and added, daringly, 'Never let it be said that I interfered with your love life.'

She raised her eyebrows but said nothing. The trouble with Margot was that she kept her emotions so well concealed I never knew what she was thinking.

I became serious. 'No, thanks! Honestly! It is kind of you. But, no thanks! If I don't show up this evening, they might think I have something to hide.' And I might miss a message on my machine!

'Unlikely, I should imagine.'

'I have to go back some time, so it may as well be sooner, rather than later. Really, I am not in any danger. She looked at me in an appraising way, but made no comment. 'The long arm of the law is still outside, I expect. Especially as they want to interview all the people who live in the building.'

'Well, if you are sure.' She did her best to keep the relief out of her voice. Why should she take me in? She wasn't a particular friend of mine; I had no particular friends. 'See how it goes. If it's too gruesome or scary, come tomorrow night. Bring some things with you in the morning, so you are prepared for a stop-over.'

Impulsively, I gave her a hug. 'You're very good.'

I had another reason for not going with Margot this evening. The Police had said they would speak to me again, and I had no wish to divulge my guilty secret in Margot's presence. I was in more control in my private domain in my own flat.

So, here I was, in a silent, empty house where a grisly murder had taken place not much more than twenty four hours ago. Who had made that telephone call to the police? What was I to say about Michael?

I checked my answer 'phone. Nothing! I made a cup of tea with the last tea bag. I put it on the draining board to save for next time. I ought to go to the supermarket and buy some food. I looked in the 'fridge. Very little! Forcing myself to think positively, I sat down at the kitchen table and made a shopping list.

Bread, low fat margarine, some form of convenience meal, chicken or fish, something that would cook in twenty minutes without any input from me. I sat back, nibbling my thumb-nail. What else? Tea bags, of course. That was the reason for going in the first place. Milk. I had half a pint left, but might have to water the Police Force when it decided to swing into action. It was a wonder they weren't already knocking at the door. No doubt a speedy message had been passed on regarding my return. Perhaps they were waiting for some of the others to come back so they could kill more than one bird with one stone. God! How many wise saws contained the idea of death and dying? (And why was I so robotic, predictable and cliché-ridden? So bloody boring! Was it on account of the programmed, educational input force-fed to us at schools and universities? Or was it the inevitable result of my regimented love life?)

Well, in that case, they may have to wait some time. Jason and Archie were a law unto themselves, and no doubt they had been performing for the Media all morning. I regretted my refusal to look at the television at lunchtime. I had passed a number of screens in shop windows as I traversed Oxford Street but had been disinclined to linger with the other time-wasters.

I pulled on a sweater and picked up the list. I would buy something extra, some little treat to make up for my having such a rotten life. Perhaps inspiration would come once I was amongst the shelves.

I had never before noticed the gloomy aspect of the staircase. It had only a couple of small windows and a dim central light. Weren't staircases supposed to be well lighted in boarding houses? The carpet was sludge-coloured and could do with a good clean. I wondered if Michael had remarked its condition on his weekly ascents. I wondered if Mrs Margoloys had been gazing up at it as she was struck down from behind. Why did I think it was from behind? She could have seen her assailant. She could have known him! And all the poor old lady had wanted had been a bit of companionship: just a vicarious slice of our frenzied, useless existences.

I banged the front door behind me. Anything to defeat the silence of the deserted house!

'I'm just going to buy some food,' I informed the young policeman who again courteously held up the blue and white tape. He nodded. 'Can I bring you anything back?'

'No thanks, Miss! We are due to be relieved soon, so we can go to the canteen.'

'Right, then! I won't be long.'

I started down the street, then turned to him again, as though on an afterthought. 'Has anyone else come in?'

'Not so far as I am aware, Miss. Could have, before I arrived.'

'I see! Okay! Thanks!'

'Can I ask where you are going, Miss?'

'To Sainsbury's. It is only just round the corner, off Baker Street.'

The supermarket was crowded with after-work shoppers. I meandered round the aisles for what seemed an age, trying to decide what I wanted to eat and locating the items I needed with difficulty. They seemed to have done yet another relocation of essential foodstuffs: keep the staff busy, if not happy.

The convenience foods were no problem to track down. Long racks of brightly coloured wrappers shrieked for attention. But I walked up and down for some time before I found milk, margarine and bread. I picked up a packet of cereal

I didn't need and put it in my basket. I stopped in front of the rows of alcoholic drinks for several minutes, ostensibly reading the labels on the wines and taking in nothing of what I read. Should I bother?

I was about to take my purchases to the check-out when I felt a gentle tap on my shoulder. I spun round sharply and came within inches of the apologetic, wistful face of Specs. He was wearing the same old, navy blue anorak and looked as unkempt as when he had floundered into the seat next to mine at Wigmore Hall.

I drew in a deep breath. 'Well!' I said.

'Isn't it funny how we keep bumping into each other?' he said.

I strode away from him towards the cash desk. He tripped along beside me, trying to keep up amidst the dislocation of other shoppers and their trolleys.

'Have you heard about what happened in my house?' I spoke curtly over my shoulder as I joined the shortest queue.

'No!' he said. He appeared to have lost his perky exuberance. He's lying, I thought. But if he had anything to do with it, he has a nerve, approaching me again.

'The old lady downstairs was murdered.' I said this as though I were telling him that frozen peas were 99 pence a bag.

'No!' he gasped.

The man in front of me, who was stacking food on the conveyor belt, momentarily raised his eyes to look at us, before continuing with his task. Specs stood by my side, his face partially obscured by his hood. This struck me as suspicious.

'Why do you wear your hood up in here?' I asked. 'Aren't you hot?' I noticed he was not carrying a basket. 'Haven't you bought anything?'

'Not yet,' he muttered. He pulled his hood back. His face had turned a greenish grey. 'What happened?' He appeared scarcely able to speak. If this were an act, it was a good one. However, I was too preoccupied with my own predicament to concern myself with Specs' state of mine. The man in front moved up and I began stacking my goods ready for check out.

'If I were you,' I told Specs, as my hands busily placed the packages, 'I would go to the police and let them know you were in the building. It will look better than them finding out later.'

I was now beyond the till. I ripped a plastic bag from its container and started to pack my cartons and bottles into it. Specs followed me along the counter, his eyes popping behind the thick spectacles.

'Why should I do that?' he asked.

I shrugged. Should I warn him I had mentioned him to the Police? He may have an unpredictable temper and start thumping me around the head right there by the cash register. 'It's up to you! Suit yourself!'

I filled two bags, handed over my credit card and waited to sign the slip.

'There are two policemen outside the door,' I said. 'Of course, they want to know who has been in and out of the building.'

He pushed past me and almost ran to the exit. I caught a last glimpse of him scurrying down the steps of Baker Street Underground Station as I turned the corner into Marylebone Road. I smiled grimly. He obviously didn't relish the thought of the Law.

Two different officers were now on duty at 19A. I was checked on their list and allowed through the tape. I felt more sanguine. The encounter with Specs had cheered me up.

Inside my flat, I switched on the oven and unpacked the plastic bags. I was hungry and thirsty.

'Damn it to buggery! I had forgotten the tea bags.

* * *

I had the convenience meal in the oven before I looked at the answer 'phone. The little red light was blinking. Drawing a deep breath, I pressed the recall button. The caller didn't identify himself. He didn't need to! I would have known those thrilling resonances if he had been on the moon rather than two miles away, across the darkening city.

'I want to see you!' How often had I imagined those magical words during the past couple of years, ached for them with anguished intensity? 'Come to the Embankment and wait by Cleopatra's Needle. I will be down some time after the ten o'clock vote.' The machine clicked. The message ended.

Blood pounded through my veins. From the dim depths of the hall mirror, glittering eyes in a flushed countenance stared into mine. At last! For two years I had been waiting for this. The summons! Meet me! Come to me, my darling!

I closed my eyes. Suppose I hadn't checked my messages! I could have been out. Only heard the blessed command at midnight! What a bloody nerve to commandeer my presence in that peremptory manner! I wouldn't go. No, do you mind, if it is convenient, please or thank you. How fucking rude for a charming man! I wouldn't go!

I looked at my watch. Ten past eight. I would see him in just over two hours. Not a word about how I was! Not a thought for my well-being! Or my feelings following the murder in our building. Did he know? Of course he knew! And what did I expect? The next time he showed any consideration for me would be the first. I wouldn't go! And if he questioned me afterwards, I would tell him I hadn't seen his message until it was too late.

Not least in my determination was the thought of passing the police again. Another officer, perhaps, but what explanation could I give for leaving the house at that hour. Ten o'clock would be about right. The counting and telling of the vote in the Commons would take some time and Michael then had to walk from the Chamber to the assignation place. I shivered at the word. It wouldn't do to loll about on the Embankment for too long. It wasn't far from the druggies and dropouts dossed down under the bridge near Charing Cross.

But the homeless would not have the strength to mug anybody, even if they demanded money with menaces.

I chewed my fingers distractedly. My flat suddenly seemed warm and cosy. Ten o'clock wasn't so late. Many people left home for an evening's entertainment after that hour. They visited cinemas, restaurants, night clubs. This was Central London, for God's sake, not far from the entertainment grounds of Leicester Square and Piccadilly.

But would it be politic for me to leave the flat, conspicuously alone, when my every move was being watched and recorded? Would the officer on duty nod in jealous approval? An attractive girl about town, he would imagine. Now, where is she off to? Obviously a goer! Make a note to ask her tomorrow about her movements tonight. Still, I wasn't going, was I?

The oven timer pinged, making me jump. I had been standing and staring at the telephone for twenty minutes. I took the meal from the cooker and turned the runny, yellow mass on to a plate, found a fork in the cutlery drawer and sat down at the kitchen table.

It tasted better than it looked and my plate was almost empty before I well realised I had begun the meal. It smelled strongly of cheese and garlic. Should I have eaten it if I were meeting Michael? Not to worry! He won't come within a mile of you in public! In public! God, this would be the first time I had been outside with him, if he turned up!

If he turned up! My stomach contracted and I concentrated on trying not to vomit. What a bastard! I wouldn't go! I staggered to the sink and pushed the dirty plate under running water. What a fucking bastard! I rubbed the back of my hand across my clammy forehead. I won't go!

I bowed my head and gave way to the inevitable. Grow up, Bonnington! Of course you will go! And you will stand and wait there all night, until they find you in the dawn light slumped lifeless at the foot of Cleopatra's Needle by the side of the ever-flowing river.

At nine o'clock I went into the bedroom and changed my business suit for dark trousers and a grey polo-neck that I seldom wore. With my black leather jacket, I would shade admirably into the background. I was wearing the uniform of most of the crooks around.

I stared at my pale face in the bedroom mirror as I applied mascara. I didn't have to go. I was only changing my clothes in case I decided to go. I put on black boots. Did I need a woolly cap to cover my hair? I slammed the drawer shut. Don't be so damned stupid! Would he recognise me? Or would he walk past me and think he was being propositioned by some desperate hooker?

At nine twenty I sat in the living room in my disguise gear watching the clock's slow progress. Have you noticed how time lags when it is observed? I repeatedly checked the clock against my watch to make sure it hadn't stopped.

At twenty to ten, I could bear it no longer. I slung a bag containing a mugger's wallet with a five pound note in it over my shoulder, put my travel pass in my pocket and left the flat.

The officer who lifted the tape made no comment on my departure. He was no doubt very bored by his duties. I murmured my thanks and set off down the street. Maybe he thinks I am looking for clients. If they have checked on Francesca, they probably assume that this is a house of ill repute and that Mrs Margoloys was the madam. She was stabbed by a dissatisfied customer because she refused to return his fee.

My ridiculous musings could not distract me. Michael! Michael! Michael! beat in my head in response to my stride in the macho boots. The perpetual lump in my throat intensified its presence and a vague queasiness lay across my stomach. I kept seeing and smelling the yellow puddle of my recent meal.

What the hell was I doing? What a deranged, foolhardy idiot I was! I was in enough shit without this little adventure; I was in ordure up to my armpits.

Think of something else! I imagined Dickens walking the London streets, observing the countless miseries of humanity. I empathized with Van Gogh and his constant vigil outside his beloved's house as he waited in vain hope for a glimpse of her.

The train had the dusty, half empty desolation that permeates it at certain times of day, when workers are home, drunks are still incarcerated in noisy taverns and revellers are not yet returning from evenings on the town. I sank into a corner seat and closed my eyes. I half expected Specs to come and sit beside me. After all, I had seen him scuttling into the Underground less than two hours ago. He was probably hiding behind a pillar, waiting to pounce.

After I had sat solitary in the carriage for ten minutes, the train began to move. Good thing I had allowed plenty of time. Ten minutes to ten. I would reach the Embankment at ten o'clock. Not stupidly early. I would be in position at five minutes past the hour if I didn't loiter. I shouldn't do that in that area, although it would not be long before the concert-goers from the South Bank swarmed across the footbridge.

Regent's Park! Oxford Circus! Doors opened and closed. A few passengers alighted. Leicester Square! Piccadilly! No delay when I would have welcomed one.

Michael would be walking through the lobby. Camaraderie with colleagues. Soon he would be responsible for others doing the same. Soon the tellers for the day would march forward and pause before Madam Speaker. Announce the voting figures. The Chamber would be packed or half empty. But Michael would be there. Quick chat. Clap on the shoulder. Good night! Who goes home? Not my Michael. Not yet, anyway. The crafty bastard! He wasn't slipping out in the middle of anything. His absence wouldn't be remarked. He had chosen a time when it would be assumed he was leaving for the night. And the place he had chosen was far enough away from the Commons to make it unlikely that he would be noticed talking to a young woman. Especially as we would no doubt be leaning on the parapet, watching the dark water, a spot where many young people halted to take in the panorama of St. Paul's and the London skyline. He had shown no concern about any inconvenience to me or, indeed, any danger I might encounter.

The train pulled into the Embankment Station and a number of rollicking young rowdies piled in past me as I stood waiting to alight. They swarmed up the carriage. I put my hands in my pockets and huddled into my coat collar as I walked up the platform. Should I take the first train back?

Once I was around the corner, I found the Embankment festooned with lights, strings of them adorning the trees above the promenade. Pinpoints of radiance gleamed in the depths of the river.

'All the haft sparkled with jacinth work,' came from the recesses of my mind. I was relieved to see a number of people in twos and threes and fours, walking along the pavements. I walked amongst them towards the Houses of Parliament, half a mile away. Its Gothic towers and pinnacles were sharply illuminated against the night sky. Everything was bright. A moon, almost full, floated to the right of St. Paul's. The river appeared motionless, liquorice black below me.

I turned and made my way back towards Cleopatra's Needle. I stopped just short of my objective and leaned on the parapet. I looked at the skyline. Oh, Thames! Flow softly till you hear my song. How innocent I was when I read those lines, before I arrived in my personal Waste Land.

Time passed. A drunk stumbled by and lurched against me. I recoiled as I realised the Embankment had become almost deserted. How long would I wait? I refused to turn and look at the clock on Big Ben. But I heard its distinctive tolling. First the quarter, then the half hour. If I had decided to take that job in the House of Commons, I should have heard that time division every quarter hour of every day, its inexorable round in spite of war and famine, scandal and disgrace. I wondered if, after a time, I would have ceased to register its distinctive tones.

There was a muffled cough behind me. I turned, half expecting another drunk requesting largesse.

Michael stood a short distance away, rubbing his hands, although it was not a cold night. I supposed he was noticing the coolness of the river breezes after the warmth of the Commons chamber.

'Hi!' I said. 'I came at your command.' I always attempted to disguise my ecstasy, my profound joyous turbulence at his presence, with a cover of flippancy. Some caustic quip would emerge from my mouth, apparently without my volition. He perhaps assumed I had been standing there thinking up some put-down just to be malicious: that is, if he thought of me at all. He was wearing a dark suit, against which his pale shirt glowed in the gloom. He looked superb, every inch the political animal, with his bulging briefcase by his side.

'Now, Frances,' he said. 'We haven't much time. Somebody could come past who knows me.' Hadn't I heard that before? We can't go out because somebody could notice and recognise me. What about anyone who knew me?

He came and stood beside the parapet at least a metre away from me. It would look more natural if you were closer, I thought. However, I said nothing.

'Have you told the police about me?'

'No!' Then the devil made me add, 'Not yet!' I bit my tongue. It was, after all, true.

'Well, don't!' He snarled the words as I gazed down into the black water beneath us. Not a word of commiseration, of sympathy for my plight! No expression of shock or revulsion at what had happened! All he was showing was a pathetic determination to save his own skin.

My chin went up. 'I have to see the Police again,' I told him, non-committedly. 'Not all the people living at 19A were home, so the Police will come back.' I would not be threatened. Destroyed, perhaps! But I would not be intimidated.

'Look, Frances!' he blustered. 'Don't be a fool. Don't try and be clever about this. Reputations are on the line here. Have you told anybody about us?'

He moved nearer and clasped my arm, his fingers pressing and pinching my flesh.

'No!' I tried to shake him off.

'Don't lie to me!' He grasped more tightly. A noisy crowd passed behind us, perhaps theatre-goers from the Savoy, lately discharged into the night air. Happy and laughing! Why wasn't I with them?

I pulled away from him. He followed and pressed close. 'Neither have I,' he hissed in my ear. Then he spoke the following words quickly, and a temporary bleakness fell over us as a cloud sailed across the bright disc of the moon.

'We must finish here and now. The situation has changed. I have my career and family to consider.'

A crimson fury obscured my eyes. The lights and the darkness merged into an inchoate mass. I wasn't looking at him but I knew he preened and drew himself up a little. He self-consciously fingered his tie. 'I now have a job, you know. I have been in the Whips' Office all day.'

If the arrogant bastard thought he was impressing me, he was wrong. 'I am sure the electors will take due note,' I said.

Suddenly I was sick of it all. Tired of Michael Rutter and his crass self-satisfaction. Hundreds of better men than him were sleeping in their plastic bags not two hundred metres away. The death of Mrs Margoloys, an old woman for whom I had felt a superior pity and an irritation at her kindly attempts at friendship, had panicked me and pitched me back into the real world: the world where fantasies and fairy stories aren't for real and we have to face up to the consequences of our actions.

I saw myself for what I was, a silly woman pointlessly wasting her life, skulking in the shadows with a lover who had ended a two year relationship without one affectionate word or any semblance of regret. When his head and his loins were at odds, his head would win every time! His heart never had a look-in!

I tasted bile, bitter in my throat. It was my own fault. I should not have been so supine, playing to his rules, acceding to his unreasonable demands, while he held me in less esteem than his dog, if he had one. I didn't even know that. I had been the biggest fool in Christendom! When I held myself in such low regard, how could I expect him to do otherwise?

But this self-awareness was overlaid on the knowledge of the intractable pain that would come as our relationship ended. The dread I had lived with constantly for the past two years had covered me with its dark wings. My reason for living was taken from me. My other half, the fulfilment that made me whole, was from henceforth to be absent from my life. I would not see him again. He had never had any idea of his importance to me. His shallow understanding could not contemplate such a profound, undying love.

I knew at that moment that my life was ruined. If I lived to the middle of the next century, I should never find such another one who touched my heart, my body, my soul, as he did.

I turned and walked away from him. Away from the Houses of Parliament with its soaring Gothic spires, towards Charing Cross and its hidden subterranean tunnels.

'Frances!'

I ignored him and walked on. My boots thrust and struck the tarmac and urged me forward. He did not follow.

CHAPTER FIVE

There was a note under my door, a single sheet of paper folded over. I picked it up. It was covered in Archie's flamboyant scrawl:

P.Cs. to the right of them. P.Cs. to the left of them. Poor, dear Mrs M! Want to talk?

Archie had signed his name with a flourish and filled the remainder of the page with extravagant X kisses.

I looked at my watch. Seven minutes past eleven. Did I want to talk to Archie? Or did I want my bed? One thing was certain: I didn't want any heavy sexual shenanigans. I wanted nothing so much as kind oblivion, quietude of forgetting, alone in darkness and peace. However, I knew I would not find it in my own bed tonight. I would relive my walk down the Embankment until eternity doused the stars.

I picked up the telephone and rang downstairs.

'Archie! Hi! I've just come in. Is it too late for me to come down?'

'No! Of course not! Never too late!' There was a slight pause. He sounded uncharacteristically wary.

'Is Jason there?' I asked.

'No, darling! By myself! In my jim-jams.'

'I won't look,' I promised. Nothing was so important to me at that moment as to get out of my flat, away from myself and my frantic thoughts. I was still numb from my encounter with Michael and had no recollection of the journey home. But I knew the melt-down would begin soon and the resulting bends would be unbelievably painful. At least with Archie I would have to push it into the background as I awaited the descent into the great chasm of my private nightmare.

'Right! On my way down.' I replaced the receiver before he could change his mind.

His door was half open. He was waiting for me on the other side and took me into his arms as he kicked the door closed with his foot. He was wearing pyjamas, just the bottom half, and I was held firmly against his naked chest.

This was no way the brotherly hug and kiss we had been in the habit of exchanging previously. In spite of myself, I began to salivate and pant. His mouth came down hard on mine, his hands cupping my face and his half open eyes staring into mine. From somewhere the treacherous idea came into my head that this was how they were taught to kiss at drama school.

The bottom half of our bodies locked and we gyrated slowly like demented mayflies. I found my hips rocking against his as tiny moans issued from my throat. I was worse than a bitch on heat.

Archie dropped his hands to my waist and urged me into the sitting room. We were on the couch, he had undone the zip on my trousers and discarded his own, before I was well aware we had moved. All the time, he was kissing me, my face, my neck, my shoulders. And my hands were on his body, his superb form without fat or flab. His skin was smooth, lightly tanned, over rippling muscle that was not apparent when he was dressed.

He caressed my breasts. We rolled together as he pulled my sweater over my head. 'Nice!' he murmured. 'Nice!' as it fell to the floor to join his pyjama trousers. He unhooked my bra and ran his fingers lightly over my body.

After a time he picked me up and carried me to his bed. Slowly, slowly, he slipped my knickers down and off while my gasps and groans reverberated in my ears like a mini-earthquake. It had never been like this with Michael!

Archie put his fingers on my mouth and gently shushed me as he came hard inside me. Our bodies moved in perfect unison as we climaxed together. It was oblivion. It was heaven.

After he rolled off me, I still held on to him as though I would never let him go. He pulled the sheet over us and held me against his shoulder.

'My!' he said. 'We needed that!'

Suddenly, we were laughing like loons. We were sticky and sated, heat pulsing between us.

'Darling! My darling!' He pulled me close to his side. 'Why have we wasted so much time? All these months, when we could have been in paradise every night.'

A dagger of pain, physical in its intensity, smote my heart. All these months I had spent so much time anticipating Michael's arrival. I buried my face in Archie's shoulder and wished to remain there forever. But, even then, I knew I would pay for this indiscretion.

'Ciggie?' Archie's packet of Marlborough was on his bedside table. I didn't smoke. Nonetheless, he lit two cigarettes and we puffed in silence for a while.

'Isn't Jason coming back tonight?' Already our recent coupling seemed remote and irrelevant.

'Don't know what he's doing, darling. We don't enquire too closely into personal affairs.'

'Where's Chloe?' I asked next. I had genuinely forgotten her existence as Archie and I reached for each other. I wasn't particularly interested in the girl's whereabouts, but wondered if and how Archie would explain away his disloyalty.

'Working, I think.' Archie flicked his ash butt into the saucer by his side. 'Dancer!' he said, laconically.

'Oh!' I said. That noun covered a bevy of possibilities.

'She wasn't too happy about what happened to Mrs Margoloys.'

I said nothing. It was an obvious statement. None of us were over the moon about the fate of the poor old lady. But it would affect Chloe less than any of the residents at 19A. She had no emotional involvement in the matter. Why should she be worried?

'Don't know,' Archie said carefully, 'if she has had any previous dealings with the boys in blue.' I remembered the little pantomime I had witnessed on the street outside as Chloe noticed the police presence outside our house. 'Or if she has some dark secret she doesn't want exposed.' He spoke lightly, but in a way that discouraged further questioning. Was the girl into drug dealing or dodgy receiving? If so, Archie was skating over dangerous ground.

He kissed the side of my head. 'I may be reading too much into it,' he said, 'but I get the impression she isn't keen to continue our relationship just at present.' Especially with the police buzzing round the place, I silently completed for him.

'I suppose we will be interviewed again,' I said. 'Damn' nuisance!'

'Sure thing, darlin'!' Archie crushed out his cigarette in the makeshift ashtray. Then he came into me again, his penis stiff as a guardsman on parade.

'You on top, this time!' He lifted me above him and I sat across him. We fucked again, gloriously, savagely. I jumped up and down on his cock until he rolled me over, positioned my heels on his shoulders and entered deeply inside me as my vagina shortened to accommodate him.

Afterwards, we fell apart and dropped into sleep in each other's arms. It was getting light when I opened my eyes. Archie lay beside me fast asleep, looking like a little boy with his long, dark lashes sweeping his cheeks. I switched off the lamp by the bed. The room appeared to have been trashed by marauders. My clothes were in a procession leading back towards the sitting room, ample evidence of the progress by which they had been discarded. All around hung the sweet, sour smell of sex.

Carefully, I eased Archie's arm from across my breasts and slid from the bed. Gathering my garments, I pulled on trousers and sweater, stuffed my underwear under my arm and collected my shoes from beside the sofa. As I crept to the door, I noticed the message board on the wall. Taking the attached chalk, I wrote, 'Thanks for last night!' with the decorated exclamation mark underneath the words. If Jason saw it and wondered, I didn't really care.

I scurried up the stairs and gained my flat without meeting a soul. Not too likely at six in the morning.

My mouth was foul as the bottom of a ferret's cage, and I drank three glasses of water straight off. Then I ran a deep bath of steaming water, poured in a good measure of Night Jasmine and soaked in it for a long while.

It was Thursday! And today there would be no Michael to look forward to. He was not coming any more!

The police rang me at work to ask what time that evening would be convenient for a further interview. I toyed with the idea of telling them that no time was suitable; then changed my mind.

'I normally get home between 6.30 and 7,' I said. Margot raised her eyebrows. That was near enough to the truth. 'Unless I work late.'

'Shall we say 7.30, then? Give you time to have something to eat before our officer calls.'

'All right! Fine! I'll expect him then.' I replaced the receiver, put the tips of my fingers together as I stared into space. Margot looked up.

'The Police want to talk to me again' I said, as I prepared to resume my work.

'Hard luck!' she said. 'Surely they can't imagine you had anything to do with it.'

'God knows!' I opened a folder marked, For Urgent Attention. 'But I do appear to have been the only person in the building when Mrs Margoloys was found.'

'If you were guilty, no doubt you would have scarpered.'

'Unless they think it was a double bluff.' Margot shrugged in disbelieve.

'I don't even know if she was still alive when I got home.' I was speaking slowly, my voice beginning to crack. 'If I had checked on her, she may not have died.'

'Come on! You don't know that. More likely she was already dead!'

Margot began typing her report. I looked at her bent head. Sometimes she could be most exasperating. She must be dying to talk about the crime and the set-up at our building. Just when I needed to get something off my chest, she was restraining her curiosity in consideration of my sensibility. We were paying the price for our habitual reticence. Or perhaps she genuinely wasn't interested.

It seemed straightforward enough to an outsider, no doubt. A defenceless old woman battered by an intruder for a few pounds. So much violence in London these days! Cut and dried, really. But I would have liked to talk the matter through to clear my mind before I had to face the police again. However, our habit of reserve was too strong to be broken. We had never confided in each other at an intimate level. I had a guilty secret. Perhaps Margot had, as well. And now it was too late to begin afresh.

Michael, you bastard! You've fucked up my shitty life. You've stopped me having normal relationships with my own sex, as well as yours.

I was glad to get into the case of Micro Foods, even if for the most part I was staring at meaningless words and turning pages at random. My last encounter with Michael had left me pulverized, ground down with a giant pestle into a fine powder that was blowing in the wind. Yet I became hot when I recalled my frolics with Archie. A warm glow travelled up my spine as I remembered our ecstasy. I couldn't regret it. I would be analysing it before long. Why couldn't I sink into my skin and live as thoughtlessly as everybody else?

What the hell was I going to tell the police? My problem was not Mrs Margoloys, but Michael. However, whatever transpired, he couldn't terminate our relationship. He had done that already!

The interminable day passed in a flash. All too soon I was again unlocking my front door. It was ten minutes before seven. I had left the office at six fifteen. No way did I wish to sit fidgeting as I awaited the appointed time. I knew my stomach was too churned up to accept food.

I met nobody on my entry into 19A. I had not seen Francesca, the music students or Sammy since Mrs Margoloys' demise. Jason neither, now I came to think of it. Had the Police located them? Had they been to the music college, or had the students returned to their families? Parents wouldn't be too happy about their teenage daughters residing in a murder house. Only Sammy's absence appeared to be without guile. And he was probably helping himself to spares lying around his building site! Nobody would relish police probing – Francesca perhaps least of all.

Michael, you bastard! My jumpiness is all your fault. And had he shown the slightest regard for my safety? No! He was too busy trying to save his own shitty hide.

I hung my jacket in the closet and tidied the flat, plumping up cushions to give a cared-for look and throwing out the dead flowers that were listing sadly in the hearth.

Punctually, at half past seven, there was a knock on the door. As I went into the hall, I realised I had not checked the answer 'phone. The red light winked ominously as I opened the door. It could be Michael or Archie. Too late to do any-thing about it now! Endeavouring to position my body between the restless red light and the eye span of the person outside the door, I found myself confronting the pretty face of a young policewoman. She smiled.

'Come in, please!' I ushered her quickly into the living room. It looked naked now the flowers had been removed. 'Won't you sit down?'

She took the chair with her back to the light. I hovered. 'Would you like some tea or coffee?'

'No, thank you! I've just had a cup – one of those awful polystyrene ones from the stall at the end of the street.'

'Do you know this area?' I asked. Make conversation. Act normally.

'No! Not very well.' She took a notebook and pencil from her top pocket. No recording machine, then. I took a deep breath.

'Please sit down.' Instructed to sit in my own home, I perched on the edge of the settee. I was full of heat and guilt. I looked at her. Fair, longish wavy hair, pulled back. Hazel eyes. If they expected me to bond with a young woman, they were barking up the wrong tree!

'I expected the other officer,' I said, inanely. She ignored my remark and started to question me in an overtly sympathetic, yet penetrating, manner.

'You live here alone,' she began, more a statement than a question. Had she spoken to Archie already, queried my life style? Archie would have opened up to this female. 'Must have come as a shock to you.'

I nodded.

'Did you know the old lady,' she checked her notebook, 'Mrs Margoloys, well?'

'No! Not well at all. I told ..' She glanced up. Was there sexual tension between the police officers? In any event I had no clear recollection of what I had said to her colleague, except that I had gone on about Specs.

'No!' I repeated. 'I would speak to her if I saw her in the hall when I was coming and going.' A ludicrous remembrance of 'Diary of a Nobody' came into my mind and Pooter's neighbours, Mr. Cummings and Mr. Gowing.' With an effort, I suppressed a nervous titter. Pull yourself together, Bonnington! Wouldn't do to get hysterical in the presence of this efficient young woman. What's so funny, anyway? A poor old woman has been murdered, alone and friendless, when she should have been surrounded by a loving family, or at least been safe within her own four walls.

'Did you visit her in her room?'

'No! Never!' I sounded a callous bitch. 'Not until Monday evening, that is.'

'Why did you go and see her then?'

'She asked me to.'

She wrote in her little book. Was she writing in shorthand? Were they expected to learn shorthand these days, the Police? She looked up. 'Yes?'

'She left a message on my answer 'phone,' I elaborated, 'asking me to call and see her.'

'Yes! We have run the messages.'

So why had she asked me then? To test my veracity? Thank God Michael had never left messages! Not until the dreadful summons yesterday. Were they aware of that? Of course they were! They were aware of everything that was totally irrelevant to the enquiry. In spite of a reputation for bungle and inefficiency, the police would be ferreting around in my affairs with a fine toothcomb. I longed to scream, to shout, to smash crockery. Quietly, I leaned further back on my old sofa with its smart new cover and tried to steady my nerves.

'What did she want to talk to you about?'

'Well, she was rather odd,' I said slowly. The young woman gave me a look of enquiry but kept her pen moving. Like everybody else in this house, she was probably thinking.

'Odd, in what way?'

I wished she wouldn't bloody well repeat everything I said. Were they trained in interviewing techniques?

'Well, she always appeared a bit eccentric. But she wanted to confide she had seen a strange man in the house. She told me to be careful.' Tears pricked the back of my eyelids. 'That was peculiar in itself,' I went on to cover my emotion. 'She saw everyone as a friend.'

'She didn't know, or say, who the stranger was?'

'She gave me the impression she didn't know.' What the hell! They knew anyway. 'The woman downstairs, in the flat below, has callers sometimes. Often,' I amended. Francesca would have to watch her own back. It was everybody for themselves in this scenario.

'Yes! We have talked to her,' she said, shortly.

Really! Had Francesca been in her apartment all the time, lying low? Was she too terrified to put her nose outside the door? I felt hilarity threaten to overwhelm me. The whole situation, Michael, Archie, Francesca, Specs, began to appear to me as surreal as Modern Art or one of Archie's second-rate plays.

'Tell me about your own visitors.'

The question, inevitable as it was, sobered me. Now we were getting to the nitty gritty. Adrenal pumped and my stomach butterflied. I launched into a somewhat incoherent explanation of my dealings with Specs. 'He seems to appear everywhere,' I finished lamely. 'He was even at Sainsbury's when I went there to shop.'

'If he lives nearby, that would be a reasonable thing to do,' commented the officer. Bitch! 'Who else comes here to see you?'

Now, we had come to it. The moment of truth!

'My mother, sometimes.'

My mother had last visited me five months previously, during the Christmas holidays. 'My sister lives in Canada, but she has been here once.'

'What about friends? Boyfriends? Do you have a regular boyfriend?'

The term seemed ludicrous, old-fashioned. I wouldn't have imagined Michael had ever been anyone's boyfriend! Nevertheless, this was crunch time. I swallowed over the hump in my throat. If I didn't mention Michael, it was bound to come out. Did they know already? Had they run his message on the tape? And it would look suspicious, as though we had something to hide. Which we had, of course! It was a wonder the baying Press weren't in full cry outside. Much better to tell the police openly about our affair, than have them confront me with their knowledge. And what loyalty did I owe to Michael in view of his reprehensible behaviour?

If I told them, it would be just another affair indulged in by yet another lecherous Member of Parliament. And Michael wasn't a household name: not high profile, at all. His name had only recently been mentioned in the News. Unfortunate timing! But, let's face it, how many people would have noticed it?

The silence grew. My tongue was too big for my mouth. I was as parched as if I had spent six hours in the desert. The young woman began to appear impatient. She hadn't all night to wait for me.

'Boyfriends?'

Ach! To hell with it!

'Yes!' I said. 'I am having an affair with a Member of Parliament.'

I realised it wasn't true. It was over! No flicker of emotion crossed her attractive face. Or was there a slight tightening of the lips that could imply contempt?

'Name?'

'Michael Rutter.'

Now there was an awareness of the name. Was she wondering where she had recently heard it? Without excusing myself, I went to the kitchen and poured a glass of water. I gulped most of it down before I returned to her.

It was done! Now all hell would break lose!

'Does he come here?' she asked. A routine murder enquiry was livening up.

'Sometimes.' I confined myself to answering the questions she put to me without adding any information. Let her work for it! A great fiery pit had opened at my feet and I was calm in the face of my danger. Michael had called time before I had opened my mouth. What had I to lose? His good opinion? Perhaps I had never had that. Nevertheless, I felt as though I were gasping inside. A great bellows was pumping back and forth within me, although my voice sounded calm and rational enough.

'When was he last here?'

'Thursday.'

'Last Thursday? A week ago?'

'Yes!'

'And he has not been here since then?'

'No!'

She closed her notebook with a small slap.

'Thank you, Miss.. ' pause, 'Bonnington.' She rose to her feet. 'That will do for now. We will want to talk to you again, of course. You are not planning on going away anywhere in the near future?'

I shook my head. I wanted to do nothing except crawl into bed. And stay there for a long, long time.

'Thank you.' She moved to the door. 'We'll be in touch.'

I stayed on the sofa as she let herself out. Going to inform the Press, I thought. And she hadn't pursued the boyfriend query. For all she knew, Michael could have been one of a string of lovers. The whole house could be a bloody brothel!

What a mess! What a total, fucking, bloody mess!

I went to lie on the bed, where I tossed and groaned for a time. Then I got up, combed my hair and poured myself a thick slug of brandy. I put slices of bread under the grill and mixed the ingredients for a Welsh Rarebit. What the hell! If the shit was going to hit the pan, I needed to be fortified.

She was not my only visitor that evening. The smell of grilled cheese still hung in the kitchen when I heard a faint tap on my outer door. I went into the hall.

'Who is it?'

'Francesca!'

I opened the door. She appeared to have shrunk. She normally wore very high heels. Now her slim, elegant feet were thrust into house mules, and I found myself on a level with her eyes. Her face was bare of make-up. Unadorned and ill-defined, she looked terrible.

'Francesca! Come in!'

She appeared distracted. 'You are having supper?'

'No! I've just finished.' I urged her into the hall and closed the door. Without her war paint she looked her age, which must have been nearer forty then thirty.

I took her into the sitting room. 'Would you like some coffee? Or a Whisky?'

'Whisky would be very nice. Thank you!'

She had a faint, musical intonation that could have been acquired. Now I looked at her properly for the first time, I realised she was of Middle Eastern appearance. I had always assumed she was Italian.

I poured a generous measure of Whisky, realising that this was the longest exchange of words we had ever had in two years of close neighbourhood. She nursed her glass between her hands, occasionally sipping from it and grimacing slightly.

'Would you like some water? It is malt.'

'No! No! It is fine. You are very kind.'

I sat opposite her and waited. Now I was in the chair the young policewoman had occupied not long ago. Had Francesca been interviewed before she climbed the stairs to my door?

'I am so worried!'

I resisted the temptation to prompt her. She placed her glass on the table beside her and put her hand on her brow, shielding her eyes. I wondered if she was crying, if I should go and put my arms round her. But she looked up and appeared composed.

'You see, I have a little difficulty. I have a friend.'

'Yes?'

'Man friend.'

'Yes!' What could I say?

'I haven't known him very long.' Her voice broke slightly.

'No?' I sounded parrot-like, even to myself.

'I think he keeps bad company.'

I groaned inwardly. First Archie. Now Francesca. The police would find our house interesting, to say the least. Murder never solved, but numerous petty felonies cleared up.

It is no more than I would have expected, Francesca. I would have imagined it would be obvious to you that at least some of your clients are on the thin edge of the right side of the Law. Only those engaged in dodgy enterprises would have the spare cash needed to pay your exorbitant fees. They would be in the twilight underworld of criminality where prostitution was a part of everyday life.

Francesca wasn't a low class tart. She would be dealing with the big boys. In another age she would have been a courtesan. Was she cognisant of the crime-related, drug-soaked sub-culture we know exists in every corner of the land? Were her clients furious, as Michael must surely be, at the police invasion of our building? Worse still, was one of them the killer who had battered Mrs Margoloys? No wonder Francesca looked raddled. It dawned on me that Francesca's problems were greater than my own.

'What are you worried about, Francesca?' I asked, gently. 'Do you think one of your friends may have been involved in Mrs Margoloys' death?'

She gasped. 'No! No!' She picked up her glass and drained it. 'Do not say such things.' Again I wondered if her rather stilted expressions were acquired or natural.

She stood up. 'I should not have bothered you.'

Bugger it! Now I had frightened her with my insensitive enunciation of what must be in both our minds.

'You aren't bothering me at all.' I stood up also. She seemed small and vulnerable. 'Through no fault of our own, we've all been dropped in the shit. We are all in this together.' I picked up the Whisky bottle. 'Have another drink.'

But she had changed her mind about a girls' only confessional. She almost ran into the hall and wrenched at the door. I followed her, turned the catch and opened it.

'You know where I am if you want to talk,' I said to her retreating back as she stumbled down the stairs, the loose mules impeding her progress. The only answer was the faint bang of her door as she closeted herself once more inside her own domain.

I sighed. Damn! I was exasperated at my own clumsiness. How stupid to have voiced that question straight out! She must suspect that one of her clients could be the guilty man and have screwed up her courage to come and see me. What had she intended to say? What had she told the police? It occurred to me that if she did know anything, her own life could be in danger.

Fuck! Fuck! What an imbecile I was! Why hadn't I kept my mouth shut? Fancy scaring her away like that! She must be terrified. These big shot criminal types are not noted for their magnanimity. I remembered a short, stocky man I had once noticed entering her flat, hat pulled down a la Al Capone. Compared to Francesca's troubles, mine seemed akin to those of Mickey Mouse.

I made sure the bolts and chain were in place on my door. I would not open it again to anybody tonight. For the first time, I was grateful for the police presence at the outer door. I felt exhausted by the events of the evening. A sleepless night, followed by an amorous one, had played havoc with my resources.

I undressed, made a milky drink, didn't bother with toning or moisturizing, and fell into bed.

* * *

The newspapers were on to it quicker than a dose of clap. The Sunday tabloids, surprise, surprise, went berserk over the story.

Murder House, where M.P. Met His Lover, screamed the headlines on the News of the World, above a picture of our modest dwelling. M.P's Tryst at Murder Scene announced the Mail on Sunday, its huge letters filling the front page. The Times, more discreetly, put the item at the bottom of its front page: Clandestine Affair at House of Death. All of them carried photographs of Michael, in the inner pages, if not on the front.

The irony of the situation did not escape me. Michael obsessively craved publicity and had never received much of it. Now it was being tipped over him in cartloads.

The Press were back in force outside 19A. Their vehicles and equipment extended the length of Nottingham Place. I examined my tiny balcony, but concluded it would be sheer folly to attempt to climb down to the back yard from the third floor via a fire escape that terminated on the floor below. Obviously the fire regulations were being flouted. But I had to go to work on Monday morning. I would have to brave the pack!

In the event, it wasn't as bad as I had envisaged. I moved quickly and passed through the crowd at the same time as an old lady who was holding forth across the road had grabbed their attention. When I reached my work premises, I walked smartly along the lower corridor, but nobody tried to detain me. Of course, not everyone spent their weekends catching up with the news, especially the younger generation. If they had, they would probably have thought that this was yet another Member of Parliament behaving in the usual way. Their own concerns were more pressing.

'A bit of excitement at your place,' Margot remarked laconically as I arrived in the office, slightly out of breath.

I groaned. 'You can say that again!' I slumped into my chair without bothering to remove my coat.

Margot rose and busied herself with the coffee cups. The kettle came to the boil so quickly, it must have been previously heated. I closed my eyes. I wished that just for once she would stop being diplomatic and be curious and bitchy. 'What have you been up to then, you sly boots?' Why can't she make it easy for me, just once in my life?

I opened my eyes as Margot placed a steaming cup before me. The heat and strong aroma swirled upwards and hit my nasal buds. God! I felt sick! As usual! Margot went to her desk drawer and removed a small bottle of rum.

'Reserved for emergencies!' she said. She poured a measure into my coffee. 'Have a slug of this. It will buck you up a bit.'

'Uugh!' I tossed my head from side to side. 'I don't think anything will do that, Margot.'

She went back to her own desk, added rum to her own mug and sat with her hands cupped round it. 'I have some in the evenings sometimes,' she said. 'Urgent job. Needed yesterday. No time to do anything properly. It helps to put things into perspective.'

I imagined Margot at her lonely desk, knocking back the foul liquid.

'I know the feeling,' I said.

We sat silently, sipping our coffee. Margot had not gone back to her keyboard. She is giving me a chance, I thought. Time to talk, without intrusive questions to upset me.

'You're a good pal, Margot,' I said eventually, embarrassed by the unfamiliar camaraderie.

She shrugged, smiled with a tiny grimace. 'Not good enough!' she said. 'We should have made more time for each other.'

'Oh, God! Margot, no hair shirts! Don't start blaming yourself. I am more than capable of making a fool of myself without any help from anybody.'

'Well, if it's any consolation, I am in a similar position.'

I stared. My suspicions had been right, after all.

'The chief difference is my 'friend' isn't quite so high profile as yours. But the shit would still hit the pan if we were found out.' She laughed mirthlessly. 'Or if there was a murder next door.'

'Oh, my God! It's so horrible! Horrible!'

I was weeping, unexpectedly and uncontrollably. Somehow, tension had eased and tears were streaming down my face. Margot gave me her box of tissues, switched the 'phones over and put her arms round me.

'Oh, Margot! How many of us? How many?'

After a few minutes I calmed down, wiped my face and blew my nose. Margot had been holding my hand. Now she went back to her own desk.

'Come home with me tonight,' she urged.

I shook my head. 'The Police want to see me again. Anyway, I don't want to get you involved.'

A pencil thin line of a frown bisected her eyebrows.

'I don't like to think of you alone in that house,' she said.

I gave a short laugh. 'Oh, I'm not alone! My high-class gentleman's friend neighbour called up to see me last night. The first time I have said more than four words to her. And she is terrified of something.'

'Really? Well, I suppose she could have a reason to be. What did she want?'

What did she want? I realised I didn't know. Francesca had run away before she had made much sense.

'Just to talk, I think.'

Margot twiddled a pen in her fingers. 'Have you spoken to any of the others?'

'Only Archie,' I said. 'There has been no sign of Jason or the music students. Or Sammy either, but he was never home much, anyway.'

'I suppose any of them could be potential suspects,' said Margot, slowly. 'They could be keeping out of the way. Have you any idea as to who or why?'

'No! I can't imagine any of them..' I trailed off. What do we ever know of the real lives of our friends and acquaintances? 'What motive could there possibly be for..?'

Margot didn't comment as I stopped speaking. For the first time I attempted to run the scenario through my head. It resembled a silhouette which jerked along like an old fashioned fun-fair peep-show: the victim, a shabby old woman shuffling around the hall of a residence where half a dozen rooms and flats were let and leased. She was at home, in her own home, the only home she had. She had no idea of danger or concealment. She was kindly and tolerant. She knew and liked all the people who lived there. I tried to swallow the egg-sized lump in my throat. And clear my thoughts for Margot's benefit.

'Not Jason or Archie, I am sure,' I said. 'They are both a bit feckless, histrionic, but good-hearted lads. Neither would have harmed a hair of her head.'

But was I sure about that? Did their pantomime cover dark secrets? Jason had hinted at a murky past that he did not explain. I had dismissed it as an attempt to be mysterious and interesting. There was his first marriage and his obvious distress over his separation from his sons. But that was a common enough plight these days.

The music students? I knew virtually nothing of their personal lives. They had each other for company and were out most of the time. And why would two young girls wish to hurt an old woman?

Sammy? The few times I had spoken to him, he had appeared cheerful and uncomplicated. He had a bantering word with Mrs Margoloys when their paths crossed. 'Hi! Mrs M.! Are you going for the Olympics this time? You'll have to get practising, you know.'

And Mrs Margoloys would be delighted at the exchange. 'Get on with you! You should be doing that yourself, strong young man like you!'

Sammy had laughed and patted his beer belly. 'You could be right, Mrs M. But I think I'll leave it till next year.'

Surely not Sammy!

That left Francesca! Did she know something? Was that the reason for her panicky call at my flat last evening? Was one of her visitors a V.I.P. who had more to lose than Michael? Had he bludgeoned a defenceless old woman to shut her up?

Margot was still sitting quietly, waiting.

'One of Francesca's clients,' I said. 'Possibly.' My head throbbed. 'Oh, I don't know! The whole thing is crazy! To hell with it!'

'An intruder?' suggested Margot. 'Did she disturb an attempted burglary? Someone thought the house was empty. They hit her to silence her when they discovered their mistake.'

'A phoney gas man or electricity employee?'

I put my head in my hands, but Margot's generous measure of rum plus lack of sleep was doing the trick. I felt groggy and unreal, detached from present circumstances. Nothing had registered sharply since my meeting with Michael, in spite of the drama of current events. What was he doing? Skulking in the corridors of power, discovering who his friends were, as they deliberately avoided him or rushed to interrogate him on his amorous activities.

'You randy bugger! Butter wouldn't melt in your mouth while you've been getting your leg over all these months!'

Would he glare at them in icy indignation, or smirk sheepishly at their grudging admiration? Whatever he was doing, it was nothing to do with me! And what would he say to his wife? Sorry dear! A man's gotta do what a man's gotta do.'

'Sorry Margot!' I said. 'My head's thumping. I don't know what to think. I suppose the best thing I can do is try and sort out the Psalter case.'

'Right!' Did I detect relief in Margot's voice? 'But take it easy! Don't do too much!'

Not a lot had been said, but I felt we understood each other better than we had ever done. So, Margot had a lover! Married, no doubt! What fools we women were! Attractive, intelligent females, unable to find suitable partners! I sighed as I opened up the Psalter case on my computer. One thing was certain. This job was not going to receive my undivided attention.

In order to clear my head and give myself a change of environment, I left the office at lunchtime and walked down Oxford Street, anonymous amongst the teeming crowds. As usual, Michael came with me, walking by my side, talking to me, commenting on the unfortunate fallout of the situation. Who had ruined his life? He, himself? Or had I done so a long time ago, with my flaccid acceptance of his rigid, capricious rules governing our relationship? Not to mention the unknown killer who had catapulted us all into notoriety!

Or could it be poor Mrs Margoloys, with her habit of popping up like a rabbit from a hat where she was neither wanted nor welcomed? Was she the culprit as well as the victim? And what about my fellow flat dwellers, with their compressed, convoluted existences? Michael would insist any or all except himself were culpable. But, my darling, it was you who decided to play the game according to your own tawdry standards.

I glimpsed Michael's distinctive features in the faces of the crowds around me. I shook my head to clear my eyes. I was going mad! A television screen in a shop window on my left displayed a large close-up of Michael's face. I pushed my way through the knot of spectators gathered round the plate glass window. They gave way, good-naturedly. Michael was being interviewed by a BBC reporter! It was not possible to hear the exchange. My stomach lurched into its usual plunge that any sight of him occasioned. He appeared calm and unfazed, his handsome features arranged in a polite smile as he established a rapport with his interlocutor.

'Another one of them at it,' grumbled an envious voice to my right. 'Dirty sod!' There were sniggers from those who heard the comment. I leaned my head against the cool glass. I felt very nauseous.

'Are you all right, love?' Two middle-aged, well-dressed women were looking at me with concern.

'Yes!' I lifted my head. Thank God my photograph hadn't been published. 'Just came over a bit dizzy.'

'Come with us, love, and we'll get you a cup of tea.' She nodded towards the café nearby. One of the women was holding my arm as the crowds surged around us.

'No! Thank you very much! My office is just round the corner. I'll go back.'

Would my face appear on the screen? I must get away from it. Would reporters begin to congregate outside my building? The directors of our discreet organisation would not be best pleased.

The women insisted on accompanying me as far as Edgware Road and watched me from the corner.

'You went real whey,' one of them said. 'I thought you were going to faint.'

'Have you had any lunch, love?' asked the other. 'Young people don't always look after themselves.'

They watched my progress down the street. 'Do you think she is pregnant?' Perhaps I imagined this last remark as I turned to wave my thanks before I walked through the door. I skulked inside the lobby for a minute or so, fiddling with my handbag as though I had forgotten something. When I thought they had gone, I emerged again and joined the throng outside. I managed to cross the intersection before the lights changed.

What could I do? Jump in front of an underground train? Throw myself off Westminster Bridge? I turned down the side of John Lewis, where it was quieter. I passed through the side door and wandered round the Fabrics Department, registering in a detached way rolls of sumptuous brocades and gleaming velvets. As I stood intently inspecting swathes of cream lace panels, an assistant approached and asked if I needed help.

Eventually I took myself back to work and managed to negotiate the afternoon. Margot left early to meet a client. When she had gone, I got up from the computer and wandered round the room. Why weren't the Press outside? They must have sussed out my office. It was a relief to be able to give up any pretence of industry. I would take the files home and work on them this evening. Anything was better than sitting staring at my own four walls with my fears beating against my skull.

Oh, to turn the clock back one week to the time before Specs appeared in my life and Michael had kept his appointment in the Whips' Office! None of it seemed to matter now. Would this murder ever be solved? How many killers were walking the streets, sitting beside us on trains and trying to strike up friendships? I hated the thought of going home, running the gauntlet of the Media again. So much injustice endured by so many innocent people every day!

Sighing deeply, I collected my things together. Don't forget the files! Business woman to your finger tips! It had to be done. I had better get going. Once back, I needn't open my door again. I would be safe!

Yet I lingered around, clearing my desk, making sure all my papers were in the correct files. Was my instinct telling me something? I retouched my make-up in the office, reluctant to risk facing any quick-change Friday nighters in the cloakroom. It was the beginning of weekend jollity. And it was exactly a week since I had gone to the concert at Wigmore Hall and endured the unwelcome attentions of Specs.

By now the building was quiet. After a few shouted good wishes that floated up faintly from the ground floor, silence settled like a deep pall over the premises which had been so animated a bare quarter of an hour earlier.

What was Michael doing at this moment? It was no longer my concern.

I took my jacket from its hanger and had it half on when the telephone rang. It cut through the silence sharp as a razor. I jumped violently. Leave it! I should have been out of the office by now, anyway. It continued ringing, its shrill insistence boring gimlet-like into my skull. I stared at it in a mesmerized fashion.

I picked up the receiver. An unknown female voice began ranting in my ear. I couldn't follow a word she was saying. Was she from the Media? I had not been bothered in the office previously. The switchboard had shielded me from intrusions. But this was my private line, the number known only to a handful of close friends and colleagues.

'Who is this?' I asked.

'Who is this?' she mocked, and now her voice was more intelligible. 'Who is this, you fucking little slut!'

I stood bemused. If it was a tabloid journalist, why was she being so abusive? Was it a wrong number?

'You never gave me a thought all these years, all these fucking awful years, did you?' The voice was low, harsh with congealed fury.

I put the receiver down on its rest. I was shaking. Michael's wife had somehow found out my office number. I picked up my briefcase and left the room, locking the door behind me. As I started down the corridor, the 'phone rang again.

I was still trembling when I reached the street. I realised I hadn't left my keys behind at the security desk. Gavin, who manned the desk in the evening, was missing when I passed through the lobby. He was probably checking on the ground floor offices or filling his kettle in the Gents' loo. I ought to go back and leave the keys. But the thought of that distraught woman coming through again on the main switchboard was too much to risk. Sod it! The keys only affected Margot and myself. Margot had her own set and wouldn't be standing on one leg awaiting my arrival on Monday morning. The key to the outer door should be left at the desk, but in view of all the trauma of the past week, I could be forgiven for forgetting it. I decided I really couldn't face Gavin's inquisitive leer or his attempts at bonhomie. Not after that telephone call! The venom in the woman's voice had been unbelievable. She sounded as though she cheerfully would have murdered me. She couldn't have sneaked into 19A and battered Mrs Margoloys in the mistaken idea she was me, could she?

I passed Bond Street and walked down to the Oxford Street tube. I needed to walk to clear my head before facing the claustrophobic confines of the underground. Shoppers barged straight at me as though I were invisible. If I didn't move aside, they banged into me and then glared as I automatically apologised. I had meant to dawdle by the shop windows,

CHAPTER FIVE

Selfridges, Evans, John Lewis, but all I wanted now was to reach home, my own safe haven, and lock myself in, away from prying eyes.

The train was packed and I swayed in discomfort between the seats, squashed against the vast bosom of a sweating woman, overwhelmed by the onion smell wafting from her armpits. With great relief, I pushed my way out of the carriage at Baker Street station and stepped on to the escalator up to street level. I contemplated the reviving Darjeeling and the perfumed tub that would be mine in ten minutes.

As I came over the top, I spied a most unwelcome distraction. Specs was standing near the ticket machines. He looked like a fixture. He was stamping his trainer-shod feet and peering at the faces of the passing travellers. He should have been holding an identity board. I tried to ignore him as he fell into step beside me.

'I want to talk to you,' he said.

I stopped abruptly. The crowds behind parted and flowed on around us like water swirling about boulders in a fast current.

'Talk then,' I said.

'Not here.' He was still shuffling his feet. For God's sake! 'Come for a coffee.'

There was a coffee house right next to the station.

'Five minutes,' I said. Pointedly I looked at my watch. I strode away from him, up the steps and towards the café. Once more, he was trotting at my side.

I ignored my companion until we were sitting facing each other at a red formica-topped table with our coffee before us.

'Forgotten the sugar,' he mumbled, and got up to fetch some from the trays beyond the till end of the counter. What an inept, aggravating bugger he was!

I looked at my watch. The five minutes were already gone. Should I leave? Walk away? It seemed childish now I was here. Anyway, if I did so, he would no doubt follow me to Nottingham Place, making a spectacle of himself. I smiled. Specs making a spectacle! I sipped my coffee and waited.

'Can't drink it without sugar,' he said as he slipped into the opposite seat.

'Some people can't,' I said. I gave him my underground stare, which I have perfected for times when travelling near gawping passengers on the tube. He looked away as he made a business of breaking open his little packet of sugar and tipping and stirring it into his coffee. God, I was sick of him!

'Well?'

He jerked about on his seat, twitched his shoulders inside his anorak. He didn't answer. I swallowed my coffee and picked up my handbag.

'If you have nothing to say, I'll be getting home. It's been a long day.' I rose to my feet.

'No! Wait!' He reached out and grabbed my hand. I pulled it away as though his were scalding hot. But I sat down again. I tried to calm down. It was obvious that my antagonism was making him nervous.

'Look, if something is bothering you, you really should go to the Police,' I said.

He spread his stubby fingers with their bitten nails on the top of the table. Circles of condensation showed their resting place.

'I came to your house,' he said.

'I know. I saw you.'

He looked surprised, as though he had forgotten the incident.

'Look!' I repeated. 'I know what happened to Mrs Margoloys was a terrible shock to all of us. I don't see you have anything to worry about if all you did was walk up the stairs to my flat and then walk down again.' His perpetually anxious expression did not change. 'Of course, it would be better if you told the police. If they have to chase you up, it will look as though you have something to hide.'

Again I gathered my things. A noisy group of teenagers waited at the counter. I longed for my gently steaming bathtub. This time he placed his detaining hand on my arm. I shook him off.

'Come on, Specs!' I said, my use of my nickname for him not entirely involuntary.

'My name's Paul,' he said. Then he spoke so softly I could hardly hear him over the hubbub beside us.

'What?'

'I do have something to hide,' he said in a clearer tone.

One of the girls at the counter glanced in our direction and said something to her companions. They all sniggered. My cheeks grew hot. They must imagine I was scraping the barrel with my choice of boyfriend. Enquiringly, I raised my eyebrows at Specs. Get on with it!

'I saw that old woman before I came to your room,' he said.

'Oh!' I thought a minute; then shrugged my shoulders. 'Well, she was always wandering round the hall.'

'She was my aunt,' he said.

I gazed at him in amazement.

'My Aunt Ada,' he added.

I wasn't sure whether to believe him. Mrs Margoloys had never mentioned a nephew. But then, I had never had any lengthy conversations with her. If he were her nephew, he couldn't be the strange man she had confessed to me. And as a close relation, he had every reason to visit her. Obviously, the Police would want to interview him. Was he telling the truth? Or inventing a plausible excuse for entering the building? If so, it was a stupid lie, as it could so easily be checked and verified.

This had completely altered the parameters of the case. I had to get away from him for a minute, away from his thick-lipped grimace and his owlish blinking. The loo was probably disgusting.

'I'm going to get another coffee,' I said. 'Can I get you anything?'

He shook his head. I escaped to the end of the queue. His aunt! For God's sake! I had never seen him before the concert.

Was he hoping for a legacy and had finished her off to speed things up? I remembered I had not expressed commiserations for his loss.

'Yes?' The snake of people had moved too quickly.

'Cappuccino, please.' I wanted out. Another tendril connecting me and Mrs Margoloys was too much to bear. What a rotten thing that Specs had sat next to me last Friday evening! I was in enough shit anyway, without this added complication. Whatever Specs' problems were, they had nothing to do with me. As I handed over a note and waited for change, I wondered if the music student, Emily, knew that Specs had the seat next to hers. And couldn't stomach the idea of sitting beside him. No! I was going crazy. I had handed in the spare ticket at the box office. Anybody could have bought it: unless it was on the other side. I had assumed the empty seat belonged to my ticket. I tried to recall who was sitting on my left at the concert. I had taken my seat and buried my head in my programme. The places on that side were full. I had imagined the people sitting there were all together.

I resumed my seat at the table. 'Have you visited your aunt before?' I asked. It seemed a bit late now to say I was sorry. He shook his head.

'Only just moved to London,' he said. 'At college here. She's my aunt by marriage. My mum asked me to see if I could find her and how she was.'

He said no more and sat staring gloomily into his empty cup. I drank my fresh coffee and waited in silence. I didn't want to know anything about him. I imagined him leaving some rundown Northern or Midland suburb, while his mother fussed around him, terrified about his safety in the big, bad city. If he was in this thing up to his neck, it was nothing to do with me. It was up to him to do something about it. All I wanted was the heat off Michael and myself.

A great explosion of laughter from further inside the café hit us like shell fire. I replaced my cup on its saucer.

'Well, I really must go. Things to do.'

'Are you going away?' he asked dully. 'Leaving London?'
'Not to my knowledge,' I responded, as I rose to my feet.
'I do have a job here.' If this were a film, I would be stroking
my gloves down my fingers as I looked at the top of his head.
His hair was thick and needed attention from a good barber.
'I hope you get things sorted out.'

I wondered if he would be involved in the administration
of Mrs Margoloys' estate, although the term seemed a joke.
I remembered I still hadn't given my condolences on the death
of his aunt by marriage. It was too late now.

'Go to the police,' I said. 'Tell them the position. That's
the best advice I can give you.'

I turned and walked smartly out of the door of the coffee
house and crossed the road at the traffic lights without looking
back. I had no doubt that Specs would still be sitting exactly
as I had left him. I dreaded what might be waiting when
I arrived at my road, but the street was deserted. No police
vehicles or burly cameramen with the bulky implements of
their trade. Had they decamped to Northamptonshire? Had
that put the venom into the voice on my office 'phone? The
treasonous thought jumped into my head that she deserved
Michael more than I did.

* * *

At last, I was home. The Press had gone. The street was
empty. I threw my things down in the hall and immediately
went to turn on the bath taps. I poured a generous amount of
Elegance foam into the gushing water, took my white towelling robe from its hook and went into the bedroom to undress.

I remembered the occasion when Michael and I had bathed
together. Black candles glowed from every surface, reflected
and gleaming in the silver bucket containing the Champagne.
We romped and rolled in the tub like a couple of porpoises.
That was about the extent of our dalliance. I thought it daring
and joyous but, as I recalled it now, Michael had been

somewhat embarrassed at our antics. Gloomy, furtive sex was more his style.

As the bath filled, I moved to the kitchen and made a cup of tea with lemon. I pondered whether to take the telephone off its rest. I decided against it, but I certainly wouldn't answer it. Let it ring its tiny heart out! It could be Mrs Poison Ivy again. If there were anything urgent or important, no doubt a message would be left.

I dropped my robe round my ankles and climbed into the fragrant water. It seemed an age since I had been able to relax, to let go on all the stresses and pain encompassing my life. What a difference a week makes! Harold Wilson said that a week was a long time in politics. Well, a week was a long time in my fraught existence at Nottingham Place.

Now mercifully departed, the Press gang had stretched from Marylebone Road to Marylebone High Street. A la Diana, I had put my head down and marched through them uttering not a word. When I reached my front door – happily still protected by two stalwart policemen – I turned to them and threw them two words: no comment.

I began to seriously consider Margot's offer to stay with her for a few days or, better still, find an anonymous hotel for myself (I had even left one morning with a half-filled suitcase to confuse them). Now, the street was empty. After all, what was it but a run-of-the-mill murder and I but one of many M.Ps' mistresses?

With a little shock, I now realised that the Police had moved on also. During the week there had been another two murders in London. The body of a young girl had been fished out of the Thames and a fatal stabbing had occurred in Fulham.

Archie had appeared as I left one morning and thrown his arms around me with great dramatic bravura.

'Poor darling! My poor darling!' he crooned in my ear. 'What must you be suffering, beautiful sweetness'.

I pushed him away with some brusqueness. Our frolics seemed a million years ago.

'Don't, Archie!' I implored. 'Please!'

'Ah! She wants to be alone,' said Archie. He didn't appear miffed. But he didn't come to my room again. I remembered his remarks about his girlfriend and her wariness over the police presence at 19A. Could it be he was involved in repercussions in that area? Drug-pushing, say? And, after all, what was I but a jilted mistress? I couldn't be locked up for that.

My work colleagues regarded me with renewed interest, but nobody questioned me. It seemed there was a tacit agreement to leave me alone. And what was there to tell? Just another bloody silly woman making a fool of herself over a married man. And what a dated attitude that is in today's permissive climate! Somebody else gets there first! So what! Take what you can grab and enjoy forbidden fruits. Women since the dawn of time have been doing likewise. But don't get involved!

Yes, it had been one hell of a week! And I was dreading the weekend. I closed my eyes, sank down to my chin in foam. What was Specs about? What a coincidence he had tried to pick me up when his aunt – by marriage, my tired mind insisted – lived in the same building! Or did he engineer it to have an excuse to enter the premises? Was he lying? Or was he merely mistaken? He had called her Ada. They had said Rosa in the television report. However you looked at it, he was certainly a peculiar young man.

If anyone knocked on my door, I would ignore it, the Police or whoever. I had too much to sort out. Why the hell had I performed with Archie? It was all grist to the mill with those two young thespians. Our relationship had been so straightforward before. Well, no doubt it still was as far as they were concerned. They probably jumped into bed with different women a dozen times a week.

What the hell were we all searching for in such desperation? A meaningful relationship? Love and affection? I was done with all that. I had achieved nothing from my crazy, dangerous liaison. And yet my dilemma seemed small beer compared to the sins of the world. Just another sordid, self-indulgent, messy affair! Well, from now on, things would change!

After a long time, I climbed out of the bath. The water was cooling and I was in danger of falling asleep. I remembered a young woman who died of hypothermia in her own bathtub as the water chilled icily around her. It was widely supposed that she was drunk.

I wrapped myself in white towelling and went to sit in front of the television. It was just on ten p.m. I would not watch the News. I had enough news to last me all year. There would be something more entertaining elsewhere.

I switched on BBC1. Problems between India and Kashmir. A further difficulty with spin doctors in the Department of Transport. I wondered if the elderly ladies in their cubbyholes followed the antics of the spin doctors. When was that phrase coined? They were a new breed as far as I was concerned. I was weary to death. I really should find something to eat. Cheese and biscuits in a minute.

I awoke with a start. The hands on the little ormolu clock pointed to thirty five minutes past midnight. Damnation! Fuck it! I had been asleep for more than two hours. Now my sleep pattern was out of cinch. I felt woozy. The flat was a tip. I switched the lamps off, stumbled to the bedroom and pulled my nightdress over my head. Tomorrow was another day. I would cope with things tomorrow.

On the verge of sleep, I seemed to remember a tiny noise had awoken me. A footfall on the stair? Somebody prowling outside in the street? Should I get up and check the lock on the door? No! I recalled fixing the bolt and chain. Anyway, I was too tired. I pulled the sheet over my head and slept.

CHAPTER SIX

Saturday morning! I was dreading the weekend. The Press had left Nottingham Place, but there was no knowing when they would be back.

If I had hoped for a glimpse of Michael on the box, I was not disappointed. He appeared in a photo call with his handsome, smiling wife. At least his children were not present. He had learned something from David Mellor. Michael gave an admirable, restrained performance as he resigned from his newly-appointed position. Poor Michael! He had barely put his foot on the slippery ministerial ladder before it was kicked away from under him.

But that was the least of my worries. Early on Saturday morning, the Police rang. I knew it was going to happen. Nevertheless, it was gut-wrenching when it did. Would I present myself at the police station? Very polite and courteous. Would I like a police car to pick me up? I declined the offer. Said I would be there by eleven.

My interview was extremely relaxed, more like a cosy chat than an interrogation. I was closeted with another attractive policewoman who looked younger than me. Perhaps they thought that if it were girls together I would be more confiding. A mistaken assumption on their part! I have always gelled better with men; girly camaraderie has never been my scene.

I was offered coffee and biscuits. We sat in an empty office rather than one of those bare interview rooms with a recording machine on the desk and a grim faced officer at the door, familiar from television dramas.

'I thought you might prefer this to a visit to your home.'

Sensitive and sympathetic! We were sitting in low chairs in an office tastefully furnished in terracotta and black.

'We do appreciate you dropping by,' said the young woman, as though I had any choice in the matter. She had removed her jacket and looked cool and confident in her crisp white blouse. 'I hope it hasn't interfered with your plans for the day.'

'No!' I said. 'Not at all! I hadn't arranged anything for today.' Now I thought about it, this tidy office was a welcome relief from Nottingham Place. And I had lost my taste for wandering the streets where Specs seemed to hide behind every façade. 'How can I be of help?'

'Well, we just wanted to know if you had remembered anything that might be relevant. People do sometimes recall some small occurrence that could be useful. For instance, have there been any unusual callers at your building recently? Have you noticed any strangers in the public areas?'

'The only public areas are the stairs and hall,' I answered her. 'I told the other officer about the young man I met at the concert.'

'Ah, yes!' The young woman turned and picked up the folder lying on her desk. 'Paul Mansell!' She glanced briefly at the papers inside it before returning her gaze to me. 'You didn't know him previously?'

'No! But he seemed to be following me after the concert. And I appear to bump into him everywhere these days.'

She said nothing, but looked at me enquiringly.

'He was waiting at Baker Street Underground when I came home last night.'

'Oh?'

'Apparently he is Mrs Margoloys' nephew.'

She raised her eyebrows. Was I telling her something?

'So he informed me last evening, anyway.'

She picked up the folder again and made a note at the bottom of the sheet.

'I don't know whether it is true.' I spoke as she was writing. 'He seems rather a strange young man. But it would

explain why he was in the building. I assumed he had just followed me home.'

'Hmm! Not very pleasant for you.' She tapped her fingernail lightly on the folder. 'Have you seen anyone else?'

'I don't think so. Oh! Archie brought a new girl friend in.
But she was with him all the time, I imagine.'

'And your friend, Mr. ...?' She paused again and consulted
her notes. Was it possible she hadn't registered Michael's name?

Now we had come to it! Michael was to be discussed. The
previous queries had been part of a softening-up process. This
wasn't going to be easy. Whatever he was, Michael wasn't a
friend. Lover, liar, lecher, manipulator, adulterer, exploiter,
deceiver! Friend! What a joke!

I waited as she went through the charade of checking
Michael's name. As if she hadn't slavered all over the tabloids
during the last two days! I drew a deep breath and became
aware that the pounding of my heart was gently lifting my
shirt. Up, down. Up, down. I took a gulp of coffee. She was
still reading her notes.

'Mr. Rutter,' she said at last. Now she looked at me. 'Was
he a regular visitor?'

'About once a week.' My voice sounded reasonable, calm,
as though I were speaking about an insurance collector or the
window cleaner. You bloody fool, she was thinking. Or, you
lucky bitch!

'And for how long had he been visiting you,' - was there a
slight hiatus in her sentence, or did I imagine it, 'once a week?'

'Two years,' I said. In spite of my resolve, my eyes watered,
either with loss, shame, humiliation, or all three of them.

'And when was the last time he came to your building?'

'A week ago last Thursday.' I bit my tongue to prevent
myself from blurting out that he always came on Thursdays.

'And you've not seen him since?'

I bent my head. I didn't answer. My last painful meeting
with Michael was no business of hers. It was nothing to do
with Mrs Margoloys' murder.

There was a knock on the door and a police officer put his head round it. She looked up, shook her head with a slight frown, and he withdrew.

'You've not seen him since?' she persisted.

Ought I to tell her? Otherwise, I could be deemed to be perverting the course of justice. It is no business of theirs, the voice in my head insisted. Whatever I said would no doubt reach the Press. Last tryst for jilted lover! Why the hell should I do their work for them? They would get it wrong anyway! No doubt Michael had kept his mouth shut and nobody else knew about our assignation on the Embankment. It was private. The last thing between me and Michael. Nothing whatsoever to do with the murder enquiries!

'No!' I said. What the hell! They couldn't imprison me for being economical with the truth. There had been enough titillation at my expense. Enough ignorant comments by strangers across breakfast tables. If pressed or found out, I could say I thought she had meant at my flat.

'Sure?' asked the young woman. Her attractiveness had disappeared. Her grey eyes boring into mine were pale as icicles. Why was she making an issue of it? Had Michael panicked and told them everything in his chagrin? In which case I was exposed as a liar. I nodded my head.

'Tell me about your conversation with Mrs Margoloys the last time you saw her.'

Thank God, she had changed tack!

'Well, she said she was worried about a stranger in the house.'

'Was she a woman of nervous disposition?'

'Not at all! She was very sociable and friendly. Rather lonely, I thought, when she was left behind at home as we all went about our own concerns.'

It sounded heartless. It was heartless.

'You knew her well?'

'Not really! I just exchanged a word with her when I was going in and out.'

'You didn't know she had a nephew?'

'No! She never mentioned him to me.'

'Well!' she said. She tidily aligned her papers. 'Can you think of anything unusual that has happened in the past week or so? People hanging about outside, say? Anything at all out of the ordinary?'

'I don't think so,' I said, slowly. I hadn't noticed anything suspicious at all, apart from Specs' persistence, which had caused me so much irritation. Why had I reacted so strongly against him? Perhaps because he punctured my self-esteem. I didn't want to be seen with him. And he got in the way of my absorption with Michael. Had I noticed anything properly for the past two years?

'Have you any leads?' I asked. 'It is such a terrible thing to happen. A poor old woman in her own home, doing no harm to anyone.'

The young officer closed the folder. I ask the questions, was her attitude. She was non-committal in her reply. 'We're working on it.' She smiled, put out her hand and shook mine. 'Thank you for coming in. We'll be in touch.'

I was dismissed. She opened the door and a policeman materialized to escort me to the outer door. The corridor was empty, as were the chairs in the lobby.

'It's very quiet,' I said.

'It is now,' answered my guide. 'If you come back tonight, it will be bursting at the seams. At least the dregs of one drunken brawl and a bucketful of sick on the floor.'

I shuddered. 'Sooner you than me!'

He laughed. 'Not a nice place on a Saturday night,' he said. 'But you get used to it.'

He opened the outer door, closed it behind me. I was down the steps and on a quiet road of North West London.

What now? What indeed! I was a liar. How long would it be before I was exposed? What had been the point? They had learned nothing more about the murder. I had told them nothing I hadn't said before, except my stupid pride had caused me to lie about my last meeting with Michael. What did it matter? He hadn't done it. For want of another plan, I made my way to the nearest bus stop and waited for a bus to Baker Street.

* * *

Back home, I sat at the kitchen table and remembered my last conversation with Margot.

'Come back with me. I don't like to think of you alone in that flat.' She pushed her glasses higher up her nose and looked at me seriously. 'After all, one woman has already been murdered there.'

'Thanks for reminding me!' My voice was sharper than I had intended. My nerves were frazzled. She looked at me quizzically.

'The murderer isn't likely to come back. We are too high profile. And I don't want you bothered by the evil practitioners of the Press.'

She shrugged, perhaps with relief, or perhaps she realised my need to be solitary, to think, to lick my wounds in private. 'Well, ring me if you change your mind. I'll come and collect you if you don't want to go out by yourself.'

'It's not as bad as that, Margot. Not yet!' But it was! I didn't want to walk the streets unprotected. 'I'll be fine! Really!'

'Well, I don't want to see you all over the Sunday newspapers.' She bit her lip. She hadn't meant it in quite the way it sounded.

I forced a laugh. 'Neither do I!'

'Well, must dash!' She began to gather her things together. 'Meeting somebody! Remember! Ring me! Promise?'

Now I moved from the kitchen to my minimalized sitting room and sat on the floor clutching a cushion to my breast. I considered joining a dating agency, considered it and put the idea on the back burner to simmer. It was not a good time.

I would attract the perverts and weirdos. Nevertheless, I could amuse myself by studying the self-seeking advertisements in newspapers and magazines. There were hundreds of attractive, interesting, solvent, romantic, red-blooded males out there, according to their own promotion. Where were they all hiding? I wondered if Specs were buried in the small print. Take your time and they will come to you! That piece of advice had come from my late father.

I wondered if my mother knew of my dilemma. I would go and see her as soon as the Police allowed me out of London. I would go and relax and vegetate on the wild Norfolk coast and be pampered and cosseted by my nearest relation. I sighed and wept a little. Why were we all so far away from each other?

I sat there a long time. I dwelled on the fact that two floors below me a defenceless old woman had been battered to death for God knows what reason. And that very likely the crime would never be solved! I felt the terror and injustices of the world.

At last, when the room was in darkness and the window was reduced to a dull glimmer reflected from the light outside, I rose, switched on the table lamps and drew the curtains. I peered from the kitchen window at an empty street, apart from a solitary cat padding along the far pavement. 'When cats run home and night is come!'

I made a cup of Instant coffee and sat down opposite the television set with the remote control in my hand.

Michael's face was on the screen. God help me! I was going mad! What was he up to now? The camera panned back and showed him escorted by two police officers. He was being helped into a police car, his head solicitously guarded from contact with the door frame.

Reality receded. The image changed. A newscaster mouthed unintelligible words. Why were they arresting Michael? For God's sake, why was Michael being arrested? Another story began.

I stared uncomprehendingly at the screen. Had my eyes deceived me? It wasn't news time. What was happening? Was Michael being arrested or had my fevered brain imagined it? Was it a special news flash? I had no Radio Times, so could not check the programme times. Feverishly I searched through the Evening Standard for the television page. An idiotic comedy progressed before my frantic gaze.

I switched channels. Channel Five had perpetual news programmes. Again Michael's face appeared large on my set. Now I was listening to the commentary.

'Michael Rutter is helping the police with their enquiries into the death of Mrs Rosa Margoloys. (Surely Specs had called her Aunt Ada! Couldn't they even get her name right?) Mrs Margoloys was killed five days ago in her home in Central London.'

Another shot of Michael being hustled down the street and into the police car. Was that near where he lived in Northamptonshire? 'This is breaking news,' intoned the impersonal voice. 'We will return to it when we have more information.'

Shaking, I pressed the button and shut off the transmission. I tried to think, tried to assess what I had just seen, what it could mean.

Michael! My darling! Why have they arrested you? What bungling idiots have decided that was the thing to do? What fools law enforcers are! They arrest an innocent man while the real culprit is roaming free!

Michael! Michael! What have I done to you? No wonder the Press had disappeared from Nottingham Place. They must have received a tip-off about the forthcoming arrest. They had no doubt hot-footed it to Northamptonshire and were even now scoffing tea and sandwiches outside his house. Or were they waiting at his London flat? How the hell could Michael be a suspect? He had not been to Nottingham Place for ten days! Thursday was his day, not Tuesday when Mrs Margoloys had been murdered. I had seen her alive and well last Monday evening and no doubt the other residents had seen her at the weekend.

Michael never came to the flat without my prior knowledge. But he had no intention of standing waiting on my doorstep. That was why he had his own key. Since then, I had seen him fleetingly at our last traumatic meeting on the Embankment.

I ought to ring the Police and tell them those facts. As far as they knew, I was the last person to see Mrs Margoloys alive. Timing was so important in these matters. It was so easy to get it wrong.

I had stomach ache. Perhaps I was developing appendicitis. If I rang the Police, would I be taken seriously? I had been his girlfriend for a long while. His girlfriend would cover for him, wouldn't she? Of course I would!

And I could be a suspect myself? Was that why they had picked up Michael? Was it a ploy for my own entrapment? Would he drop me in the shit to save his own skin? What a stupid question! Of course he would!

I longed for somebody to talk to, for some impartial advice. Me? Strong-willed, self-reliant, independent woman? How about Jason or Archie? Neither of them was an ideal choice, but I couldn't think of anybody else.

I put my head out of my door and listened. The house was silent. No voices or music. Dim lights glowed on the stair well. Had everyone packed up and left the premises? Were they even now laughing and joking with friends and relatives? Hadn't I walked out of the house carrying a suitcase in order to deceive the Press? One thing was certain: either the house was empty or the other occupants were making as little noise as I was. I closed my door again and leaned on it. Was I alone in the building?

Anyway, were any of them safe to confide it? We were all potential suspects since the arrest of Michael was a joke. Francesca had her Mafia-style customers, Archie his dodgy girlfriend. I hardly knew the music students. How about Jason? Effusive, good-natured, damaged. Sammy, seldom present. Had Sammy slipped in, done the dastardly deed, and then disappeared back to Tufnell Park? Had any of them wielded the murder weapon?

With a pang, I realised that Mrs Margoloys had been the only stable element amongst us. And she was the one who had been cruelly cut down.

I had been deluded into thinking the publicity was dying. It wasn't. Now it would flare up again, particularly as far as I was concerned. The absence of the Press hordes was the lull before the storm. For some reason, the film, Zulu, came to mind. The gallant band of defenders were surrounded. However many times the tribes were repelled, more and more appeared in their place, flowing like lava down the hillsides in a symbol of diligent black death.

I locked and bolted my door. This was going to be all over the newspapers tomorrow. And it wouldn't be long before I was part of it.

* * *

Michael had not been detained. There was a quick flash of him on the News Update. He looked grim and pale as he climbed into a car outside the police station where I had been received with such courtesy.

As for me, what now? My life had fallen apart, just as his had done. Not with so much publicity but, nevertheless, I was bereft.

On Sunday afternoon, I sat on my sofa, clutching a cushion against my stomach and assessed my possibilities. I had the feeling of a great void underneath my feet. If I moved less than cautiously in any direction, I would fall into it. My life had been so bound up in Michael, how would I survive now that his prop had been removed from me?

I had resisted the desire to put the Whisky bottle on the table before me. Now I fetched it from the kitchen and poured out a generous measure. Alcohol and breast cancer? What the hell! I took up the glass and examined its ancient amber colour against the light. The nectar of the gods! I took a sip, grimacing at its bitterness.

Well, Michael was finished as far as I was concerned. Michael had involved at most two hours a week. The rest of it was all my fantasy. Anyway, I didn't have much choice. Apart from everything else – the raw publicity, the ridicule, the fury of his wife – he would never forgive me for the ruination of his brilliant aspirations. He was not a forgiving man. In his mind, I would be identified as the author of his troubles. He would not wish to be in the same room as me, ever again. Probably not even in the same country.

So, what was I going to do about the rest of my life? Get over him, that's what! Not next year, not five years hence, but perhaps in twenty years' time I would only intermittently think of him. I buried my head in the cushion. No tears came. I was as shrivelled, dried out as an old pea pod. I took another sip of Whisky.

I would throw myself into work and study. I could change my job. Red light! Don't do anything rash on the spur of the moment. Hadn't I said that to someone not long ago? I had a good degree; I could do research and gain additional qualifications. It would do me no harm, even if it did me no good. Did I wish to spend the next three years with computers and old books? At my age? No, I didn't! My job was stressful, but my employers were supportive. If I informed them that it was not possible to do an efficient piece of work in the time available, they would not be unduly censorious. Not a light consideration, these days!

I thought about joining a dating agency, and put the idea on the back burner. Now was not a good time. I would only attract the ne'er do wells. I had realised that before. Nevertheless, I could study the self-seeking advertisements in newspapers and magazines. There were hundreds of attractive, interesting, romantic, red-blooded males out there, according to their own promotion. Where were they all hiding? I wondered if Specs were buried in the small print. Take your time and they will come to you. My late father had once given me that advice. I wondered if my mother knew of my dilemma. I would go and see her as soon as the police allowed me out of London.

Was there life after Michael? That was the million dollar question! I could enhance my leisure interests. Have a damn' good time! I could go to a gym. The consequent adrenalin would pep me up. I could learn to tango or line dance. I could take up intellectual pursuits, learn Russian or Arabic or Chinese. I could broaden my mind at the same time as I reduced my buttocks.

I picked up the Whisky and gulped it down. The glass was empty. I refilled it. The contents of the bottle were going down fast. Don't drink alone, I admonished myself! It is so joyless and pathetic.

How quiet the house was! How empty! Sunday afternoon! The time for leisure and recreation! I thought of poor Mrs Margoloys, desperately trying to waylay us as we dashed about on our own business. What a way to end up, in this unfriendly house! She should have been in a sunny country cottage with two sleek cats for company. Perhaps one day she had been young as me, lamenting a lost love.

I told myself I was being a fool. Life has endless possibilities for the fearless. When you are knocked off course, you pick yourself up and struggle on. I was still young, comparatively. I had the advantage of a good education. Hadn't I turned down the opportunity of working for a Member of Parliament only a few days ago? I began to laugh, amusement spilling tears down my face. The perception and the reality of what it meant to work in the Houses of Parliament were so different. Those elderly ladies fresh from their batteries must be so proud of their achievements. Good luck to them!

My head was aching. To hell with it all! Lies and reality, deception and fantasy! Too many of us spend our time in the Far Away Tree, in order to render our battles bearable.

I flung the cushion across the room. I needed air to breathe. These four walls were too constricting. I would go for a walk. I would join tourist London on the rampage.

* * *

My prospects were not as rosy as I imagined. On Monday morning I was called into M.U.'s office, given a month's notice and offered a generous settlement. Obviously they wanted no trouble with the Unfair Dismissals Tribunal.

'It isn't my decision, Fran,' said a noticeably embarrassed Managing Director. 'Your private life is none of our business as far as I am concerned.'

He trailed off. I was stunned. More so, since in all my cogitations, I had not envisaged this. I had always taken it for granted that the decision as to whether I went or stayed in my employment was under my own control. I was captain of my fate, etc. What a fool! Of course, adverse publicity, unlike that for celebrities, was not beneficial for client relationships. We operated on our good name. An unsavoury murder, even by association, was not permissible. My predicament vis-a-vis Michael was good for a giggle but not for building confidence in the integrity of the firm. I felt my face burn. My mouth had been open to protest. I closed it again.

'I quite understand the position, Mr. Jarvis,' I said with as much dignity as I could muster. It came out snottily and cold. He rose and held out his hand.

'You appreciate we have no problem with your work,' he said. 'In fact, I feel we have been fortunate to have had your services over the past few years.' He fiddled with his paper knife and avoided my eyes. God knows how many other employees were doing what I had done. 'You have always worked efficiently, with dedication and loyalty to the firm.'

Past tense. It was over. And I was sick of this protracted leave-taking.

'No false eulogies, please,' I said stiffly. The big boss had obviously come down hard on M.U. She must go. And the sooner the better. Or could it have been, What do you think we should do about her? A quick consultation over a game of golf as they dissected my life. M.U.: Yes, I think she should be asked to leave. Pity! But the good name of the firm is paramount. A lot of competition these days. And the Chairman, Well, she's not exactly a whizz kid. Competent enough, but not too difficult to replace, I would imagine. And back they went to their putting and swings.

'I won't take the month's notice,' I said. How could I possibly keep coming here for that length of time, suffering Margot's sympathy and the curious glances of the junior staff? Perhaps one of them would apply for my job. 'I don't think that would be appropriate.'

'No?' said M.U. He must be relieved.

'I would like to go at the end of this week,' I said. Untrue! I would like to walk out now. The unfairness of everything smote me hard. After all the late night hours I had put in to keep abreast of difficult cases, while those in charge swanned around the cocktail circuit. Tears of rage or self-pity stung behind my eyelids. I turned to go.

'I will make sure my workload is comprehensible to my successor,' I said, as I envisaged packing the files with misleading information and false trails. 'I will let Margot know if anything needs particular care and attention.'

I opened the door and fled. Miss Plaice in the outer office did not look up. Was I crying? No! I was shaking with shock and fury. Sod the lot of them! I went into the loo on the top corridor and took some deep breaths to try and calm myself. After a minute or so, I went down to my office.

'I'm leaving,' I said without preamble to the top of Margot's bent head. Had she known, or suspected?

'What?' She jerked upright and stared at me.

No, she didn't know. I realised that my departure would make a difference to her life. She would have to share the office with a stranger.

'What are you talking about?'

'I've been requested, no, ordered, to go!'

'No! You're joking! The rotten shits!'

She wasn't play-acting. She was genuinely shocked, as taken aback as I had been in M.U.'s office. 'After all the work you have done for them. The rotten shits!' she repeated. 'Talk about kick a dog when he's down! You must have worked harder than any of us.'

'I have become an embarrassment, a liability,' I said bitterly. 'Adverse publicity is not welcome in this establishment.'

'Well, the ungrateful bastards!' Margot was almost spluttering in her disbelief.

Absentmindedly, I took a plastic bag and began stowing in it the contents of my drawers: make-up, a small towel, tissues, hand cream. She watched me.

'You're not going now? This minute? Surely they have given you some notice?'

'End of the week.' I stopped my labours.

'Is that all they gave you? Unbelievable!'

'No! M.U. suggested the end of the month.'

'But you told him to stuff his job? Good for you!' She came over and put her arms round me. I realised she was crying. I hugged her hard.

'Come on, Margot! It's probably a blessing in disguise. I can appreciate their point about negative publicity. We run on good name and good will.'

We broke apart. I sat down at my desk. 'I had been thinking about making a move,' I said slowly. 'This is the kick up the ass I needed.'

'Oh, Fran!' said Margot. 'I didn't realise. Well, take your time. Look around. You're too good to throw yourself away.'

She meant with regard to employment, but her remark could equally well apply to the rest of my life. 'Have a holiday,' she added.

I smiled. Who the hell would go on holiday with me? My life was not a romantic novel where old friends materialized from the West Country at the stroke of a pen.

'A week will give me time to get things up to date.'

'With overtime?' asked Margot, laconically.

'Then, say Thursday afternoon, if that suits you. I could go over my cases with you, so there is no hiccup in the changeover.'

Margot gave what could be interpreted as a snort. 'You are too conscientious,' she said. 'If I were in your position, I would be throwing files out of the window. I certainly wouldn't be doing anything to make life easier for them.'

Words, words, words, I thought wearily. If you were in my position, Margot, you would be doing exactly what I am doing now.

We said no more. But that afternoon, it became obvious that somebody on the top corridor had a similar suspicion about what I might do with my work-in-hand. A telephone call from M.U.'s secretary, the icy Miss Plaice, instructed me to gather together all my cases and take them to the office of the Vice Principal. They would be inspected and I would be called upon if my presence were required for clarification. Would I hold myself in readiness for the rest of the week? I gained the impression that Miss Plaice was enjoying her role in this little melodrama.

When I conveyed the gist of this conversation to Margot, she went scarlet with anger.

'What a bloody cheek! Those little Hitlers up there daring to pronounce on your cosseted clients! What a fucking nerve!'

In a way, it was a relief. Now I could walk out with a clear conscience. I began stacking the work-in-progress, taking folders from my desk drawers and filing cabinets.

'Well!' I said. 'This way there can be no suggestion that I damaged any of the company's property. Or that I refused to comply with reasonable requests from Management.'

Margot sniffed.

'Then, I'm leaving. Perhaps you would help me carry these upstairs, Margot.'

I made sure the software was up-to-date and ran a computer print-out of the latest developments I had been working on. I regretted the schoolgirls in Chelsea. I had enjoyed that encounter.

'I didn't really want to hang about all week,' I said. 'This gives me an excuse to go straightaway.'

Margot's eyes again filled with tears. She was much more emotional than I had realised. I clipped the print-out to the top folder and picked up an armful of files. A lesser pile waited on my desk.

'Coming?'

'Fuck them!' Margot muttered as she gathered up the remaining folders. 'Fuck them!'

'I'll write my memoirs,' I promised, ironically.

We took the lift, which was mercifully empty, to the top floor. All the doors up there were closed, apart from that of the Vice President's secretary.

'Oh, thanks very much, Fran.' She avoided my eyes. She was another middle-aged woman with neat grey hair, always dressed in suits of neutral colour. I had never before given her a thought. Well, it wasn't her fault, whatever happened to me.

As she took the files from me, I noticed she wore a wedding ring. Was she happily married, then, or a childless widow? I had no idea. She put the folders on her desk, before taking Margot's bundle from her. Neither of us spoke. As we walked back to the lift, we heard her office door close.

'And much good may it do them,' grumbled Margot. 'They won't understand a word of your subtleties. You had the relationships with the clients, not them.'

'Leave it, Margot! Nobody is indispensable.'

Back in our office, I quickly packed the remainder of my belongings, while Margot clucked round me like a broody hen.

'You will keep in touch, won't you?' And then, 'Aren't you going to say goodbye to anyone? Not that I see why you should!'

'Just Albert on the front desk, probably. I pass him on the way out.'

She made me a cup of coffee. 'They will regret it,' she said. 'Just you see! When you've gone, they'll find out just how much you did.'

'I wouldn't bank on it!'

I was glad I had never treated the office like home and filled my space with little treasures. I took a travel poster off the wall and stuffed it in the waste paper basket.

'Shall I leave the calendar?' I asked. Monet's water lilies floated above the month of June.

'Yes, of course! Unless you want it.'

Margot was wringing her hands. I had never seen anyone do that before. Soon my belongings, my work trappings for the last four years, were in plastic bags. I took a sip of the cooling coffee.

'Thanks, Margot! You've been a real good mate!'

'We will keep in touch,' she promised, as she threatened to dissolve into tears again. Why had I ever imagined her to be hard and steely and self-contained?

'God!' she burst out. 'It is all so unfair! A mugger murders an old woman and other people's lives are ruined.'

I was calm, controlled. Must be my training with Michael, I thought with cynical detachment.

'Do you want help with the bags? I could come to the Underground with you.'

'No, Margot! You have done more than enough. But I would sooner say goodbye here, honestly!'

She hugged me again. 'Okay! If that's how you want it! But don't disappear! Keep in touch! Promise!'

'All right,' I said. 'Of course, we'll keep in touch. We have been part of each other's lives for a long time.'

I hugged her back. I picked up the plastic bags and left my office for the last time. Margot watched me to the lift, blew a kiss as it arrived. The doors opened, I stepped inside and was borne down to the ground floor. Albert was on the telephone when I passed his desk. He barely glanced at me.

'Goodbye, Albert,' I said.

He nodded in reply, obviously thinking I was merely going about the day's business.

I was outside. Out and down the steps. Red buses, taxis, people rushing about. Bustling London! All as usual! And I could shake the dust of A.J. Properties off my shoes for ever.

* * *

Walking out to make a gesture was all very well, but what was I going to do now? I hadn't discussed the terms of my settlement. Had I forfeited their goodwill by my precipitate departure? I would have to ring up, tell a white lie, say I had been too upset to stay. I would probably have to return to the premises to see A.J. In that case, I would swan in, dressed to the nines, as though I were a wealthy client.

I had to get home. I would not walk the streets any more. I seemed to have been walking London streets for the past millennium. I wanted peace, quiet and tranquil reflection. I prayed the Police and Press had not returned to Nottingham Place.

They hadn't. The road was empty as I made my hasty way to my own front door. Again, the house was preternaturally silent. Were the hell were Jason and Archie? I scuttled up the stairs as had been my habit when I was endeavouring to avoid Mrs Margoloys.

I locked myself into my flat. Strange, being here in the middle of the afternoon. Sunlight slanted across the floor in barred diagonals. I made a cup of coffee. Margot would just be filling the kettle in our cloakroom. Odd, how she had appeared to be really distressed at my departure. I had never imagined she had much surplus affection for me, although we had rubbed along together well enough.

All this time, Michael had been constantly bobbing around in the back of my mind where I had resolutely pushed him. Now he came back to the fore with sickening urgency. I sat down at the kitchen table. I must think. I must think hard. Right this minute!

The trouble with instructing yourself to think is that it is counter-productive. All sorts of rubbish churn through the mind, but constructive thought in such difficult circumstances is elusive. Nevertheless, I must try.

First, by the end of the month, I must find myself gainful employment. I would be all right financially for a few weeks if A.J. Company honoured its word and paid a month's salary and a severance settlement. But I couldn't wait too long before I began looking for work, since the inevitable time lag would occur before I received any salary from my new employment.

Michael was standing before me, shaking an admonitory finger. You silly woman, he was mouthing. You always leap before you look. Give yourself room for manoeuvre. Never cut off your line of retreat. Like you have done for the last few years, I mocked, and whether I was mocking myself or him, I wasn't sure.

Okay, that was number one priority. Find a job! So what was number two? Another man?

I could sit still no longer. I rose and prowled my flat from end to end, as though I might find one hiding behind the curtains. I wondered if Francesca was in. Did she stay in bed all day, or did she watch endless videos while wearing a satin kimono? Perhaps she had daytime employment. I wouldn't know. But if she was asleep downstairs, my lengthy peregrinations might awaken and scare the shit out of her. I was, after all, supposed to be working. Why didn't I join the ladies of the night? I was sure she earned a great deal more than I did.

Michael was shaking his head violently. He was about to explode. No, I couldn't stand the idea of another man, not for a very long time. So, what else was there to consider? My life?

Yes! Just the simple matter of the rest of my life! Where was I going now? My life had been boring and meaningless for too long. I had even been impatient of giving the time of day to a poor, harmless old woman. Oh, the arrogance of the young! I must improve my behaviour. How about joining Voluntary Services Overseas? But I wasn't a nurse or a teacher. What skill had I to offer the unfortunate sufferers of the world?

I sighed deeply; I poured myself a glass of water. I had only been in the flat twenty minutes. It was a quarter to four. What was I to do with the rest of my life? I put my head in my hands. I understood why people turned to drugs and alcohol. Foolish! Foolish! Foolish! But how the hell did we cope otherwise? As Charles Dickens realised, life is a perpetual battle. Write a book? What had I to write about, except two pathetic, inadequate human beings who spent a little time together, messed everything up and then fell apart. I hadn't even had an unhappy childhood. No excuse there!

I sat stiffly on the hard chair. I realised I was waiting for something to happen: a ringing telephone, a knock on the door. Every time I had tried to come to grips with my predicament, I had been interrupted. I should not be here, of course. I should be at my office. If I were murdered in my flat, how long would it be before I were discovered? In present circumstances, nobody would miss me. Would I lie here until I began to stink?

I listened with intense concentration. Nothing! If someone had been breathing in the hall, I would have heard him. I opened the kitchen window. Muted sounds of traffic from Marylebone Road came to my ears. I fancied I could hear children at play in Regent's Park, but surely that must be my imagination. It was too far away. Perhaps they were running by the shops in Marylebone High Street.

London was pulsing and beating below me – the throbbing heart of an indifferent city. What were they all doing? Why had Mrs Margoyloys been done to death? Was it just because she was in the wrong place at the wrong time? Had she seen something, someone, she shouldn't have? I laid my face against the window pane. A cooling draught blew through he opened sash.

What I needed was a cat. Lonely women always kept cats. Why hadn't Mrs Margoloys had a cat? Sociable and independent, a cat would have been an ideal companion for her. Well, it was all too late now!

I threw away the cold coffee and made some more. I considered knocking on Francesca's door, just to see if she were there. I could ask her how she was and what she thought about our situation. Events, dear boy, events!

I slipped downstairs and knocked tentatively on Francesca's door. It was a bigger door than mine. This was the first floor: more imposing. If she were asleep, she wouldn't hear that tap. I knocked again, louder. I suspected she wouldn't be charmed to see me, but I rapped again, anyway. All was hushed behind the door barrier. Losing my nerve, I fled back up the stairs and closed my own door quietly behind me. Francesca was either out or pretending to be. Surely she didn't have a client at this time of day?

All things considered, it was probably just as well she wasn't home. What, after all, had we to say to each other? If we did not communicate, the Police would not suspect us of collaboration.

I concocted a scenario where everyone in the house was somehow involved in the crime – like Agatha Christie's Murder on the Orient Express. Archie engaged Mrs Margoloys in conversation while one of the music students bashed her head in as Sammy pinioned her arms. Or was it Jason who was talking to her as Francesca wielded the hammer? She couldn't stand her spying on her gentlemen visitors any longer. Had she a stash of cash hidden away that Specs could not wait to grab? Or had I felled her in a drunken stupor as I staggered back upstairs following my orgy with Archie and Jason?

God! I was going mad! She was just an inquisitive old woman who had got in the way of some opportunist burglar, whom she had surprised at his tricks. She probably offered him a cup of tea.

I rubbed my hands over my eyes. I hoped to God the Police made some speedy progress in their investigation of the crime.

As for me, life would go on. I would have to do something, make some plans. I could not sit around like a zombie for the rest of my days. I would go out and buy newspapers so that I could check the Situations Vacant columns. And have a look at the Lonely Hearts columns on the way through. Perhaps it was only little girls who dated on the Net!

I slipped on a sweater. It was chilly outside. And while I was about it, I would book myself a holiday. I deserved a little diversion after all I had endured. I would go somewhere fantastical and luxurious. How about the Orient Express?

CHAPTER SEVEN

The Police were grudging about my proposition.

'Not a good time to go away, Miss!'

I was silent as I held the telephone slightly away from my ear, as though I feared contamination from the other end of the line. I could still hear blurred background talk as my request was discussed.

'How long are you planning to be away?' A different voice.

'Only a week. It is a short holiday. I can't afford to go for any longer.'

'Have you considered a break in this country?'

'I like Italy. I am sure it is easier to get lost in the wilds of Scotland than on a train with hundreds of other people.'

This was considered as I waited.

'Italy?'

'Yes!'

'A week?'

'Yes!'

Yet another voice came on the line. I thought the Police Service was under-staffed!

'That will be perfectly all right, Madam. A short break sounds like a good idea. Wish I could do the same. Let us have a contact address, will you?'

'Yes. I believe we have a hotel booked in Venice.'

But I had no intention of doing so. It would be easy enough for them to find out if they were desperate. I had done nothing wrong. If I sat at home by the telephone for a week, doubtless there would be any approach.

'Well, have a good time,' said the anonymous voice briskly. 'I envy you.' And the 'phone clicked as the receiver was replaced.

I had expected more of a battle. Feeling deflated, I replaced my handset. I would be out of touch of Michael also, as if that were relevant. He had no thought of ringing me, I didn't doubt. Damn and blast him! I realised at that moment that I really didn't want to go. How could I put more distance between us than there already was? I sat down and wept.

* * *

Three days later I was standing at Victoria Station in my glad rags, with a snazzy little suitcase by my side. (Where the hell did I pick up these vile expressions? My vocabulary was as barbarous as my battered, churned-up life! I ought to return to university for a B.Ed. and teach English!)

I eyed the other passengers as the Paris Pullman drew into the station. An elderly lady with a younger couple – probably a son or daughter, stood nearby. Further away, a middle-aged man and woman, he red faced and ill at ease in a jacket and tie, she with the weather-beaten appearance of a market woman who spent a lot of time battling the elements. Perhaps they had won the lottery! Snobbish, Fran! Stop it! They had a huge suitcase. The brochure advised that only a small holdall would be suitable in the carriages of the Orient Express. Large cases would be placed in the hold. They had cocked it up before we started!

Standing near them was a young couple who had eyes only for each other. Honeymooners or illicit lovers? I was too far away to see whether the girl was wearing a ring. No doubt all would be revealed in the next few days.

Who else? Where was the tall, dark and handsome young man who should be hovering behind the bookstall? There was an elderly man, alone. He was dapper, smart, at ease, carrying his evening clothes in a suit carrier. He obviously knew what he was doing. Perhaps he took a break on the Orient Express every year.

The train, a symphony of pristine paint and gleaming brass, drew in and came to a halt. Some tired workers must have spent the night shift scrubbing it to its shiny perfection. Smiling attendants appeared at the bottom of the steps to check our tickets and help us on board. What the hell was I doing, including myself in this elaborate charade? I would be closeted with this disparate group for the coming seven days. I couldn't see myself emphasizing with any of them. At least we got to stay in a hotel in Rome and Venice. Then I could go off on my own.

'Welcome on board, Madam!'

I had reached the bottom of the steep steps leading into the train.

'Thank you!'

The attendant gave me his hand as I negotiated them. My heels were too high for this.

'Careful! Don't slip!' He had a charming smile. In fact, he was the best looking amongst us, and his voice carried the musical intonation of a native Italian speaker.

I walked down the corridor and found my compartment, three down from the entrance. I put my bag on the floor and sat down to look around. The cubicle was incredibly small. Thank God I had one to myself. That larger suitcase I had seen would totally fill the floor space. Unlike my little bag, a case that size would no way fit on the luggage rack. No wonder the brochure had stipulated no large suitcases! Lucky I had put my evening skirts and tops in a suit carrier. The elderly gent and I were the only passengers to do so.

Now, I hung it on a convenient hook and opened the polished mahogany doors of the corner cupboard. As I thought, the washbasin was concealed there. Immaculate while porcelain, with little packets of soap, toothpaste and perfume wrapped in dark blue paper, with Orient Express in gold lettering printed on it. It was very nice!

I kicked off my shoes, pushed my feet into the soft shuffle slippers that had been provided, leaned back and closed my eyes. I could get used to this. Pity the WC was down the corridor!

I looked at my watch. The train was due to leave in twenty three minutes. I had been here for five. What was I to do? Why the hell hadn't I booked a self-catering cottage in North Wales, where I could go for long walks in the lonely hills? But I knew why. The Police were uneasy about my leaving the country, so I was determined to do so. I looked at my watch again.

God! I could do with a drink. No doubt the bar would be closed until the train started its journey. I should have brought some with me. I could have bought more than a hundred bottles of Scotch for the price I was paying for this jaunt.

I stuck my head out of the door. The attendant was rushing around in a great hurry, trying to sort out the problem of the luggage, but he still had time for a beam in my direction.

'Is everything all right, Madam?'

'When does the bar open?'

'When we leave, Madam! Can I bring you anything?'

A cup of coffee would have been lovely, but I hadn't the heart to distract him from his duties.

'No! That's fine, thank you!'

He probably thought I was an alcoholic who couldn't wait to get her fingers around a glass. I pulled my door closed to shut out the sight of more anxious travellers, and sank down on the seat. Oh, Michael! My darling Michael! If only we were together here! This cramped little compartment would be ideal for us.

My mind ranged over my fellow passengers. If I had been unconsciously hoping to meet a rich businessman, I was in the wrong place. I suspected the middle-aged couple could be thinking the same thing. I had seen them sitting disconsolately in their coach, with their legs awkwardly arranged around the obstacle of their great suitcase. He looked like an outdoor worker, in the building trade, perhaps. They seemed out of their depth in the midst of this miniature opulence, and were possibly now regretting their choice of holiday in the same way I was.

The couple with the mother were more at ease. They were used to dinner at Simpsons or the Savoy Grill, I would expect. The old girl had stared haughtily at her fellow passengers, even while attempting to assess our social standing. Obviously she was a throw back to an earlier age. All nouveau riche, she was probably thinking. Nobody worthy of my attention in this little group! Those three would keep themselves to themselves, pointedly ignoring the rest of us. Well, that was no great loss!

Now, the elderly man appeared much nicer. He had genuine class, if I was not mistaken, and I had some practice in such matters, owing to my client appraisal. Eton, Oxbridge, the Military perhaps, or some equivalent. Years of dealing with A.J.'s contacts had left me with a certain instinct in that direction.

There was a knock on my door. The handsome attendant stood in the corridor with a cup of coffee in his hands.

'Thought you might like this,' he said in his beautiful, careful speech. 'The start of a journey can be a little unsettling.'

'Why, how nice! Thank you very much!'

He came into the compartment and turned down a neat gadget by the side of the window, which became a convenient table.

'I didn't do the whole tray,' he said. 'It is so busy before we leave.'

'So I'm noticing!' I said. 'This is lovely. Thank you very much.'

'Lunch is served from 12.30. Dinner is served from 7,' he said. He gave his dazzling smile and withdrew.

I sat down by the table and took up the cup. I was parched. There were so many kind people in the world. Why had I picked an out and out bastard as my soul mate? I gulped the coffee in gratitude. It was hot, strong, just as I liked it. Slowly I was recovering from the trauma of my arrival. Until the train actually departed, I could not believe that uniformed officers would not materialize at my side, with the words, 'Would you just step outside, Miss!' They were playing cat and mouse with me, giving me permission to leave, only to withdraw it when it suited them. Even now it could happen. Were a number of officers on the train at this moment, searching the immaculate compartments, disturbing the snooty threesome and agitating the great suitcase pair? What the hell had they got in there, anyway?

Again I checked my watch. How much longer before the bloody train started? Another eight minutes before we were off towards the Surrey countryside! Of course, they could wait until we reached the coast and take me off the train there, make sure I didn't leave the country. Would the Media have been alerted? I found myself counting to sixty, whiling off the minutes in my head.

Don't be so bloody stupid, Michael would say. Why should they want you in custody? You haven't done anything. You have told them all you know. Haven't you? You have certainly told them about me. His mouth set in a grim line and his eyebrows drew together. Yes, you have definitely put the boot in, as far as I am concerned.

Slowly, slowly, I wasn't imagining it, the train was beginning to move. I opened my eyes as we slid through the environs of Victoria, through the grimy grey walls to the seemingly endless suburbs of South London. We were off! I drew a deep breath.

God, how could I stand my own thoughts for the next seven days? How lonely I would be! At least, there were other people around, even if the most pleasant of them was the young attendant. And he was only doing his job. No doubt at the end of the day his face ached with all his smiling at tiresome passengers. Did he even notice them any more? Were we to him like a frieze on an ancient monument, forever in motion and forever still, real yet unreal, just part of his working life, like my computer and files?

Perhaps the cottage would not have been a good prospect. Too much introspection would have been involved. At rock bottom, I was a survivor who had picked the best option in the circumstances. I would be pampered and cosseted. I had no decisions to make for a week, apart from choosing what I would eat and drink. I would endeavour to make the best of it, even if I could not expect to enjoy it. I was paying enough for it, wasn't I?

'Didn't we see you on the television?'

The weather-beaten woman was peering into my face as I sat alone at a table for two in the dining car. She was elegantly dressed in a black evening gown, the well-filled bodice of which was heavily sequinned. Her husband hovered behind her, obviously uncomfortable in a new dinner jacket.

In the panic of the moment, I lied. 'I don't think so,' I said, with a forced laugh. 'Someone who looked like me, I suppose.'

'By yourself, dear?' persisted the woman, her pale blue eyes sharply penetrating.

'Looks like it,' I said, shortly. I picked up the menu. 'Plenty to choose from.' I pretended to study it. 'Enjoy your meal.'

I had dismissed them. They passed on down the carriage. They would not understand why their friendly overtures had been abruptly rejected. That had been stupid on my part. No point in antagonizing anybody so early in the holiday. If she did recall seeing me pestered by the Press in Nottingham Place, she could start dropping hints that I was involved in the murder enquiry. And perhaps all she meant was that I resembled someone in East Enders.

Aware of my burning cheeks, I buried my face in the menu, imagining that the other diners would see guilt written all over me. Two white-coated waiters stood impeccable and imperturbable down the gangway. As the contents of wine glasses diminished, they materialized like pale shadows to replenish them. Had they taken note of the little exchange?

Damn! Damnation! Fuck it! I had come here to get away from my turbulent anxieties, and now some interfering bloody woman could ruin everything for me. And it is all so fucking expensive! Mentally I groaned as my eyes roamed unseeing over the French nomenclature. Above all, the claustrophobic nature of this extravagant train began to appal me.

Think! Think! I must dredge up some plausible explanation. Then I could speak to her again in a friendly fashion. Would she be satisfied with that? Or did she very well remember seeing my frantic face on the small screen so recently? I had no way of knowing.

'Do you mind if I join you?'

I looked up. The elderly man, travelling alone, was standing before me. He had been absent at lunchtime. Now he was immaculate in white dinner jacket and perfectly arranged bow tie. Some feat in the confines of the narrow compartment! I had noticed one man getting dressed in the corridors as I made my way to the dining car. Obviously his partner had demanded the available space.

I smiled at him. If I could have chosen my dinner companion from our little group, I would have chosen him: a kindly, courteous, grandfather figure.

'Please do!'

He sat down opposite me behind the crisp white linen and sparkling glasses. A small posy of carnations and white roses decorated the centre of the table. Immediately the attendant was by his side with the wine list. Why hadn't he brought one for me? Obviously he had imagined a lover or husband was to join me. Gender equality did not exist in these Edwardian surroundings.

'Would you like something to drink before we eat?' my companion enquired.

'No, thank you.' I was dying for a drink. 'I'll just have a glass of wine with the meal.' I really must keep my wits about me in my present situation. 'But, please, you go ahead.'

The wine waiter was bending reverentially over the list in the old man's hand.

'Very wise,' he said. 'I'll do the same.' He looked up at me over his neat spectacles. 'If you would help me drink a bottle of wine, I should be honoured.'

'Well, yes! Thank you. On condition that I buy the wine tomorrow.'

He waved his hand in courteous dismissal of my suggestion. Of course, he was from the era of the Old School when women were pampered and protected. It occurred to me that he was the only one of our group who fitted his surroundings.

The elderly man and the waiter were murmuring together about the merits of the wine. I bet it cost an arm and a leg. Were the prices quoted? Perhaps I shouldn't be over insistent about paying my share.

I glanced over my shoulder at the other occupants of the dining car as this exchange was taking place. I wanted to see how far away my erstwhile tormentor was seated. I noticed that the rough-looking pair had opted for water, which was being carefully poured for them by their waiter. They hadn't won the lottery after all! Or perhaps they didn't know what to order. They probably feel as uncomfortable here as I do. You rotten snob, Frances Bonnington!

'A bottle of Beaujolais? Is that all right with you?' My companion was addressing me. 'It is quite light and refreshing.'

I nodded. What did it matter?

'Oh, I am so sorry.' He removed his spectacles. 'I should have checked what you intend to order. Of course, it won't do with fish. But then, we could have a half bottle with the earlier course.'

'No! I wasn't planning on having the fish. The wine you have chosen sounds fine to me.'

'Well, perhaps we will have a bottle of white as well. Our first evening, after all.' He picked up the menu again. 'Undoubtedly there is a fish course. And then neither of us will be restricted in our choice of main meals.'

'Please don't order another bottle on my account.' The words came out stiffly. I couldn't imagine Michael giving me so much consideration if he were sitting opposite. My companion gave his order to the wine waiter, who nodded and began to move away. The dining car was nearly full.

'Oh, and please would you remove the cork from the bottle of red, now?'

'Yes, sir! That is standard procedure.'

My companion put his spectacles away in their case and regarded me with a benign expression.

'I am so sorry to neglect you,' he said. 'The man arrived so quickly I didn't have time to introduce myself.'

'Frances Bonnington,' I said, extending my hand. 'Good evening!'

'Tom Lomax,' said my companion, as he shook it. 'I am extremely pleased to meet you.'

I relaxed. What a change from Michael who, like as not, would not greet me before he fucked me!

'My friends call me Fran,' I amended.

'Then I hope you will count me among them,' said Tom. 'But Frances is a beautiful name. If you will permit me, I shall call you Frances.'

'As you wish,' I said.

Why was such a charming man alone? Was he recently widowed? Was he gay?

'My wife suffers from Alzheimer's Disease,' he said, as though reading my unspoken thoughts. 'These last few years I have had to get used to travelling alone, after nearly fifty years of congenial companionship.'

'I am so sorry!' What could I say about such a situation? 'Do you have any children?'

'One son, who is very professional and busy. Two young boys. Delightful children!'

He sighed a little. And he doesn't see much of them, I thought.

'I am very fond of them,' he added.

'I am sure.'

The wine waiter arrived with the bottle of white and poured a little into Tom's glass. He tasted it without ostentation, then nodded his head. The waiter half-filled our wineglasses and withdrew. Tom raised his in an early toast.

'Here's to you, my dear! Happy holidays!'

'Thank you! I will certainly drink to that.'

The wine, suitably chilled and slightly astringent, hit the back of my throat and flowed warmly to my stomach.

'Young people appear to lead such stressful lives these days,' said Tom, apropos of his earlier remark regarding his son. 'I'm sure we didn't operate under the same pressures.'

I drank some more wine. 'You're right about stress,' I said, in what I hoped was a nonchalant tone. 'I am just taking a little break from my fraught existence. None of my friends were free to join me.'

Tom leaned forwards, his hands clasped before him on the table, where the cutlery gleamed and the white linen napkins shone. Fine, strong hands on which spots of age showed starkly against his tanned skin. Once, this man had been full of youth and vigour.

'You are quite right,' he said. 'It is amazing how often one's friends are not free.'

I laughed. He joined in my laughter.

'Well, it is rather expensive,' I said. 'I had to break open the piggy bank to come.'

'I am spending savings,' he said. 'Rupert doesn't need it and Muriel is well cared for in her nursing home.'

We had a convivial evening. I gathered that Tom had worked in the Insurance industry all his working life. For the last few years he had cared for his wife, until she became too difficult for him to manage. Now she was in a Surrey nursing home where he visited her every week.

'She hasn't known me for almost a year,' he said. 'It is as though a curtain comes down to block out the personality.'

'I am so sorry,' I said again. 'How distressing for you!'

'Well, she doesn't appear distressed. A blessing in some ways, not to remember.'

If I had Alzheimer's, would I forget Michael? Never!

'We were very lucky.' Tom took a sip from his glass. 'We had a good marriage. But let's not be morbid!' He poured more wine. 'Have you been in the Piano Bar yet?'

'No! I just unpacked after we arrived. Then the nice young man brought me a cup of coffee. I came for lunch and have been reading all afternoon.' That was a lie. I had been gazing out of the window.

'Well, perhaps you will join me for a nightcap after we finish this excellent meal.'

He was easily pleased, I thought. Michael would have been grousing about something or other – the food, the wine, the confinement.

'Well, perhaps for a short while,' I said. Out of the corner of my eye, I saw the rugged couple get up and leave the dining room. No doubt they were going to the Piano Bar. Faint musical sounds reached us as the door opened.

'They work very hard, the pianists here,' said Tom. They are expected to play virtually from morning till night, or even early next morning. Seems hard on them when we are all on holiday.'

I wondered how he knew about the working practices of the pianist, but I picked up his point about our holiday and replied, 'Waited on hand and foot. And perhaps the pianist enjoys it. Surely he wouldn't do it, otherwise!'

Some time later, we were sitting in the Piano Bar with brandies before us, listening to lively melodies from Oklahoma and the Sound of Music. Again, Tom insisted on signing the chit for our drinks.

'Tomorrow, it's my turn,' I said. 'After all, I am a working woman.' As the words left my mouth, I realised they were not true. No job was waiting for me when I arrived home.

The woman who had spoken to me earlier was sitting further down the carriage and I frequently noticed her eyes on me. Was she trying to remember the programme where she had seen my face? She probably assumes I'm a fortune hunter, I thought. With quantities of alcohol inside me, it seemed incredibly funny. I have spent the last two years gaining precisely nothing at all. Sweet F.A. Anyway, I hope Tom manages to tell her he has a wife. But it was a strain. Any minute I expected her to come rushing down the coach, exclaiming loudly, 'I know where I saw you. You was on the News!'

Suddenly, I was yawning and exhausted.

'You will have to excuse me, Tom,' I said. 'I am dead on my feet. I am going to go to bed.'

He rose as I gathered my wrap and bag.

'It has been a delightful evening,' he said. 'Thank you so much for your companionship.'

'Thank you! Don't forget, it is my turn to do the honours tomorrow.'

Thank God I didn't have to pass the raggle-taggle passengers on the way out. They were talking to the young couple, who were listening politely but not contributing much to the conversation . They obviously wanted to be left alone. I'll bet they turn in soon, I thought. I smiled vaguely in their direction as I turned to go. I would be glad to be solitary at last in my tiny cabin with my own thoughts. I was dead beat.

* * *

Venice was fantastic, bursting into brilliant light and shimmer in its broad expanses and mysterious as an opal in its shaded alleyways and canals. To my right from St. Mark's Square I saw bouncing gondolas, frisky as thoroughbreds, tethered to the striped poles of endless photographs. On the left were magnificent Mediaeval buildings redolent with history. From this city, young Marco Polo set out on his extended journeyings, and in the buildings behind me the Red Priest schooled his young maidens in musical arts. In spite of myself, my spirits lifted.

I had visited Venice previously, when I had noted not much more than the canal stink and the pulsating crowds. Now, earlier in the year, the crowds were thinner and the sheer beauty of the city could be better admired as I explored its delights in the company of Tom, whose knowledge of its art and architecture was formidable. For the first time in years, Michael faded to a pale spectre in my background. He ceased standing at my shoulder with his perpetual interjections. Rather, he was hovering behind me, making feeble observations that I ignored. He was no expert on Venice or, indeed, on anything remotely cultural. Now why had I never realised that before? But I had! It had been a niggling anxiety at the back of my mind. I had merely refused to acknowledge it.

Meanwhile, I relaxed. I became just another committed tourist. Mrs Margoloys was a dull, regretted ache, still there but not so troubling; while Michael was a painful sore which was slowly healing. I was in one of the most beautiful and exhilarating cities in the world, with a charming, undemanding escort, and I felt alive again.

It was not to last! There was a message for me in the hotel lobby when we returned from a long day's sightseeing in time to dress for dinner. At this stage of our holiday, the pleasures of the Orient Express had been exchanged for a small hotel overlooking the Grand Canal.

'There is a message for you, Madam,' the desk clerk informed me when we collected our keys. My stomach plunged as I took the note. Please ring .. it instructed, with a number I didn't recognise. Was it the Police or the tabloid press? I rather felt it was the Police. After all, I had given the hotel contact to nobody else. What the hell now? Couldn't they leave me alone for just one week?

'Not bad news, I hope?' Tom was looking at me with concern.

'No! No!' I lied. 'Just asking me to 'phone. Business!'

'What a shame, on our holiday! Perhaps it is nothing pressing.'

I parted from Tom at the lift. I couldn't wait to reach my room and make the call. Perhaps they just wished to inform me that someone had been charged with the murder. Pray God it wasn't Jason or Archie! But surely it was too soon! Neither of them had been taken in for questioning, as far as I knew.

The telephone was answered immediately. I recognised the voice of the officer who had interviewed me. I identified myself and waited.

'Sorry to break into your holiday! But we are going to have to ask you to come back.'

'What?' I was flabbergasted. Then furious. Why would they want my return? Why had they sanctioned my departure in the first place if I was so indispensable to their enquiries? And for this to happen after such a brilliant day! I could have wept. I drummed my heels back against the bed in mute frustration.

'But I am only here till Saturday,' I pleaded. 'Can't it wait till then?'

''Fraid not! If you don't agree to come back voluntarily, we will have to send someone over to pick you up.'

Bastards! My mind bucked at the idea of two heavy-footed Police Inspectors, recognisable in spite of their plain clothes, waiting in the hotel lobby, tramping about as I packed my case. What on earth could I say to Tom, after all his kindness? It didn't bear contemplation.

'I'll take the first available flight in the morning,' I said stiffly. 'Is that soon enough?'

'Good!' replied the disembodied voice. 'It will save a lot of hassle. We have booked you a ticket on the 10.20 flight from Venice airport. That should give you enough time.'

How the hell had they managed that at such short notice? Pulled a few strings, no doubt! Would the airport staff be looking out for a dangerous felon? But, at least, I would have time for a last dinner with Tom.

'Would you like a car to meet you at Heathrow? Or would you prefer to come under your own steam?'

'I'll make my own way.'

'Till tomorrow, then.'

I replaced the receiver and tried to still the trembling in my body and limbs. What had I done to deserve this? Surely I could not be a suspect in their murder enquiry? What had Michael said about me? If they suspected my involvement, they would have arrived to arrest me, not sent out a half-baked message requesting my return.

There was a light rap at the door. I dragged myself across the room and opened it. Tom stood in the corridor.

'I thought I would check you haven't received bad news.'

'No! No!' I hoped I didn't sound as distracted as I felt. 'But I have to go back to the U.K. in the morning. Something unexpected has come up.' How trite that sounded!

'I am so sorry! I shall miss you!' He seemed genuinely upset.

'I shall miss you, too!' I felt weak. I was holding on to the door surround for support. I tried to smile.

'Well, what a shame for you, spoiling your holiday! But I hope we will still be able to have a pleasant dinner this evening.' Tom raised his eyebrows in enquiry.

I wasn't hungry, didn't think I could eat, but I should eat, and I didn't wish to sit in my room all evening with my tormenting thoughts for company.

'You look a little pale,' said Tom. 'Distressing to have your holiday curtailed. Why don't you lie down for a little while before we have a drink? We walked around quite a lot today.'

Tom was nearly half a century older than me. I smiled at him. 'I'll be fine,' I said. 'But I do feel a bit done in. Perhaps I will lie down for a while.'

He checked his watch. 'Quarter past eight in the bar? Would that suit you?'

'Sounds just right! Till then!'

When he had gone, I sat in the bedside chair with my head in my hands. Was I a suspect? Surely, surely, surely, they couldn't imagine I had any input into Mrs Margoloys murder?

Rosa, they said on the News. Specs had said, My Aunt Ada. Was she Rosa Ada? Or Ada Rosa? Or was Specs up the creek and she wasn't his aunt, anyway? However much I argued with myself, I could not deny the fact that I had been in the house at the time. I appeared to be the last person to have seen Mrs Margoloys alive. All the other residents had been out or had alibis. I had been in my flat upstairs when she had been struck down so callously. Or at least before she had been found.

I lay down on the bed and closed my eyes. All the terrible events of the previous few weeks swirled over me in a vast, macabre dance. They gathered around, leering grotesquely, and bore down upon me.

Eventually I got up, splashed water on my face and applied fresh make-up. I pulled on a long, flimsy, deep pink skirt and a white skimpy top and went to the bar to meet Tom. Heads turned as I walked across the lobby. I would go out with a bang, rather than a whimper!

* * *

Once again, I was at the Police Station. It seemed I had never been away. Tom and the fairy tale fantasy of the Orient Express faded as though it had never been. Tom had pressed my hand on parting from me the previous evening. He had given me his card which I had put in my bag without looking at, he had assured me I had enhanced his holiday, fervently wished me well and pottered off to his room. At least, there were fewer complications with elderly gentlemen.

I considered returning to the bar for another quick drink – a nightcap would do no harm – then thought better of it. I would need all my wits intact for my encounter with the Police next day. Instead, I went to my room and packed my suitcase and hand luggage. I had already alerted Reception of my departure early the following morning. They promised my account would be ready and informed me the times of the waterbus to the airport. I was to collect my ticket there. It seemed that numerous anonymous people were making sure I arrived back in London without hitch.

In spite of my protestations, a car was waiting for me at Heathrow. But it was all discreetly managed.

'Miss Bonnington?'

'Yes!'

'Your car is waiting, Miss.' Plain clothes! No uniform! An identity pass was displayed. Metropolitan Police! My heart sank. But at the same time I was relieved to be spared the hassle of the airport, the aggravation of the underground as I dragged my luggage up and down escalators.

'What about my case?'

'No sweat, Miss! We'll collect it before we leave.'

All under control, obviously. Mercifully, the bags from my flight were already cavorting round the carousel. With my escort by my side, I stood and watched it. Perspiration beaded my brow. The airport seemed extremely hot. I ignored the temptation to question my companion. He wouldn't answer me in any case, even if he knew the reason why I had been dragged back to London three days before the end of my holiday. I thought of Tom strolling alone around the sights of Venice, and hated the whole of the British Establishment. I would sue them for wrongful arrest! Arrest?

'Am I under arrest?' I queried in a pleasant manner as we watched the endless parade of near identical suitcases tumbling from the chute. He glanced at me. He was young, not much more than a boy.

'No! Of course not!'

'Why have you met me, then?' I stared ahead, tried to keep my face and voice expressionless.

'To save you time and trouble,' he said. 'It can be the devil getting out of these airports.'

Especially when there is a burly young man by your side, I thought. Should I make a dash for it, leave my suitcase to its endless waltz? No! He would be on me before I had gone ten metres. Why make a scene to no purpose?

My bag glided into view.

'There it is!'

The young man lifted the case from the rotating belt as easily as if it was a pack of Four X.

'Is this all?'

'Oh, yes! I travel light.' I was carrying the holder with my evening frocks.

'Looks as if you've been dressing up. I hope you didn't miss the party.'

'No!' I said shortly. I had no intention of discussing my curtailed holiday with him.

'Okay! Let's go!'

We negotiated the terminal surprisingly quickly, his broad shoulders ensuring that the crowds parted before us. Doors were opened and officials waved us through. God! They knew him! And what did they think I had done. Perhaps they thought I was his girlfriend.

So now, once again I was sitting in the same chair in the same room. By myself! Fifteen minutes ticked by as I waited, like Patience on a monument. Was this delay meant to soften me up? At this moment I could have been exploring the intriguing back alleys and little churches of Venice with Tom. I wondered if he had found himself another companion. There had appeared to be plenty of solitary people wandering about Venice. He was elderly, dapper and frail, without menace. He was probably at this minute pointing out the nuances of the stones of Venice to interested American tourists. Why were Americans more involved with historical niceties than us Brits.? I sighed, closed my eyes. God! What was I doing here?

'I hope we haven't spoilt your holiday!'

I opened my eyes. The young woman of my previous interview had been replaced by a friendly-looking, middle-aged man. Nailem had entered the room silently and was standing behind the desk, regarding me with some concern.

Still involved in my daydream, I merely stared at him. It was a pointless remark, anyway. If they had taken account of my welfare, they would not have recalled me.

'Sorry you have been kept waiting.' He sat down. 'Coffee?' I nodded. Helping the Police with their enquiries! What a silly euphemism! Meant you were guilty, didn't it?

A young woman appeared at the door.

'Two coffees, Sharon, please!'

Nailem looked at me as the door closed.

'Sorry about your holiday,' he repeated. 'But we did think it was necessary for you to come back.'

I nodded again. I felt infinitely weary.

'Normally you wouldn't have been allowed to leave the country.'

I raised my eyebrows. 'Really! Am I a suspect?' I enquired icily.

'Everybody and nobody is a suspect, Ma'am!' His irony was not lost on me. 'But in your case, there are new developments.'

I could feel cold moisture under my armpits. For the first time I was seriously frightened. The Police were so incompetent! Were they trying to pin on me a crime I had not committed in order to boost their success figures? Would I become familiar with the inside of a prison before my next birthday? Whereas previously I had been irritated by the inconvenience and intrusion of the Police investigation, now it was borne in on me that they could positively think I was guilty. I didn't do it, you stupid shit! I screamed at him inside my head.

'Oh!' I said.

'New information has come to light concerning Michael Rutter,' he said, his face and voice deadpan.

Michael! Michael! Michael! What have you done? Was the officer joking? Was he testing me in some way? Did he imagine we had planned the crime together? How the hell could Michael be in any way involved? I had myself spoken to Mrs Margoloys after Michael's last visit a fortnight ago. Was this political? Had he enemies in his own Party? I had the bizarre picture of a shadowy Labour Whip handing over money in a brown envelope for the Police Benevolent Fund.

Were the Police as corrupt as rumour sometimes painted them? That sort of gossip was usually discounted on the grounds of improbability. Michael had been on the threshold of joining the Government. Did a disaffected rival know some Chief Inspector at an intimate level? Were dark forces at work here? But, however you looked at it, an evil crime had taken place in my building.

The Officer was watching me closely. I shook my head to clear it. My fists were clenched until the knuckles whitened.

'Oh, yes!' I said. My voice was shaky. The Officer scrabbled with papers on his desk, came up with one. He scrutinized it before laying it down again.

'We have to ask you some questions about your relationship,' he said.

'I've told you,' I said wearily. I was sick of this, this raking over the ashes of my consumed affair. 'We were lovers for over two years. I knew he had a wife and family. He didn't deceive me.'

The Officer looked up. He was old enough to be my father. I was glad there wasn't a young woman constable impassive by the door, as always seems to be the case in television police dramas.

'Your relationship was on-going?'

The door opened. Coffee was brought in, a tray with percolator, cups, milk and sugar.

'Thanks, Sharon!' A click as the door closed behind her.

'Milk and sugar? Your relationship was on-going?' He repeated the question as he poured the coffee.

'No! No, it wasn't.' I felt defiant. I had imagined I wouldn't divulge this information. Only Michael and I knew about the conversation by the Thames. But of course he would have spilled the beans. Whiter than white Michael Rutter had seen the error of his ways! Why should I take all the opprobrium?

'No! It finished more than two weeks ago.' I raised my head and looked the officer directly in the eyes. 'Mr. Rutter informed me our ..' I hesitated over the next word. Affair was accurate, but I didn't like it. Friendship was inappropriate. Intimacy I would not use. The officer was watching me, waiting, mildly enquiring.

'Liaison,' I said. 'He informed me our liaison was over.'

Les Liaisons Dangerousness skipped through my head. Ours had certainly been dangerous, especially in the light of present events.

'Really?' asked the Police Officer. 'This happened quite recently, you say?'

'Oh, yes! Two weeks ago! After he was given a post in the Government.'

Whips aren't members of the Government. Did the Officer know that? He remained as expressionless as I hoped I was. He scribbled a note on the page he had extracted.

'And when was this, did you say?'

Wasn't he listening to a word I was saying?

'Two weeks ago, last Wednesday.'

He made another note.

'And where did this conversation take place?'

'On the Embankment. Near Cleopatra's Needle.'

A fleeting expression of amusement crossed his face. Or had I imagined it?

'Well, Miss Bonnington, I don't think we need detain you any longer.' He stood up. The young woman appeared at the door.

'That's it?'

'That's it. For the time being. Yes!' He smiled for the first time during the interview. I was dismissed.

'You mean you have brought me back here, back from Venice, just to ask me a couple of questions?' I was almost spitting in my fury and disappointment.

He looked at me. 'Very important questions,' he said.

Fuck you, I screamed inside my head. I swallowed. No way must I give them the impression that I was prone to irrational anger.

'Couldn't they have been asked over the telephone?'

His eyes had slightly narrowed. The young woman waited. 'We don't work like that,' he explained. He gestured to his colleague, who stepped forward.

'I haven't drunk my coffee yet,' I complained. Fatuous words to make them think I was an idiot.

'By all means, stay and finish your coffee.' He left the office without looking at me again.

'Oh, for God's sake! I don't want it.'

'Okay!' said the young woman. 'Bit of an ordeal coming in, isn't it?' She held my jacket for me to slip on. 'I'll show you out.'

I found a taxi to take me and my luggage to Nottingham Place. Then I spent the afternoon at the cinema. I had to get away from the house, the telephone, my memories, everything.

I sat in the dark, in the almost deserted auditorium, taking in nothing of the complicated plot. The speech was inaudible, the violence gratuitous. I closed my eyes. At least I was safe and anonymous here.

I came out at the end of the film into the harsh neon lighting and strident traffic of Leicester Square. I wished I had spent the afternoon in the park. In order to stretch my legs, I walked back to the flat, dreading my arrival there. When I reached Nottingham Place, the street was empty. The Media circus had moved on. Perhaps they had been tipped off that I had gone to Italy.

Fumbling awkwardly with my key, I eventually unlocked the heavy front door and stepped inside the dim interior. A figure was standing at the end of the downstairs hall. For one mad moment I thought it was Mrs Margoloys come back to life. My hand flew to my heart and a tiny scream escaped my mouth. As I stood trembling inside the doorway, the figure advanced.

'I didn't think I was that bad! You look as if you have seen a ghost.'

Archie came forward, smiling, his teeth gleaming white against his tanned skin. I leaned against the door, trying to still the shaking of my legs.

'Archie! How you startled me! I thought ...'

He came to me, held my hand and kissed me lightly.

'You thought I was Mrs Margoloys. I didn't know we were so alike!'

He laughed softly but, was it my imagination, or was there a hint of menace in his easy veneer?

'What are you doing in the hall?' I demanded.

'Well, it is a free country. I could ask you the same. I thought you were on holiday.'

Who had told him that? I had divulged my plans to nobody except the Police.

Archie was standing quite close to me. He was tall, over six feet and he towered above me. I had always considered him slim and weedy, not much more than a boy, but since our intimacies, I knew there was powerful brawn beneath his shirt. I imagined him with a weapon in his hand, battering Mrs Margoloys about the head. Was Michael to be blamed for what Archie had done?

I felt sick. I must get away from him. He was now standing between me and the front door, which was shut. As usual, the house was silent as the grave.

'Hey, I was only joking! Are you okay? You are white as a sheet.' He was regarding me with a mixture of curiosity and concern. I remembered our night of passion and marvelled at my own crassness. Did the Police know about that, as well?

'Come downstairs with me. I'll make you some coffee.' He took my arm. I shook him off, pushed past him to the stairs.

'Don't feel well!' I muttered. 'Lie down for a bit.'

I rushed up the stairway, afraid he would follow. As I turned the corner at the top of the first flight, I saw he was still standing there, looking up at me with a questioning expression. I fled upwards, grasping my keys, reached my door, wrenched it open and fell inside. I was gasping for breath.

I leaned against the wall until the wild race of my heart slowed a little.

I dropped my bag, drew my bedroom curtains and lay down on my bed. This time yesterday, I had been in Venice. It seemed a lifetime away.

Had Archie been as surprised to see me as I had been to see him? Who had told him I was on holiday? I had told nobody in the building that I was going away. What had he been doing, lurking about in the hall? He had no reason to be at the end of the corridor, not far from Mrs Margoloys' room. Was he trying to erase evidence? Had he unlocked the back door to let someone in? Had Mrs Margoloys seen something she shouldn't have? Had Archie and his girlfriend become involved in a drug-dealing racket? The girlfriend was certainly jumpy at the Police presence near the house. If Archie thought any evidence had been overlooked, he was a bit late! The building had been done over with a fine toothcomb.

My head ached and throbbed, courtesy of my early rising and the trauma of the prospect of renewed Police questioning. I certainly felt ill. I had not lied to Archie on that front.

There was a gentle tap on the door. I ignored it. I could manage without Archie's ministrations. It came again, more insistent. I buried my face in the pillow. I was opening the door to nobody tonight.

After a time, I heard the faint sound of retreating footsteps. Was it Archie checking on my welfare? Or an unknown intruder? Or Specs on one of his unheralded appearances? My skin crawled. How much longer did I have to suffer this terror?

For the first time I became aware of how vulnerable residents were in this type of building. There was no way out if the stairway were blocked. Fire regulations were apparently being breached. Yet Mrs Margoloys had been in the downstairs hall, only yards away from the street and safety. But she was a frail old lady! What chance would she have had?

After a time, I got up and made my way to the kitchen to make some tea. My throat was parched, my mouth dry.

A slip of paper lay in the hall. I picked it up – a folded over sheet torn from a diary.

Sorry I frightened you, Archie had written in his flamboyant script. I was checking the back door was secure. It's no laughing matter. Underneath were three large exclamation marks and his distinctive signature with a curlicued final e, followed by a P.S. Have a good sleep! See you soon.

As I sat in my kitchen, swallowing bread and honey, I heard the muffled thud of the front door. I looked out of the window, but the street was empty. If Archie had gone out, he must have turned left towards Marylebone High Street. There was a Rising Sun pub. in that direction. Or he could have gone to the laundrette at the end of the road.

On the other hand, someone could have come in. I watched for a couple of minutes, but the street outside was deserted. Quiet as the grave! How I wished I could get that phrase out of my head.

I could see into the lower rooms of the houses opposite – one of the reasons I preferred the top floor. Not that I wished to spy on others, but I had no desire to be overlooked myself. They were equally deserted. I sighed heavily, and my breath left a smear on the windowpane. God! London was teeming with life, heaving with bodies, and I lived in a place that was devoid of them.

Perhaps Jason had returned and he would amuse Archie for a while. I wasn't interested what they got up to, as long as I wasn't dragged in on their dubious activities.

* * *

The next few days passed in a haze of inactivity interspersed with periods of frantic busyness, feigned to lull me into the conception that I was making a conscious effort to pull my life together.

I scoured the situations vacant columns and diligently applied for jobs. None of them filled me with the slightest sliver of enthusiasm, but I deceived myself into thinking that I was doing something about my future.

I would wander around the flat, exploring tactile surfaces, hugging a soft towel and stroking and caressing fruit in a bowl. I spent a lot of time dozing or lying on my bed in a semi-conscious state, not thinking much about anything, just enduring the anguish of my prolonged separation from Michael. Then, full of a self-righteous fury, not least at poor Mrs Margoloys, whose unseemly demise had ruined my life, I would find myself storming round the rooms, viciously thumping up the cushions.

I saw no-one. The other residents had certainly gone to ground. Occasionally I heard the distant slam of a door, but nobody came to mine and I met nobody on my infrequent trips to the outside world.

I slept, sometimes for a long time when exhaustion caught up with me. When I woke, I would shop for food, even though I wasn't hungry. Once I opened my cookery book, found an exotic recipe and went round the corner to Marylebone High Street to track down the ingredients. I spent hours in the kitchen, marinating, then chopping and mixing and blending, only to find at the end of all my exertions that I couldn't face the meal. I barely swallowed a mouthful before tipping it into the trash can. I wonder if Mrs Margoloys would like it, I thought, before I realised with a stab of shock that Mrs Margoloys was no longer with us.

I wanted to drink myself stupid, but managed to resist that temptation. It may have been that I thought the Police were biding their time and were waiting to pounce once more. I couldn't risk making a fool of myself in front of them. My liberty could be an issue here.

And I was beginning to find my residence threatening. After my strange reaction to Archie, I felt I needed my wits about me at all times. After all, the murderer could still be at large in the building. I never knew who was in or out. If I had to leave my flat for any reason, I would cautiously open my door, peer down the stairwell to make sure nobody was on the stairs, then creep down the top flight. Then I scuttled down the remaining steps to the front door and dragged it closed behind me.

I was afraid. I was incredibly afraid. My freedom, my very life, could depend on my behaviour now. I ordered myself to be cool and collected at all times. But most of the time I lay soporific on my bed.

There were no messages. Then, on Sunday morning, a telephone call came from Margot, checking on my welfare.

'I tried last week,' she said. 'When there was no reply, I thought perhaps you were staying with your mother.'

I chatted brightly to her, telling her about my job applications and my truncated holiday in Italy. I told her I was relishing my unexpected release from the daily drudgery of A.J. Partners. She may have suspected I was lying, but was too sensitive to challenge me.

'Have a good rest,' she said. 'You deserve one. Pity about your holiday! You'll have to arrange another one when all this blows over.'

There was a slight pause. My instinct told me that Margot was uneasy. Had some mistake been found in my work?

'Margot, is there something else?'

I had not watched television, kept up with the news, for the past couple of days. I had become sick to death with the trials of the world. Had something terrible happened?

'Margot?'

'I thought you would know,' she said slowly. 'Michael Rutter was arrested last Tuesday. He has been charged with murder.'

Oh, My God! My God! My body turned to jelly. I clutched the hall table for support. My face in the mirror above it became shadowy with great staring eyes. Margot's voice receded as she continued expressing regret and concern.

'Fran? Are you still there? I thought you would know. I didn't realise you were out of the country. I am so sorry!' Her voice rose with anxiety. 'Fran? Are you all right?'

It was a mistake! It must be! They were trying to flush out the real murderer. I swallowed, somehow managed to bring myself under control.

'Yes, I'm all right, Margot.'

'Shall I come round?'

'No! I'm sure you are busy.'

'I am worried about you!'

I didn't want to talk. I didn't want to talk to anybody. I wanted no solicitous friends around me. And, in any case, Margot was not truly a friend, certainly not a soul mate. I wanted to sit by myself in the quiet dark, the peaceful dark, and not think about anything any more.

'Bugger A.J.'s,' Margot was continuing. 'They treated you badly after all you had done for them.'

No, I didn't need Margot to be here. I wanted to indulge my pain. I pulled myself together.

'No, Margot! I've got a job interview tomorrow and I want to prepare for it.'

This was a total fabrication, but it would get Margot off my back. 'In any case,' I continued, 'my relationship with Michael Rutter was over.'

I sensed her disbelief across miles of telephone wires. In the mirror before me, I saw my chin rising and my eyes gleaming. I put the 'phone down. I looked at my watch. Nearly eleven. On weekdays, this was the time of day when Margot and I would have made a cup of coffee and, if the pressure wasn't too great, have taken a five minute break.

I felt very calm. I put on my shoes and, without checking the stairs and hall, went out to Baker Street Underground to buy newspapers. With a selection under my arm I returned to my silent flat. I switched on Radio Three: soothing music and news on the hour.

How the hell had I come to miss this latest development? I had been stuck tight to the television before I left for Italy. Tom and the beauty and history of Venice had beguiled me. The enchantment of La Serenissima had made my own predicament appear tawdry and irrelevant. When I was unexpectedly forced to return, I wanted nothing to do with the miseries of 19A Nottingham Place and the self-seeking obsessions of its residents. Only poor Mrs Margoloys had been worthy of consideration.

I spread the newspapers across the floor of the sitting room and sprawled over them. The tabloids displayed large photographs of Michael on their front pages. M.P. arrested for murder! Old news now, but the Sundays were running it. Fascinated and horrified, I turned the pages. Four and five page spreads about his career, his family, his private life.

I scoured the small print. No mention of me! There must be! They must be aware of our relationship. Then, there it was. A paragraph in one of the tabloids containing a detailed list of previous lovers and the words, 'For some time, Michael Rutter has been the lover of Frances Bonnington, Personal Relations Consultant with A.J. Partners. Frances Bonnington is at present on holiday in Italy.'

It sounded as if I had absconded. Well, they were out of date. They evidently hadn't caught up with my return or my recent sacking. No doubt they had been pursuing enquiries while I was abroad. But they would have received short shrift from A.J.s office – discretion is our password – or Margot, if they had been put through to her. Shame and guilt suffused me. Thank God my mother didn't read newspapers!

If I hadn't been sitting on the floor, I would have collapsed on to it. I wasn't sure whether my concern was for myself or Michael. It certainly wasn't for his family. A desire for vengeance assured me the bastard had got what he deserved. All his life he had pursued his own selfish interests, taking no account of the effect of his actions on the well-being of others.

Remanded in custody! He was incarcerated in a police cell and that snooty wife and his uppity children would have to visit him there. Or would they? She would probably divorce him. He would be free. Well, I didn't want him! Didn't I just! My heart did a little jig. Here, steady on! He would be in prison for a long time if he were found guilty of murder.

Hold on! He wasn't guilty! How could he be guilty? Why in hell's name had he been arrested? The stupendously stupid police had pulled in the wrong man! This was another attempt to boost their success statistics.

What had I said to them on my return from Venice? I closed my eyes and sought to recreate my last interview. I had said nothing to incriminate him in any way, I was certain. That was why I was so angry that they had insisted I come back to England.

I spread open the broadsheets and read the same stories in slightly more restrained language. The tabloids were not too troubled by the Law of Libel. Imagine arresting Michael! Had he colluded in some fancy plot to give the real murderer a false sense of security? Was it all a great hoax and Michael was truly helping the Police with their enquiries?

Michael! My darling Michael! He was with me all the time in his impotent distress. He had been with me all the while when he had visited my building. And afterwards he couldn't wait to get out of it. I always watched from my kitchen window as he strode confidently down the street. And with all the other crazy suspects, Specs, Francesca's callers, even Jason and Archie, they had arrested Michael!

I put my head in my hands. Would they come for me next? They had, after all, recalled me from Venice. I looked around my sunny sitting room in panic. Did they imagine we had planned Mrs Margoloys' murder between us? I was, after all, ostensibly the last person to see her alive.

I went to the bathroom and was messily sick in the lavatory bowl. No wonder Margot had rung. She was a good mate.

Thank God I had told her I had an interview tomorrow. She could have taken it into her head to pop over at lunchtime when she was so close to my flat. However, if she repeated that claim to the Police they would put me down as a liar. I wiped my mouth with a towel and drank a glass of water.

No wonder the rest of the house had been avoiding me. They must all think I was implicated.

CHAPTER EIGHT

Michael was formally charged at a brief hearing some days later. He was remanded in custody pending trial for the murder of Mrs Ada Rose Margoloys. Alleged murderers were not granted bail.

Later that afternoon I was sitting in my flat staring blankly at the spots of sunlight piercing my walls, when the intercom buzzed. It had been out of order for most of my tenure, but recently workmen had arrived to reconnect the old wires. Now its insistent whine made me jump.

'Yes? Who is it?'

'Miss Bonnington? It's Jane Rutter. Could I have a word?'

Who the hell was this? A persistent journalist? My mind raced. As I stood hesitating, the caller spoke again. 'Michael's wife! Would you open the door, please?'

'Come up to the top floor,' I said. I pressed the door release.

I hovered in the hall until there was a knock on my door. I opened it. I don't know what I had expected, but the reality was much as I would have imagined, if I had allowed myself to think about her.

She was thin, elegant, dressed in a charcoal grey trouser suit with a cream and blue scarf arranged around her throat.

'Come in! Please!' I held the door back and she stepped into my tiny hall. She looked around with some hauteur.

'So this is where he amused himself!' she said.

I bit my lip. I had no intention of quarrelling with this woman at a time like this.

'Come in here.' I ushered her into the sitting room. 'Would you like some tea?'

'No, thank you!'

What in fuck's name was she doing here? Did she intend to pick a fight? She obviously did not want to break bread in my premises. I indicated the sofa, sat down on the chair opposite and waited.

She took her time, looking around as though she were making an inventory of my belongings. Fortunately, the room was reasonably clean and tidy. Housework is the easiest chore to tackle when the mind is distracted. She was wearing a lot of make-up on her pretty, rather worn face. Worse for her than for me, really! I was a nine day wonder! Her life would be rent apart by any squalid tittle tattle the Press could uncover. She would be endlessly photographed visiting the prison, loyally standing by her man, or not, as the case may be.

'So, where was she?' The abruptness of her question took me by surprise.

'Who?'

'The old woman! The one Michael is supposed to have murdered?'

God! What was this? Did she wish to relive the scene of the crime?

'On the ground floor. In her room down there.'

There was a silence as she took this in.

'Mrs Rutter!' I leaned forward. She must be going through hell. 'I'm sure he didn't do it. He will be found innocent. It is all a great mistake.'

She gave me an icy glare. She probably thought the residents of 19A had conspired together to frame her husband.

'How do you know? Did you accompany him to the front door when he left?'

'Well, no!'

'Well, no!' she mimicked. 'Busy putting your clothes on again, were you?'

I ignored her jibe, could forgive it in the light of her anguish.

'I saw Mrs Margoloys after he left here for the last time.' I drew a deep breath. 'Our relationship has ended, you know.'

That was very hard for me to say. In spite of my best efforts at control, there was a tremor in my voice.

'Then why didn't you tell the Police, you stupid girl?'

I refused to retaliate. She could have said bitch.

'I did.' I got up. She recoiled a little as though she feared I might strike her. Had Michael ever hit her?

'I think a cup of tea would be a good idea. I would like one, anyway.'

I escaped to the kitchen. Anything to get away from her terrible, glittering eyes! She had a great deal more to cope with than I had: her children for a start.

She followed me and came and stood in the kitchen doorway, watching as I filled the kettle and set cups and saucers on a tray. They clinked together in my shaking hands. I lifted a teapot from the cupboard. It was months since it had been used and was probably covered in dust. I tried to steady my hands and think what I was doing, but it was difficult with Michael's wife blocking the doorway. Making a pot of tea became a major operation. Pour milk into a jug! Bowl for the sugar!

'I don't take sugar,' she said after I had accomplished that task. My small kitchen began to feel hot and over-crowded. I opened the window and muted traffic sounds from Marylebone Road came faintly to our ears.

'Did it in there, did you?'

'What?'

'Oh! Never mind!'

Why the hell had she come to see me if she only intended to be offensive? To my relief, she turned and went back to the sitting room. The kettle came to the boil and I poured water over the tea bags, then carried the tray through and set it on the coffee table before the sofa.

She was examining a sand picture that a friend had once brought back as a present from the Grand Canyon area of California. Thank God Michael had never been there, as far as I knew. But then, he must have done all sorts of things I had never known about!

'Milk?' I queried.

'Milk, no sugar.' She came and sat down.

'Look, Mrs Rutter!' The words came out smoothly. 'Let's not fight! I know it must be devastating for you.' I wondered whether to tell her I loved Michael.

'You realise that?' She took a sip of tea, grimaced and returned the cup to its saucer. 'If he hadn't been coming here,' she said, 'none of this would have happened.'

Well, no! That couldn't be denied. But he came of his own free will. It wasn't all my fault.

The tea was too pale, not much darker than the milk. It hadn't had time to draw. I didn't care. She can't even make a decent cup of tea, I could imagine her screaming at Michael. Again I wondered if he had ever assaulted her. She seemed the kind of woman to invite violence. But all their private conversations were over for the time being. Michael was stuck in some grim prison. And he could be there for the next few months, if not years.

However, there was no reason why I should be insulted by this harridan in my own home.

'Michael is a grown man,' I said stiffly. 'Perfectly able to make his own choices.'

'You realise you have ruined his career? He will never be able to begin again, even if he is found innocent.'

I shrugged. I wasn't the first, and wouldn't be the last, to pursue an adulterous affair. And that was my only input. The murder of Mrs Margoloys was unfortunate for him, horrible, but nothing to do with me.

'You weren't the first, you know!' Jane Rutter was obviously intent on twisting the knife. 'Nor the only one.'

'I didn't imagine I was!'

Why the fuck had she come? I must terminate this interview. Should I order her out of my house?

'Lost your job, didn't you?'

I silently thanked some unknown god of small things for my professional training which allowed me to ignore her shafts without, I hoped, any flicker of emotion.

'Is there anything I can do for you, Mrs Rutter?' I asked gently. In spite of her hostility, I felt very sorry for her. She was unfortunate enough to be expected to play the loyal spouse of Michael Rutter. If she began divorce proceedings, she would be vilified. Her face crumpled. For a moment I thought she would cry. But she brought herself under control.

'Why couldn't you leave him alone?' She sounded immeasurably sad.

'These things happen,' I said. Indeed, what could I say? There were no words to describe my driving passion, my primeval instinct, my overwhelming desire for Michael Rutter. He, and only he, would do!

'Alone in that place,' she went on. I assumed she was referring to the Houses of Parliament with its hundreds of M.Ps. and copious staff jamming its rooms and bars. 'Easy prey for the likes of you.'

'And what is that?' Despite my resolution not to rise to her bait, I was stung by the inference of her words. How dare she come to my home and insult me? I was no doubt better educated and more professionally qualified than she was, although I was not in the same sphere socially, of course. 'Are you suggesting your husband has poor taste?'

Stupid! What a stupid thing to say! Careful, Bonnington!

'No man will fall over anything,' she said, coarsely. Her ladyship image was slipping. Nouveau riche, perhaps? 'That's what Mummy always warned me.'

'Well, your mother was a wise woman,' I said. Again I wondered if she had come to say anything specific and had not yet done so. Or had she just come out of spite and curiosity to look me over?

All at once, she seemed to sag, to shrink in her seat. This must be one hell of an ordeal for her, confronting her husband's mistress. She had obviously been to the Court proceedings before making her way to Nottingham Place.

'Are you staying in London?' I asked. 'Can I ring for a taxi for you?'

'I have a taxi waiting outside.' All this time!

She gave me a look sharp as cold steel, seized her handbag and walked from the room. Her departure was as sudden as her arrival had been. She said no goodbye, made no parting remark. She was gone.

I went to the kitchen window in time to see her climb into a black cab, which revved briefly and then disappeared in the direction of Marylebone Road.

I drew in a very long breath; let it out slowly. May God help us all! What the hell had she come here for? Had Michael instructed her to come and see me? No! He would not have done so! And she may not have had an opportunity of speaking with him. Would she report to him that I was a slut who had threatened her with the bread knife? Or was she morbidly inquisitive about the scene of her husband's amours?

I walked down the stairs to the basement and knocked on Archie's door. I needed company.

* * *

What followed were the longest four months of my life. I counted not only the hours but also the minutes until Michael's trial. My experience no doubt mirrored his, as he fumed and despaired in his Police cell, shouted at his legal representatives and belly-ached to his wife. Did she visit him regularly during his incarceration? Did she berate or encourage him? Did she stand shoulder to shoulder with him in his hour of need, or did she punish him for all his past misdemeanours?

In my hermitage at Nottingham Place, I had no idea of the progress of proceedings. I would be called as a witness – I had been informed of that, but whether for the Defence or Prosecution, I was not quite sure.

I ignored every summons for a job interview. I was not yet up to mastering another complicated, professional appointment. Time enough to secure my future after I knew about Michael's. Instead, I took a post filling shelves at Tesco's supermarket. This was physically tiring and mentally unde-manding. When my shift was over, I returned to my flat and slept. I was sleeping twelve hours a day and was still exhausted.

Most of the time, the house appeared to be empty. The young music students had left for the summer recess and prob-ably would not return. Sammy had always been an infrequent occupant of his small room. There was no sign of Francesca. Archie told me she had gone back to Italy. No doubt she was taking advantage of a client's resplendent villa, I thought with weary cynicism. She had always been a nebulous presence, anyway. She obviously hadn't been told to hang around!

Jason and Archie came and went. Indeed, they were the source of my information about the other residents. But they always had been unreliable companions, and now they were more elusive than ever. On day I noticed Jason meticulously reading the labels on tins of soup as I walked behind him, pushing a shelf stacker containing a mountain of sliced bread. He didn't see me and I didn't greet him. I was not ashamed of my occupation, but explanations tired me these days.

Margot rang once or twice, asking how I was surviving.

'Still in the land of the living, Margot!' I flippantly answered her queries.

'Disgraceful, them bringing you back from Italy,' she grum-bled. 'You really needed a holiday.'

'Well, when this is all over, I'll arrange something else.'

I couldn't think about the future. My present was too exigent.

'How are the applications going?'

'Haven't been for many interviews. Waiting to hear from one or two,' I lied. 'Bit of a quiet season now. I'll try and get my mind round it in a month or two.'

She didn't press the matter. 'Well, there is no rush. Have a rest. Look after yourself. But you are not one to sit around twiddling your thumbs!'

'I'm not! I'm catching up on the galleries and the touristy bits. All the things I meant to do and never had time for.'

Again I was lying. Why the hell didn't I tell her I was working in Tesco's?

Margot was going to the States for a month. This was her last chance to call me for some time.

'Enjoy yourself,' I urged. 'Don't worry about me. I'm fine.'

'I miss you, Fran,' she said unexpectedly. 'I really miss you! This place isn't the same without you.' She didn't say, and I didn't ask, whether my place had been filled. Perhaps there was a pushy, newly qualified graduate sitting in my chair, driving Margot wild with her incessant telephone chatter.

'Well, I'll be back in about four weeks. I can't give you a contact number as we'll be travelling around.'

I wondered who she was going with. She hadn't volunteered that information.

'For heaven's sake, Margot,' I protested, 'I don't need nannying. Just go and have a brilliant time.'

'Okay!' She didn't sound convinced. 'Are those two nice boys still there?'

She obviously remembered my occasional comments on the basement boys.

'They come and go. But one or other of them is often here if I feel in need of company.'

'Good!'

There was the slightest pause. There didn't seem to be any more to say.

'You go and enjoy yourself in the Big Apple or wherever. I am sure you will. And we'll arrange to meet when you come back.'

'Yes, we'll do that.'

I said goodbye and put the 'phone down. It seemed an aeon since I had left the flat every day for A.J. Partnership. It occurred to me that Margot was the only one from the firm who had bothered to check on my welfare. The Management had made no enquiries. I was contaminated goods in their eyes. Or perhaps my precipitate departure had pissed them off.

However, I did something positive in these turgid months, and that was to look for Specs.

I rode the Circle, Metropolitan, Northern and Bakerloo lines to various destinations and wandered around the nearby streets in a futile effort to locate him. I walked from my flat, past the park, to Wigmore Hall and loitered at the bus stop where I had successfully avoided him. I knew it was ridiculous to expect to meet him by chance, but I felt driven to try and track him down.

While previously he had popped up everywhere, since Michael's arrest he seemed to have disappeared from the face of the earth. Of course, he may not live in this area at all. I had only assumed that he did because I had first met him at the concert hall. And then he had lurked frequently near my home. Yet he could have come from anywhere in this whole, damned, polluted city.

It was exceptionally hot, that summer, and sweat trickled down my face as I tramped the hard pavements. I developed painful blisters that seemed to mirror my state of mind.

After some weeks of this fruitless activity, I realised that he may have returned to the North of England. Students were on vacation and if his purpose had been to locate his aunt, why should he stay here now she was dead? I wondered if he had spoken to her the day he came to my door. I wondered if he had killed her. Had he fled with his guilty secret? However, if evidence were found against him, distance would not protect him.

I thought of Michael, my poor darling Michael, beside himself with mortification, kicking the wall of his prison cell in impotent rage. Tears ran down my face unheeded and dripped from my chin on to the pillow. How bloody monstrously unfair life was!

Even though I concluded my search was useless, now that I was in the habit of scouring London's streets, I found it difficult to discontinue my quest. I would buy a travel card at Baker Street station and journey till I was tired of it. I sometimes changed trains three times before I alighted. Then I walked unknown streets in a state of bemused abstraction until I was weary enough to return to the station and home.

Just what was I hoping for? Did I expect Specs to confess to the murder if I cornered him? He had already told me that Mrs Margoloys was his aunt. Poor old lady! Why had she never mentioned him? She was the sort who would have delighted to prattle endlessly about her young relative if she had known of his existence.

Was he telling the truth about the relationship? Perhaps that was what I wanted to know. After all, that was a good reason for him being in the building. If he was planning on going to earth, perhaps he was relying on me informing the Police of that fact.

I sighed. The irony of the situation struck me. Previously, I would have done anything to avoid him; now I was busting a gut trying to find him. Undoubtedly, I had gone mad! Michael's defection and arrest had destroyed me.

I gave up all hope of success, but I still pursued my mindless meanderings. And then, one day, I struck lucky. I wasn't even looking for him at the time. I had run out of coffee – about the only thing I couldn't manage without. I considered popping down to the basement to borrow some from Jason or Archie. But they may not be in or, alternatively, not have any coffee. Just as easy to go to the supermarket down the road - less complicated all round. It wasn't the one I worked at. I had no wish to be recognized stacking shelves by neighbours who might commiserate with me on my plight.

I was standing waiting at the checkout with a lone jar of instant coffee in my wire basket when I saw him come in. He appeared just the same, his creased worried face peering out from behind his thick spectacles. He was wearing a crumpled dark tee shirt and scruffy denims. He had discarded the duffle coat in deference to the warmer weather.

I paid for my purchase and stationed myself near the doors to wait for him to emerge. Quite a change from our previous encounters!

'Hi!'

He would have walked past without noticing me if I had not spoken.

'Oh! Hi!' he responded, without enthusiasm.

I fell into step beside him. 'I thought we might have a little talk,' I said.

'Yeah? What about?'

The change in his demeanour was remarkable. If he had had a car waiting outside, he would have been inside it and gone. As it was, he looked up and down the street, as though searching for an escape route, before beginning to trudge down it. I walked beside him. Funny how our altered situations gave me an illusion of power!

'You know they have made an arrest on the murder of Mrs Margoloys?' I could not bring myself to say, your aunt. Perhaps I was being cruel, but Michael's freedom could depend on this conversation.

'Yeah!' he grunted. 'Hope the bastard gets what he deserves.'

I was shocked. Was that what the rest of the population was thinking?

'Well, shall we have a coffee?'

'What for?'

Damn his eyes! He had changed his tune from when we first met! Did he imagine that I was in some way implicated in the crime?

'Just to get one or two things straight,' I said firmly. I grasped his arm and urged him into a Fast Food outlet we were passing. 'You sit down. I'll get them.'

I half expected him to walk out, but he moved along and found a table halfway down, where he sat and stared vacantly into space. I went to the counter and ordered two cappuccinos and a bag of French fries. He might be hungry.

He brightened up as I unloaded the tray and gave him the chips.

'You not having any?'

'I don't usually eat chips,' I told him. 'Just coffee is fine for me.'

I stowed the tray and sat down facing him. He squeezed a great glob of tomato ketchup on the French fries before posting them rapidly into his mouth. I put my hands round my cup and regarded him. Was it possible that this clumsy, ugly boy was involved in the grisly killing of a defenceless old woman? A woman, moreover, he claimed as his aunt.

'Look!' I realised I didn't even know his name.

'Paul,' he said, through a bulging mouthful.

'Look, Paul. I am sure we all want the guilty party brought to justice.'

He looked at me as he continued to stuff down the food. I did sound unbelievably pompous.

'String the bastard up!' he said.

I ignored that shaft.

'Did you manage to speak to her at all?'

If she really was his aunt, he had every reason to feel aggrieved, even if he hardly knew her. He shook his head and I sighed inwardly. If he were telling the truth, he would know nothing. This wasn't going to be easy. Had I imagined he would divulge important information merely because I asked him to do so? Would he be likely to tell me he had bashed her over the head so he could get his hands on her stash of jewels?

'I am so sorry,' I said, gently. I hadn't said that before. 'I was fond of Mrs Margoloys. This must have been a nasty shock for you.'

I remembered he was newly arrived in London. Perhaps it wasn't so strange that he had tried to attach himself to the first solitary female he had met.

He finished the snack and crumpled the pink and white striped bag into a ball between his hands. He wiped the back of one hand across his mouth where a smear of tomato ketchup decorated his upper lip.

'Didn't know her very well,' he mumbled, without meeting my eyes. 'My Mum told me to look her up. But she had lost her address and she was dead before ...'

'I am so sorry!' I repeated. 'I'm sure she would have been so pleased to see you.'

I meant it. I felt infinitely sad for the vagaries of fate that had annihilated Mrs Margoloys before Specs had discovered her.

He did not reply and the silence extended. What the hell had I expected to find out from him as I traipsed around London? Did I expect him to wring his hands and confess to the murder, so that Michael would be exonerated and we could walk into the sunset together? Specs was right to be mistrustful of my motives. I had been uniformly unpleasant to him until now. Yet, there was no getting away from the fact that he had been to our building. He had appeared without warning outside my door. Did he know more than he was letting on?

'I wondered if you came to see your aunt when ...'

I didn't finish the sentence, but he picked up my meaning.

'No!' He looked at me, his eyes reproachful behind the thick glasses. 'No! I came to see you. I didn't know she lived there then.'

'What a pity for you both!' And what a hell of a coincidence!

He shrugged, looked around as though he was about to make a dash for the exit.

'Would you like something else to eat?'

He shook his head.

'It was only after the Police got in touch with my Mum.'

Of course! They would have tracked down the next of kin. A waitress stopped beside us and whisked away my cup.

'My Mum telephoned me to let me know what happened.' He spoke slowly, as though to a child, and stared at me as if defying me to challenge this statement.

'So you did come to Nottingham Place just to see me?'

He stood up. It was not a good idea to remind him of my reception of him on that occasion.

'Got to go,' he muttered. 'Thanks for the ..'

He had reached the door, moving surprisingly quickly for one with his usual snail-like gait. I turned in my seat to watch him. He paused for a moment in the doorway, before hunching his shoulders and setting off down the street.

I bought another coffee and sat down again. Well, that was that! A fat lot of good that had done me! I had found out nothing, except his assertion that he had not spoken to Mrs Margoloys before her death. He hadn't known where she lived. Yet he had come to Number 19A, ostensibly seeking me. What a freakish coincidence, if he were telling the truth! Could he have murdered Mrs Margoloys, not knowing she was his aunt? Did he have a violent temper underneath that dozy exterior, which erupted when he was thwarted?

I pondered on what the Police had made of it all. Specs wasn't a suspect since they had arrested Michael. My head began to pound. I rubbed my temples with my fingertips, left the cooling coffee half-finished and made my way home. Enough was enough, for one day!

CHAPTER NINE

A witness box is a lonely place. The Court observed from its ground floor vantage point appears a different entity from that seen from the bird's eye view of the gallery. The spectators sat there: the students, the vicarious, the morbidly fascinated, and the friends and relatives of the defendant.

Give your name! Hold the bible in your right hand! Take the oath! What a farce it all was! As though swearing by Almighty God would have the slightest effect on ninety per cent of those who so swore. But, as I had already discovered, murder trials can be boring, pedestrian affairs.

The Court seemed crowded and at the same time sparsely populated. The total area of the Court was taken up by legal representatives, Counsels for the Prosecution and Defence and their acolytes and officials: so many be-gowned, bewigged figures. And he archaic system of procedure was still much in evidence. The Judge wrote the majority of evidence in laborious longhand. An expert speedwriter was present, but His Honour obviously preferred his own transcriptions.

Michael in the dock was close, so close. If I had thought about it at all, I would have supposed the dock to be a small, cage-like space, but from my view in the witness box it appeared enormous. Room for half a dozen in there, as well as the burly warders who guarded the prisoners! I gave one quick glance in Michael's direction. He showed no sign of recognition. He appeared to have put on weight. My heart turned to heavy metal in my breast.

The preliminaries were over. The questioning was beginning.

'How long have you known the accused?'

'Two years and seven months.'

My voice had become a thin thread. The Judge leaned forward.

'Could you speak up a little, Miss Bonnington?' He smiled at me. 'The acoustics aren't too good in here.'

'Two years, seven months, Your Honour.'

'Thank you!' He raised his hand to delay further questioning as he made a note.

'What was the nature of your relationship?'

I had been warned of the probable questions by Michael's lawyer and so had an opportunity to consider my answers.

'We were lovers.'

The Judge looked up briefly before he resumed writing. What was he thinking? Silly girl! Lucky devil! Or, maybe, he was scraping the barrel!

'And when did this relationship ..' slight pause, 'begin?'

'On April 12th, 1999.' The date was branded in my brain. No need to check my diary!

'Very precise! And where did the meetings take place?'

'In my flat, at Nottingham Place, W1.'

I stared ahead, feeling heated and at the same time bloodless. I tried to keep all emotion from my voice. How barbaric to allow this probing! To make genuine, raw love the target of all these scrutineers! And mine was the sacrifice. I couldn't deceive myself that our affair had been more than a knee-jerk reaction for Michael, a mechanical exercise, more fun than the gym. on a Thursday afternoon before his weekend return to his wife and children. His emotions had never been involved. That was his triumph and my tragedy!

I drew a deep breath and allowed my eyes to rove the public gallery. Possibly I was searching for a friendly face. I saw the hard, wan face of Michael's wife. Her hatred was so palpable it was fortunate the width of the Court was between us. She was on trial as much as I was. She was being made to look a fool before the world and had become a trophy for the tabloid Press. She had borne and bred his children, and he couldn't wait to get between the legs of another woman. What a crazy world we live in! It was, after all, only my infinite love that made me a victim. If I could despise him now, I was not a victim at all, just a good time girl poaching on another's patch, as millions do every day of every year.

'How often did you meet?'

I didn't quite understand what our arrangements had to do with the present case. However, it was up to Defence Counsel to protest. I was not here to be difficult. If I could not get the sympathy of the jury, it would not augur well for Michael. I lifted my chin and answered the question in a stronger, clear voice.

'Once a week, on Thursday afternoons. We had no other contact.'

Counsel for the Prosecution put his head in his brief, perhaps to hide a smile. No doubt it was all grist to the mill for these chaps.

'When was the last time you saw Michael Rutter at 19A Nottingham Place?'

'The 17th May.'

'Are you sure about that?'

'Quite sure.'

'Thursday, 17th May,' he repeated slowly.

The Judge looked at his watch. 'It is nearly twelve,' he announced. 'I shall call an adjournment for lunch. Everyone will reconvene at two fifteen, sharp.'

The Court rose as one man as the Honourable Judge, with a swish of red robe, swept out, followed by his officials. The door of the witness box was opened and I was back in the body of the Court, ignored by all the gossiping legal teams, loitering in the way of those dashing for the doors and the sanctuary of the nearest pub. Michael was removed down the back steps of the dock, no doubt to partake of his stodgy, carbohydrate-laden meal. His lawyer gave me a quick thumbs-up well done, before he meandered off, surrounded by his assistants.

In no time it seemed the Courtroom was almost empty. I made my way toward the back and a policeman opened the door. An official pursued me. 'Don't go far away. You will be in the witness box again after lunch.'

I went outside and walked the streets. Would I be heavily fined if I didn't go back this afternoon? I bought a coffee from a street stall, but couldn't face food. The whole sordid shambles of this trial sickened me. An innocent man was in the dock, while everywhere the guilty were walking free.

We were all pilloried. Here they were, dissecting my private life, while the actual murderer was miles away, probably reclining on a Spanish beach, unless he were one of the witnesses waiting in the corridor where I had spent so much time recently: Specs, or Jason or Archie or one of Francesca's gentleman callers, who had all given their evidence before me. None of them had cracked, although Francesca had suffered badly. Her life had been caught in a searchlight, as well.

From the basement up, all the present residents of 19A had been called. Jason and Archie, urbane and charming, played to the gallery as though they were performing in a West End melodrama. How could either of them have battered an old woman to death? Sammy, contributing nothing, knowing nothing, hardly ever there, had the shortest sojourn of any of us. Then came the music student, Emily, testifying to giving me the concert ticket. Francesca, making out she was having difficulty with the language, was deliberately vague.

They had all come and gone. Now there were only Specs and I left in the small room. He would be called after they had finished with me.

Some of the shops were early decorated for Christmas. Tinsel and greenery were heaped in the windows. Michael's children would not have a very good Christmas this year. Perhaps their mother would take them away on holiday to Italy or the Caribbean. Probably it would be all over by then and Michael would be a family man again, and all this would be behind them. Except that it never would be behind them, any more than it would be behind me. Life for all of us had changed irrevocably for the worse. Maybe, even now, his wife was instructing her lawyer about a divorce.

With a great deal of dread, I made my way back to the Old Bailey.

'Do you see your former lover in Court, Miss Bonnington?'

The Judge raised a barely perceptible eyebrow at the Counsel for the Prosecution.

'I'll amend that,' he said, perhaps to give me time to absorb the shock of the question. 'Do you see the man with whom you had a relationship in Court?'

'Yes!' I nodded.

'Could you point him out?'

'Over there.' I looked in Michael's direction, but was unable to register his physical presence. The body of the Court swam before my eyes and I clutched at the edge of the witness box for support. With an effort of will, I focused my sight. Learned Counsel was scanning his papers, obviously trying to discomfort me by his silence. In effect, it gave me time to compose myself.

'How long did this relationship last?'

No wonder witnesses cried out in protest that they had answered the question a hundred times before.

'Just over two years.'

'Just over two years!' He looked at me. 'Once a week,' he said. It was not quite clear whether it was a statement or a question.

I inclined my head. 'That is so.'

'And was he your only lover? At that time?'

Thank God for the last three words.

'Objection!' cried Counsel for the Defence as he jumped to his feet.

'Overruled!' said the Judge without raising his eyes. They were trying to discredit me, as Michael's lawyer had warned they would. 'You may answer the question, Miss Bonnington.'

'He was my only lover,' I returned evenly.

A slight murmur reverberated around the Court – ahs! from the romantic, ohs! from the cynical.

'Rather an unsatisfactory position for you, wasn't it?' queried my inquisitor.

I shrugged slightly and made no reply. The Judge had his eyes on Learned Counsel and he rephrased his question.

'Were you distressed by the infrequency of your meetings?'

'I accepted the position,' I said, stiffly. I felt I was in a never-ending nightmare. Michael's lawyer was on his feet again. Counsel for the Prosecution sat down.

'I fail to see how the witness's state of mind bears on this case.'

The Judge's pen ceased its traverse across the paper. He looked over his spectacles. 'Make your questions relevant, Mr. Featherall, please.'

'Your Honour, I only suggest that Miss Bonnington's feelings could have a bearing on the actions of the Defendant.'

'Very well! Continue! But remember,' he admonished, 'that this witness is not on trial here.'

For a moment I floated across the Court to sit in the dock beside Michael, as Sheila Buckley sat beside John Stonehouse all those years ago. I would have been proud to have been there.

I had missed the next question.

'I'm sorry! Could you repeat that, please?'

There was a faint titter from somewhere in the gallery.

'I asked you, Miss Bonnington, to tell the Court about your last meeting with the Defendant. Take your time! In your own words.'

And who else's words could I use, for God's sake?

'My last meeting with Michael Rutter,' I said carefully, looking straight at Learned Counsel as I spoke, 'was on the Thames Embankment at 10.30 p.m. on Wednesday, May 23rd.'

'I thought you only saw him on Thursday afternoons, in your apartment.'

'Yes! That's right! This was an extraordinary meeting.' Thank God I hadn't slipped general between the last two words. The last thing that would be forgiven was levity. 'This was the only occasion on which I saw him at a different time and place.'

'In two years,' observed the horrible man who, I now noticed, had an angry-looking pimple on his chin.

I inclined my head.

'Very well! Go on, please.'

The silence in the Court was total. No coughs or feet shuffling. Everyone was hanging on my words.

'I was there first. Big Ben was striking the half hour as Michael joined me.'

I would have gone on, but the Judge raised his hand. He was noting it all down in his slow, meticulous hand. He gave me a brief nod when he was ready for me to proceed.

'He came and stood by me.' I was shaking almost uncontrollably. My lips were dry. I took a sip of water. Was it right that this torment was allowed? 'He told me the relationship had to end.'

My mouth was full of tongue. I couldn't continue. Fortunately the Judge again raised his hand to slow down my explanation. Was he a wise old bird who well understood my distress? The Court seemed to be collectively holding its breath. Why was it so important for the Jury to understand my anguish? Perhaps the Prosecution was planning to persuade them that it was at this time that we plotted together to murder Mrs Margoloys, except she was dead then, wasn't she?

'Why did he choose this time to finish the relationship? After such a length of time?' the questioning resumed.

I resisted the temptation to scream at him, the Jury and the slavering gallery, because he is a total bastard, because he was bloody sick of me. I longed to rip the wig from his smug head. Neither had I the heart for a rational analysis of my situation, such as, Ah! Who can hope to understand the vagaries of the human heart? What is desirable one day turns to ashes the next. Instead, I said, 'He had just been offered a position in the Government.'

'And wished to forestall the possibility of scandal,' Counsel finished for me. He allowed himself a glance at the clock before he spoke directly to the Jury. 'A previous affair is so much easier to manage than an existing one.'

He was a canny operator. The Jury were now digesting the fact that Michael was a total shit. And they were right, of course. But would such a man take the extra step and kill to protect his reputation? That was for them to decide. But the idea must be planted in their minds.

'No further questions.'

The Judge looked at his watch. 'I think as we are approaching four o'clock, this is a good time to adjourn for the day.' He left and the Court began to empty.

I stumbled from the witness box and was led outside. An official brought me a glass of water.

'Don't worry, love,' someone said. 'It's all a nine days' wonder as far as you are concerned.' She was right, but it didn't stop the knife going in deeper. 'Plenty more fish in the sea.'

Specs was the only witness remaining in our little room. He looked up and grunted as I walked in. I couldn't face talking to him. It seemed an age since Jason, Archie, Francesca and Sammy had been around to spread a little bonhomie.

I walked out and wandered aimlessly down the road. The few reporters hanging about on the pavement appeared not to notice me. They had my testimony, after all. I didn't know whether they would recall me. I hadn't asked if I could go. I was tired of being ordered about and browbeaten. I hadn't done anything wrong! Yet I couldn't get it out of my head that I was guilty and was being punished. Did I empathize with Michael to such an extent? In biblical times women taken in adultery were stoned to death. Much more recently, in Afghanistan, they were severely beaten.

I would not believe Michael was guilty. Yet the Jury held his fate in their hands. I had tried to look at them as I stood in the witness box. At least half were women. One black male. In spite of the evidence, what did they know of Mrs Margoloys, Michael and me? What knowledge had they of the trivia that made up our lives? What could they know about the domestic arrangements at 19A Nottingham Place? Or about a lonely old woman, desperate for social contact, living in the same building as unemployed youngsters, even if they fancied themselves as future celebrities? Did they absorb the lurid prose of the tabloids and take it all as gospel truth? What was to hinder them from making ill-advised judgements in the present case? Yet they held the fate of a brilliant man in their hands. The Law and its practitioners was truly an ass. A total, complete, undeniably, fucking ass!

* * *

I scraped my hair into a knot at the back of my head, put on a pair of plain glasses and joined the queue for the public gallery. My own time in the witness box was over. But Specs' evidence I must hear! Strangely, nobody appeared to recognise me. Everybody was too busy watching the door to see who was coming and going.

I took my seat next to an elderly woman. In a different time and place, no doubt she would have sat knitting by the side of the guillotine. I peered downwards. There seemed to be a great deal of activity in the well of the Court. A confused hubbub rose upwards. Minor officials were checking papers, putting out water glasses, standing endlessly talking together. It was a job, a way of life, the means by which these people filled their days. Spend a day; use it up! No second chance available for that day! With all the others it builds into a structure to support the remainder of the life. And if Michael were to be locked up, there would be no second chance for him for a long, long time.

There was a stir as the Jury filed in. They were reminded they were still under oath. Then Michael was brought up.

He sat down in the dock. He looked strained and irritable. I could just see his wife below me near the front of the Public Gallery. She had been ushered in after the rest of us had filled the rear seats. She held her head high and looked at no one. A woman of about the same age accompanied her – a friend or a sister, perhaps. I didn't know whether Michael had siblings. He had always discouraged personal questions. I had checked his date of birth, parentage and marital status from the M.Ps.' register, but no ancillary details were available.

Michael glanced briefly at the Public Gallery after he was brought up, but as far as I could see he gave his wife no smile of acknowledgement. Knowing the man intimately as I did, I could imagine his state of mind. He would be living in the midst of volcanic turmoil because of the injustice of his arrest. He may be blaming it all on me. I quivered and fixed my gaze on my leather boots. The woman next to me became aware of my trembling.

'Chilly in 'ere, ent it?' she remarked, companionably. I smiled back and nodded.

We were being called to order. 'All rise.'

The Judge, in his scarlet, bewigged splendour, took his seat on the Bench. We sat down again to the accompaniment of expectant coughs.

'Your witness, Mr. Dick.'

The Counsel for the Prosecution who had so harried me rose to his feet and tucked his thumbs inside his gown. I began to feel that I was living through one of the more lurid television soap operas.

'Mr. Paul Mansell!'

I imagined Specs sitting waiting in the little room, biting his fingernails to the quick. Now he would be hovering outside the door of the Courtroom, ready for his call. He was a champion lurker, that one. Was he anxious about his Court appearance? I had never noticed him show much emotion, apart from the time I had refused to meet him again.

Was he the murderer? Was I his intended victim? And when he couldn't find me, had he vented his fury on a defence-less old woman, not aware that she was his aunt? The sense of unreality was growing on me. My stomach was in a state of churn. It rumbled uncomfortably loudly.

'Didn't you have any breakfast, love?'

We were squashed closely together in the Public Gallery. I remembered childish visits to the pantomime, when staff from the Hippodrome came along the rows of cheap price benches, urging the audience to move up so that more people could be admitted. From where I sat I could see the top of Michael's head. His face was concealed, but I knew his face so well, this didn't matter. The thinning patch at the back of his head, where I had so often touched my fingers, showed white against the crisp dark waves surrounding it. I felt sick as a dog.

Specs entered from the back of the Court, following the usher towards the witness box. He mumbled the Oath when it was held out for him to read, then blinked owlishly in the direction of Learned Counsel.

'You are Paul Mansell?'

'Yes!'

'Of 106 High Street, Hackney.'

He nodded.

'Speak up!' said the Judge.

'Yes!'

That was the first I knew that he lived in Hackney. So what the hell was he doing shopping in my supermarket? It was a free country, of course.

'Tell the Court your relationship to the victim.' The Counsel paused in a rather insolent manner as he consulted his brief. 'Mrs Ada Rose Margoloys.' Surely the bastard had memorized her name?

'She was my auntie,' said Specs, as he pushed his glasses up his nose and blinked rapidly.

'In what connection was that?'

'What?' asked Specs.

'I mean, was she your mother's sister, your father's sister, or any of the other permutations?'

'Oh!' said Specs. He considered this for a few moments. 'She was my father's brother's wife.'

'An aunt by marriage, then,' resumed the lawyer. 'I understand your mother lives in Barnsley.' A quick, interrogatory glance at the witness box. Specs nodded. The Judge, busily writing, did not notice the little exchange. However, the Jury appeared to be all attention. I wondered why I had never been called for Jury Service.

'How long have you been living in London?'

Again, Specs took his time. He even checked numbers off on his fingers. Counsel waited patiently. 'Since last April,' he responded at last.

'Seven months, then,' said the Q.C. He checked his brief. 'How often did you see your aunt before her unfortunate death?'

'Hadn't seen her at all!' Specs now seemed indignant. He took off his glasses and wiped them. He sniffed a bit, as though his asthma was troubling him. I had suspected he was asthmatic, but couldn't decide whether he was genuinely suffering now or was playing to the gallery. Again Counsel waited, tapping his fingernail against the papers in his hand.

'Didn't know where she lived,' Specs added. He put his spectacles back on and stared at his interlocutor.

'Didn't your mother keep in touch with your aunt?'

'No!' said Specs.

'So what was your purpose in coming to London?'

'Mum said to see if I could find her.' Specs permitted himself a little smile. 'She didn't know how big London is!'

'Indeed! So when you went to Nottingham Place, it was to visit your aunt?'

'No!' said Specs.

My heart trebled its rate. What the hell was he going to say?

'Would you please tell the Court why you were in 19A Nottingham Place?'

This time Specs did not hesitate. 'I thought there was a room to rent there,' he said. 'When someone came out, I went in to see what it was like.' He shuffled his feet a bit. 'I don't like it much in Hackney.'

'Indeed!' The lawyer repeated himself. He walked closer to the witness box and looked Specs in the eye. Specs recoiled a little.

'Why did you think that? There was no vacant apartment there at that time.'

There were now! Two on the ground floor: Mrs Margoloys' little room and the music students' big bay. Neither had been occupied since the crime, whether from lack of advertisement or inclination on the part of potential tenants, I had no idea.

'Made a mistake,' said Specs.

My heartbeat returned to something like normality. At least the stupid boy hadn't said he was following me. I had said I had assumed he was visiting his aunt. At least I couldn't now be trawled through the newspapers, with Specs cited as a successor to Michael. We had had plenty of meetings, one way and another. Thank God, they had all been in public! Would some busybody remember us and inform the tabloids?

I must get out of the building quickly at the end of the morning. I began to feel faint. But if I pushed my way out now, I would be conspicuous. I dropped my head on to my chest and took some deep breaths.

When I came up again, Specs had been dismissed and some former neighbour of Mrs Margoloys was testifying to her open, affectionate nature, and trying to put in a plug for the care of the elderly. She was speedily cut short by Learned Counsel.

The morning dragged on in an interminable fashion. I daren't leave before the Court rose. Eventually, the Judge called the lunch break, Michael was removed down the back stairs, and the public in the gallery began a slow shuffle towards the doors.

'Boring, ent it?' remarked the woman who had spoken to me earlier. 'I thought a murder trial would be a bit juicier than this.'

I smiled, but didn't reply. My proximity to Michael had exhausted me. I resolved to get out of Nottingham Place, to leave London as soon as the case was over. Like Specs, I didn't relish my place of abode.

There appeared to be no evidence against Michael at all. How could they have charged him with murder?

I would return when he was in the witness box. But after his acquittal, London would be too small for both of us. I had some serious thinking to do.

Michael in the dock was as difficult and evasive as Michael had been in bed or, indeed, out of it as far as I was concerned.

I sat in the Public Gallery and tried to analyse his demeanour and my feelings for him: a not tall man with dark, wavy hair. Sombre eyes, straight nose, well-shaped mouth, firm chin with a cleft. Long before I reached the end of this inventory, my legs were trembling and there was clammy moisture on my forehead. Why did that particular combination of eyes, nose and mouth have such a devastating effect on my psyche, whilst other combinations did not? Forget the engaging personality, forget the charm, switched on and off at will, forget the compatibility factor. None of that mattered a jot! It was as though we had been born two halves of the same ripe apple and, as far as I was concerned, only he could make me complete. Unfortunately, by some terrible quirk, things were not the same for him. I was just another female from the harem!

But I had sense enough to know that, given my instinctive, over-powering response to his presence, it would have been impossible for me to have acted any other way after our first encounter. My tragedy was that he was not free and he had no intention of making himself available for me. Let's face it, he was just a greedy sod who wanted it all and was ready to jettison anyone or anything that got in his way.

The Press had pushed a camera in my face that morning. Fuck the whole sodding lot of them! I had ceased to care. I had to be near Michael in his hour of need.

But he was not performing well. It was odd that while I was helpless underneath my physical fascination with Michael, my mind was still able to stand apart and objectively analyse the situation. And my infatuation did not enable me to refute the fact that he was not going down well with the Jury. Their body language was clear – fidgeting, frowns, tapping fingers. A little more humility, a little more courtesy on his part to the Learned Counsels would have brought some of them to his side.

'Mr. Rutter, would you please tell the Court about your visit to 19A Nottingham Place on ..' Counsel for the Prosecution checked his brief, 'Thursday, May 17th.'

Michael shrugged. Blood pulsed in my ears to the pounding of my heart.

'Just my weekly, routine visit,' he sneered.

The Barrister raised his eyebrows. I was now near enough the front of the Public Gallery to observe such small nuances. Following my appearance in the witness box, I was now recognised by the officials and a place was reserved for me, from which I had a good view of the Court. A faint murmur of disapproval sounded around me. Perhaps some of the spectators abhorred my behaviour, but they didn't like that put-down from the man in the dock.

'So you do not claim to be in love with Miss Bonnington?'

Again Michael shrugged. What's love got to do with it, his gesture implied. I was so hot, I expected to see steam arising around me.

'Would it be fair to say you were simply indulging your carnal desires?'

'Say what you like!'

Michael's lawyer sprang to his feet.

'Yes, Mr. Featherall?' The Judge sounded infinitely weary. Counsel for the Prosecution sat down.

'Objection, Your Honour! The Defendant's emotional state is a matter of conjecture, not fact.'

'It could be relevant to the Defendant's presence or absence in the house,' said the Judge. 'Proceed,' nodding at the Counsel for the Prosecution.

'I was merely trying to ascertain the Defendant's own opinion of his motives and desires,' he said mildly.

'Just so,' said the Judge. 'Carry on!'

I wondered whether Michael's licentiousness was causing envy or amusement amongst the elderly men of the Court. They had heard it all before, of course. Because of the intensity of my feelings for Michael, I could not blame myself for my actions. Yet it seemed obvious that the Jury would be blaming Michael for his. He was doing himself no good by his insolent attitude. A cold miasma settled around me.

Why, in God's name, hadn't he the sense to pretend that his feelings for me were so overwhelming that he had no choice in the matter. That would have gained the sympathy of at least some of the Jurors. All the world loves a lover! Wasn't that so?

'You did not call at this house, 19A Nottingham Place, again after you left it at 4.30 p.m. on Thursday, 17th May?'

'No! I did not,' responded Michael. His supercilious air suggested the idea was unworthy of consideration.

'And this relationship was terminated by you a week after this event?'

'Yes!' The answer was short, terse, contemptuous in its refusal to communicate.

'Why was that?'

'Well, if it is relevant to the case and is not wasting time and taxpayers' money, I decided that I and the young lady had reached the point of no return.'

'And why was that?' asked the lawyer, silkily.

'Well, why does anybody finish with anybody?' asked Michael in an impatient tone. 'I suppose I had had enough of her.'

'Shame on you!' muttered the woman by my side.

Tears stung my eyes. I heard a sharp intake of breath, my own.

'And had nothing to do, of course, with your recent elevation into the Whips' Office?'

'Certainly not!'

Counsel did not pursue the matter. After a slight pause, he resumed, 'So this young woman, who had been pleasuring you for almost two years, was cast aside like an old shoe, when it suited your purpose to be rid of her.'

His terminology was deliberately emotive. Counsel for the Prosecution was assuming that Mrs Margoloys and I would become interchangeable in the minds of the Jury. I wanted to leave. The courtroom swam before me. But I sat where I was.

'Oh, come on! Grow up!' responded Michael.

'Mr. Rutter! Please mind your language,' interposed the Judge.

But Counsel for the Prosecution was doing well. He had exposed Michael as a short-tempered, uncaring bastard, who confirmed the public's low opinion of politicians in general. Could he be capable of murder?

For the first time, I had doubts about the verdict of Not Guilty that I had assumed would be a foregone conclusion. But surely no Jury would convict on the strength of a shitty love life and a woman scornfully treated? There were so many of us in that position, even after thirty years of feminism and political correctness.

I tottered out into the weak autumn sunshine at lunchtime and did not return for the afternoon session. I was too weak to face further exposure of my private life. I bought a sandwich; then took a bus to Westminster. Perhaps I wished to be near the place where Michael had spent so many years of his life.

I sat on a bench in St. James Park and watched the ducks and water birds. Nearby small children were chasing pigeons. Why wasn't my life different? Why hadn't Michael and I been able to bring our little ones here? I got up and walked, crossed the ornamental bridge and looked back towards the Admiralty buildings. Had Michael ever strolled in the park while he was an M.P.? For God's Sake, what was I thinking? He was still a Member of Parliament and would continue to be so after the Not Guilty verdict. He couldn't be struck off for facing trial, could he?

I walked on. I dawdled near the water, breathing in the rich smells of warm grass and muddy banks where the birds were squatting and preening. I paid for a deckchair and sat in the weak, late autumn sunlight, looking at the lake and letting my mind roam from childhood holidays with my family, to student life, and my recent Personal Relations position. I even saw myself in the supermarket, stacking interminable shelves.

After a time I left the deckchair and turned back towards the end of the park. Buckingham Palace reared greyly behind its confines. I continued along the Mall and across Trafalgar Square. Now I was weary and it seemed a great distance down Northumberland Avenue to Charing Cross tube station. I bought an Evening Standard at the entrance, jostled by the hurrying crowds.

'M.P.'s Trial. Sensation', screamed its headlines. Feeling decidedly apprehensive, I rode the elevator down to the Northern Line and reached the platform before I opened the inner sheets.

'Witness testifies Rutter lied about his presence in murder building.'

What! What surprise witness? Only Specs had been in the little waiting room when I left. Who was putting the boot in? Who was lying about Michael? My eyes struggled to make sense of the words on the blowing pages.

Mrs Ivy Atkins, who lives in the basement flat directly opposite the murder building, has come forward to say that she saw Michael Rutter walking away from the building on Tuesday evening, the 22nd May, five days after his admitted visit to his lover.

What! Who was this woman? Had the tabloids offered a large reward for information? Michael had never seen me on a Tuesday, not once in our two-year relationship.

My eyes flew across the small print, trying to take in the implications of what I was reading. Ivy Atkins, whoever she was, said she recognised Michael – she was an avid reader of the tabloids – but also she had noticed he wore Chelsea boots. She had become used to seeing them from her low level vantage point, as they hurried down the road at just gone 3 o'clock on Thursday afternoons. It was only when she read the newspapers and the accounts of the trial that she knew he was not telling the truth, as she had seen him on Tuesday. She had taken particular note because he had never been there at that time before. She noticed the time specifically because she was watching Emmerdale on the television, and that was broadcast at 7 o'clock on Tuesday evening. It wasn't on at 3 p.m. on Thursday.

'I got used to him marking the time on Thursday,' she had said. 'He was regular as clockwork.'

A train entered the platform with blast and noise. Automatically, my eyes fixated on the print, I boarded it, shoving my way in. I swayed to its motion, hanging on to the nearest strap. Just an old woman getting mixed up, my mind tried to insist. Her evidence will be discredited. Tuesday? Wasn't that the day I went for the interview at the Commons? Was I down in the basement? I wouldn't be home much before seven, anyway. If I couldn't remember my movements, why should she?

With a shock as powerful as if a bucket of icy water had been thrown over my head, I realised it was the day Mrs Margoloys was murdered. But Michael had not been in the building then! He was never there on a Tuesday! Coincidence? It must be. There must be hordes of men in London wearing Chelsea boots. Had Michael come to the flat to finish our relationship? I wasn't there. He had to go home. And then, news of the murder broke.

The train lurched into Leicester Square and juddered to a halt. People pushed and fought to reach the doors. Sweat ran down my back in the crowded, overheated compartment. I stared at Poem for the Day, level with my eyes, the words meaningless. No wonder I had been recalled from holiday, I kept repeating to myself. I could well have been locked up!

The train drew into Baker Street and the doors opened. Zombie-like, I walked out and stepped on to the long escalator to street level. I knew with complete certainty, with my clairvoyant sense regarding his movements that Michael had been in my building that evening. The unknown woman across the street had not made a mistake. The life style of such old ladies consists of their monitoring the comings and goings of the world outside their windows. She would have waited for Michael's appearance every Thursday afternoon with as much avidity as I did myself. She had lived lost loves vicariously through me. She had noticed the change in Michael's routine that Tuesday evening. She had not made a mistake.

I let myself into my flat and sat for a long time until it became dark. Only then did I move in order to switch on lights. I still did not think that Michael was guilty of the crime, but I knew that things were looking very black for him.

CHAPTER TEN

I missed a day and then went back at the beginning of the following week. On Monday morning, almost without volition, I got up, tidied the flat, ate some cereal and made my way to the Old Bailey. By this time, even the doorkeepers were nodding recognition.

Surely Michael's evidence would end soon! Whatever could they find to ask him? But, as I would discover, another blow was in store for me.

After the initial sniffing and shuffling, when the Court was soothed by the arrival of the Judge, the Prosecuting Lawyer held aloft a long, thin object covered by a plastic shield. I craned forward. What was it? It was shown to Michael as he stood in the witness box.

'Do you recognize this walking stick, Mr. Rutter?'

He gave it a cursory glance. 'No! Should I?'

'Please take another look.'

Michael went through elaborate motions of inspecting the object. Finally he looked up. 'I don't use a walking stick,' he said. 'And never have.'

I was mystified. There was an umbrella stand with a selection of walking sticks in the hallway at 19A. I had never touched any of them, although once I had seen Jason and Archie have a mock fencing match in the hall using two of the sticks. Perhaps Mrs Margoloys had taken one from the stand for assistance on one of her forays. Had it been found in her room?

'This stick,' said Counsel for the Prosecution, pausing for effect, 'was found half buried in mud near Greenwich.

It could have been dropped or thrown into the river in the vicinity of Westminster. If so, there is a possibility that it would have been washed ashore at that spot.'

'Oh, yes!' sneered Michael, putting an overload of sarcasm on the two words.

Be careful, my darling, I silently implored him. Don't be so antagonistic! The Jury won't like it. Be charming and helpful!

Michael's face was red. He was certainly losing his cool. Surely he wasn't rattled by such a meaningless piece of evidence. For God's sake, one of the boys could have borrowed it for a rehearsal, lost it somewhere and it had somehow ended up in the Thames. What connection could it possibly have with Michael?

And, if it had been in the water so long, how could they prove it came from my building? Did anyone there know how many sticks the umbrella stand held? But it would be entirely feasible to a gullible mind that someone who didn't wish to be seen could have reached out for the nearest weapon and clubbed Mrs Margoloys to the ground. Back to the unknown intruder theory of the crime! Poor Mrs Margoloys would wander about. But she hadn't deserved such an end.

'I was just calling to see Frances,' Michael could have said with his engaging smile, 'but she doesn't seem to be in.' He had enough practice in charming his constituents.

'No, dear,' she would have replied. 'Can I give her a message?'

What the hell was I thinking? I was taking the scenario before me and assuming that Michael had seen Mrs Margoloys and done the dastardly deed. I must be mad! Again, I had serious apprehensions about the verdict. Only consider all the defendants who are convicted on very flimsy evidence: all those who persist in denying their crimes and who are finally pronounced innocent after decades in gaol! God help us all! Surely it was ludicrous to use an old walking stick plucked from the river to try and pin the crime on an innocent man? If that was the sum of their evidence, what was Michael doing in the dock, anyway?

Judging from his superior attitude, he obviously thought the same. He had begun to sigh audibly before he answered a question. He was implying, why am I bothering with this legal idiot. Sometimes he took so long to respond that Counsel repeated the question. The Judge was now able to keep up his careful longhand, without trouble. What next? I became aware I was holding my breath, and let it out silently and slowly.

Counsel proceeded. Hairs from our hall carpet had been found on Michael's expensive shoes. Well, that was no surprise! He had never denied being in the building.

At the end of the morning Michael was released from his torment. Once again, I found myself walking the streets near the Old Bailey. I tried to think logically about the evidence against him. The most damning was the sighting by the old woman from the building opposite on Tuesday evening. He had said he was working at his desk in the Commons, but no witness could collaborate that. And there was no convincing explanation why he had broken his usual habit of returning to Northamptonshire on the previous Thursday. I certainly thought he did so after our regular love making session on Thursday afternoons.

He had told the Court that pressure of work kept him in the Commons on the Friday. He had an important speech to prepare. He had rung his Agent to advise him he would miss his regular Friday morning surgery. Even to my ears, it sounded thin. It was more likely he was hanging around because of the proposed reshuffle. Nobody knew exactly when it would take place. But he could have been dropped a strong hint that he was in the frame and that was why he had made his way to Nottingham Place to end our affair. Then, if he was questioned, he could quite truthfully say it was over. He wouldn't admit this to the Court as it would appear callous and calculating.

My neck muscles were tight and aching as I stepped aside from hurrying lunch hour crowds. It could be that Michael was going to be punished for what he hadn't done just because he had indulged in a heartless affair with me. Was he in a foul temper because his plans were thwarted? Or was he just shit-scared about his position? He had tried to tidy his life, as he would see it, and for once I was missing from my flat when he desperately needed to see me. He had made up his mind, no doubt perfected what he intended to say to me. Perhaps he was carrying a bunch of flowers, or a box of chocolates. And, then, I wasn't home!

He would have been furious. Mrs Margoloys creeping around the hall was the last straw. He must have met her on his way out. Because he couldn't deliver his message to me, he didn't want it known that he had set foot in the premises. So he had shut her up!

I pressed my hands against my temples. I was standing outside an antiquarian bookshop and a series of old maps were displayed in its window – beautifully crafted works of art, of exploration and discovery. How many murders and heinous crimes had occurred during the course of those expeditions?

I began to walk. I was wrong! I must be wrong! There was reasonable doubt about Michael's guilt. Of course he hadn't done it. But would the Jury see it that way?

* * *

'Ladies and Gentlemen of the Jury.'

It was another day. The Judge began his summing up. He turned in his seat and looked at their expectant faces over the top of his narrow spectacles.

'You may think that this is an involved case, but the issue before you is very simple. You have heard contradictory accounts of the events of Tuesday, 22nd May, but you have only one issue to keep in mind. Did the Defendant administer the blows that resulted in the death of Mrs Ada Rose Margoloys?'

His Honour removed his spectacles and dangled them from his right hand. He leaned back slightly in his chair.

'There is no doubt that Mrs Margoloys was the victim of a vicious crime. She was killed by a number of blows to the head caused by a heavy object. There is no way that the injuries could have been self-inflicted. She was killed in the hall and dragged into her own room. If she was not dead at that juncture, she died soon afterwards. When she was found on the Tuesday evening, the estimation was that she had been dead between three and five hours, as near as could be ascertained at that time.

'We know she was alive about 7 p.m. on the preceding day as she was seen and spoken to by one of the residents at 19A Nottingham Place.'

The Judge paused and checked his notes. The Jury sat perfectly still with their eyes on their mentor. He resumed: 'Ladies and Gentlemen, this is a despicable crime. A defenceless old woman has been attacked and killed in her own home. The question you have to ask yourselves is, was the crime committed by the man you see before you in the dock.' Another slight pause to allow the Jury time to consider this option.

He resumed, 'You may think that she could have disturbed a chance intruder. But no evidence has been found of a forced entry to the premises. There were others present in the house who resided there. You have heard their evidence about their activities on the evening of May 22nd. Let us examine the facts as we know them.'

Again the Judge paused and looked around the Court. The silence was broken by a bout of nervous coughing from an old man behind me. I glanced across to the dock. Michael was sitting, motionless and white as alabaster, staring before him.

'First, let us look at the possibility of a chance intruder, a house-breaker, looking for an opportunistic crime. But we have no evidence of any such person. Nobody, not the witness occupying the opposing premises, nor any of the inhabitants of this block, saw anyone or anything untoward during their myriad comings and goings. This hypothetical burglar was invisible.'

One of the Jurors made a note on the pad before him.

'So,' the Judge continued, 'if there was no unknown intruder, we are left with those who we know were present in the house, and who also had opportunity.'

Again the Judge paused and consulted his briefing. 'I will enumerate the residents of this building and refresh your memory as to their stated movements on this fateful evening. If you will consult your plan of the building.'

The Jury already had plans of 19A spread before them.

'Beginning with the top story,' said His Honour. 'Flat 6. Occupied by Frances Bonnington. She has told you that she did not arrive home from work until after 7.30 p.m. as she had been meeting a client in Chelsea and her transport on her way home was unreliable. Mrs Margoloys was seen alive about 6 pm. on that day.' The estimated time of death just put me out of the frame. His words reminded me of Specs falling into the seat beside me as the concert was about to begin. He was dishevelled and panting. I had assumed he had been hurrying to reach his place before the performance began. But had he had time to murder Mrs Margoloys before his arrival? He had not had a ticket. It was Emily's second ticket he had collected from the box office. It was the wrong day. I was going mad. Mrs Margoloys was still alive then, wasn't she?

The Judge was continuing the summing up in measured tones. 'Moving down a floor, we find the large flat of Francesca da Ogli. Miss da Ogli was also absent that evening. She spent a few days with friends in Naples and left her rooms at Nottingham Place on the Monday afternoon. She took a taxi to Heathrow and boarded an Al Italia flight for Italy. These facts are not in dispute.'

So that was where Francesca had gone. The building had seemed bereft without her callers. How fortunate for her that she had been away that week! But hadn't I seen one of her callers about that time, when Specs was making a nuisance of himself outside my door? No, that wasn't right. It was surely Saturday when Specs called.

'Moving down to the ground floor, three rooms were let here.' The Judge pushed his spectacles up his nose to examine the plan more closely. 'The large front room with the bay window was occupied by two young women music students. Neither of them returned to their lodgings that evening. You have heard the evidence to that effect.' The Judge glanced at the Jury to make sure they were paying attention to his words. They were.

'Behind this room and the intermediate bathroom was the room occupied by Mrs Margoloys, overlooking the rear of the premises.' Poor Mrs Margoloys! She hadn't even had a decent view.

'And opposite this, behind the staircase leading to the basement, was a small room intermittently occupied by Samuel O'Hara. He was not at home on the evening in question,' again he checked his notes, 'being at a party with friends in Peckham.' Sammy obviously had an active social life.

'Lastly,' recommenced His Honour, 'we come to the basement, occupied by Jason Turner and Archibald De Niro.' Again he regarded the Jury. 'Now this is slightly more difficult for you because neither Jason Turner nor Archibald de Niro has been able to produce firm evidence of their presence elsewhere at the crucial time. Jason Turner has told you that he spent the night with a friend, but he did not meet her until 9 that evening. Before then, he went to a cinema but he cannot produce evidence for this fact. He threw the ticket away and has no clear recollection of what he saw.'

Poor Jason, I thought. I bet he was doing something dodgy and doesn't want to admit it.

'But,' the Judge continued, 'there is no evidence to suggest that he did return to 19A Nottingham Place that evening. Archibald de Niro had no sight of him.' They would give each other an alibi anyway, I thought.

His Honour paused and there was some fidgeting around me. 'Get on with it, you old fart,' muttered someone near me.

'And so we come to Archibald de Niro.' Was that his real name, I wondered. 'Now, as far as we can ascertain, as the evidence has been presented, Archibald de Niro was the last person to see Ada Margoloys alive.'

Poor Archie, I thought now.

'Apart from the murderer,' muttered a woman who had been a constant presence in the Public Gallery.

'Apart, of course,' added the Judge, 'from the murderer.'

The woman sighed. She had apparently been much taken by Archie's appearance in the witness box. Archie wasn't on trial. What was the Judge about?

'Archibald de Niro has informed you that he spent the evening and night of May 22nd with Chloe Maxwell.' No doubt she was the girl I had seen in his flat who had been a participant in our free-ranging frolics. 'She has corroborated his account. They met at around 7.30, and ate at a bistro before returning to her premises.' I wondered where she lived. 'Archibald de Niro has told you that he spoke to Ada Rose Margoloys before he left the house at just after six that Tuesday evening. She told him to have a good time and he said to her, look after yourself, Mrs M.'

The Judge glanced at his notes again and then consulted his watch. 'I see it is nearly twelve twenty,' he said, ' so, as this seems a convenient time to break for lunch, we will adjourn and reconvene at 2.15 sharp.'

'All rise,' cried the usher. We did so and His Honour swept out with a swirl of his scarlet gown.

He was clever. His timing was impeccable. He was giving the Jury time to consider the innocence of all the residents of our building: time for his words to sink in and make an impact. That was good. I didn't imagine that any of my fellow occupants could have murdered Mrs Margoloys, in spite of Jason and Archie's dodgy alibis. What a pity Francesca had been away. Her callers were the unknown quantity.

But, on the other hand, I didn't think Michael had slaughtered her either. In spite of the dismissive comments of the Judge, I favoured an unknown intruder. Perhaps Sammy had left a window unlatched and somebody had climbed in without trouble, found nothing to steal, then been disturbed by Mrs Margoloys, who would probably call out if she thought Sammy had returned. In a fit of violent frustration, the unknown assailant had clubbed her down with a heavy stick he grabbed from the umbrella stand – perhaps not intending to kill her but to shut her up and immobilize her until he got away. Then he made sure he secured the window again to disguise his entry, before leaving by the front door. He would have been wearing gloves. No self-respecting burglar would not have his gloves handy! Nobody had seen him, but there was nobody in our building except Mrs Margoloys. And the street was quite often empty. People were away or staying out late at after-work drinking binges. Why should a stranger walking from Marylebone High Street be noticed? It would be assumed he was making his way to the Underground. In any event, I was probably in the area as much as anyone and I didn't know half of the inhabitants of the other rooming houses in the street.

So they had arrested Michael, in the absence of another suspect! Pressure on the police to solve crime as the number of unsolved murders in the capital soared! Even though, as far as I could see, there was no compelling evidence against him. If that crazy old woman from the opposite basement had not given her evidence, there would have been nothing at all to connect him to the crime. Just because she said she recognized his shoes! She was so sure, so adamant that she could not be mistaken. How ridiculous! How many men wore that type of Chelsea boot – hundreds in London, I would be willing to bet. But not too many of them walked down our road, I was forced to admit. Trainers were more usual.

'Now we come to the crux of this case.' The Judge was sterner, more businesslike. He had abandoned the playful, hectoring tone he had assumed during the morning session. 'Concerning the evidence against the Defendant: I would remind you to weigh it carefully in your minds before you decide whether there is sufficient evidence against him to bring in a verdict of guilty. If you have reservations, if there are any grounds for doubt in your minds, you must bring in a verdict of Not Guilty.'

I noticed the Judge did not look at Michael. All his attention was on the Jury. There could have been nobody else in the Courtroom except those twelve good men and true. And, really, they were the only ones who mattered now. Learned Counsels had done their best, or their worst, depending on your point of view.

Did the Judge think Michael was guilty? What he thought was immaterial. He was present to see fair play and to give an impartial summing up of the proceedings.

'Now,' resumed the Judge, leaning forward and addressing the Jury with the utmost seriousness, 'you may consider that the Defendant's actions were indefensible. You may think that, as a married man and a respectable Member of Parliament, he should not have been carrying on a covert affair with a woman young enough to be his daughter.'

Hold on! Not quite! My cheeks were reddening. Surely the Judge was not about to turn me into another naïve victim!

The Judge looked with his penetrating gaze at the men and women huddled together on their benches. 'Or you may think, in this day and age, so what! But that is not the issue before you today. The Defendant is not on trial for his morals, but for the murder of a frail, elderly woman. Try to put out of your minds the sexual licence of the Defendant, endeavour to forget his presence every Thursday afternoon at 19A Nottingham Place. What is for you to decide is whether he was there on the night of Tuesday, May 22nd. And if he was so present, did he strike the fatal blows and then callously leave Ada Margoloys to die alone and untended.'

Michael's lawyer shifted in his seat. He could not rise to his feet and roar, 'Objection!' But he might consider that the

Judge was stepping over the boundary into the dangerous territory of emotive language.

'Let us consider the evidence against the Defendant,' the Judge continued as he glanced over his spectacles at the Jury, before referring to the papers before him. 'Firstly, he was in the House of Commons on Tuesday, 22nd May and, unusually for him, on the previous Friday, 18th May. As you have been informed, it is the habit of many Members of Parliament to leave for their constituencies on Thursday evenings as, indeed, it was of the Defendant except on the week in question. However, a reshuffle was in the offing. It may be that he had been given a hint that he could be involved. That is a possibility. But, again, that is not the issue. The date to keep in mind is Tuesday, 22nd May. Did the Defendant decide to call at 19A Nottingham Place that evening to put his affairs in order? Why should he do so? Miss Bonnington was certainly not expecting him. She was late returning home after her numerous business appointments that afternoon.'

And nobody to confirm it, I thought. They could easily have arrested me. I closed my eyes.

There was total silence in the Court. It seemed the Judge was playing with us. He had white rabbits up his scarlet sleeve that he was going to exhibit in his own good time.

'So you have to ask yourselves why the Defendant should go, if indeed he did go, to call unexpectedly on Miss Bonnington on a Tuesday evening. You have heard he was a creature of habit. Thursday afternoons were the usual time he went to Nottingham Place.

'And why did he not telephone to check that she would be home before he made this journey? Could it be he wished to end the relationship in the event of his elevation to a more prominent position? Was he, so to speak, clearing the pitch for his new Government appointment? So in the event of any query about his private life, he could truthfully inform the Government Whips that the affair was behind him.'

His Honour paused to allow these speculations time to register. Then, his tone deceptively mild, he continued, 'We don't know the purpose of his call at this address, if indeed he did call. But we do know from the evidence given by Miss Bonnington that the Defendant did end their relationship the following day. That fact is not in dispute. Whether it is relevant is for you to decide.'

Motes of dust danced in the shafts of sunlight barring the Court. Everything was remote, unreal.

'But let us consider the facts as we have them appertaining to the Defendant's presence in the building. He has denied it. None of the residents saw him. But, as we have heard, they were all out.' He consulted his brief. 'Archibald de Niro was the last to leave at six p.m. on that fateful evening. He spoke to Mrs Margoloys before he left.'

One of the jurors made a brief note on the pad before her.

'The lady opposite, Mrs Atkins,' resumed the Judge (my mind clicked to the fact that he had begun to use the term, 'lady', rather than woman) is quite certain that she saw him leaving 19A at some time after seven on that evening. She is sure of the time because she was watching ..' he paused to consult his notes, 'Emmerdale. And she recognized his shoes.' Again he consulted his notes. 'Distinctive Chelsea boots. Not very usual shoes to see in Nottingham Place. And this lady, you will recall, had a very good view, the opposite, you may say, of a bird's eye view,' no-one smiled at his joke, 'because of the position of the window in her basement flat. He was, she said, carrying something in a plastic bag.' Another glance at his brief. 'Something long and thin. She thought it might be a sweeping brush and supposed he wouldn't want to be sweeping up wearing those shoes.'

Good God! I hadn't heard that piece of evidence. That must have been divulged on the afternoon I hadn't returned to the Court, the afternoon I had sat in St. James' Park watching the ducks.

'Now, to the murder weapon! We know that it was heavy and wooden because of the post mortem evidence regarding the damage to the skull of the victim.'

She had such a thin skull, I imagined Michael protesting. I pressed my hands together. I would not faint!

'We know a walking stick was missing from the hall. Archibald de Niro testified to the unusual nature of this walking stick. It had a thick bear's head at the crest. He noticed it every time he climbed the stairs from the basement. He is not sure when it disappeared, but thinks it was still there when he left the premises on Tuesday, 22nd May. He can't recall seeing it again.'

Oh, Archie! Archie! I screamed in my head. What have you done? Any intruder could have picked it up – Specs, an unknown assailant. Why was the Judge so keen to fit up Michael? I watched tiny flecks of blood appear on my palms where my nails had punctured them. After that, I heard little. But I had heard enough!

I stumbled out at the end of the session and didn't return. I knew what the outcome would be. I had always been psychic about Michael's movements. The fact that I hadn't known that Michael would come to see me that Tuesday evening had convinced me of his innocence. But such psychic certainty had no place in a Court of Law.

I found the evidence against him very flimsy. It seemed to centre on the word of a crazy old woman, who could be confused or malicious, or just publicity seeking, and on an unusual walking stick washed up on the banks of the Thames. But would the Jury see if that way?

From the six o'clock news the next day I learned that the Judge had completed his summing up and the Jury had been sent out to consider their verdict. They would be incarcerated in a hotel during the weekend, and Michael would have to wait until the following week before he knew the result of their deliberations.

Would I ever see him again? He would not wish me to visit him in prison. Ours was a liaison of a golden hour. A gloomy gaol greeting could not be contemplated.

It was the middle of the next week before the Jury were able to deliver their verdict. Even then, there was one dissenter. I rehearsed the scene in my head.

'Gentlemen of the Jury, who will speak for you?' Who had been chosen as the foreman? The large black man? That fussy-looking woman? The pretty girl or the yobbish youth?

'Have you reached your verdict?'

'We have.'

'And is it the verdict of you all?'

'No My Lord! Eleven of us are in agreement.'

'And do you find the Defendant Guilty or Not Guilty?'

My mind blanked out on the scene then. I could not pronounce Not Guilty for fear of tempting fate.

I was wretched. The days passed in a blur. I walked the streets, not knowing where I was going or how I returned home. I bought food and forced myself to swallow it. My skin was as sore as if the air pressing against it were full of barbs.

I spoke to none of the other residents in my building. I saw Francesca briefly as she paid off a taxi and struggled with her luggage up the outside steps. Of Jason and Archie there was no sign.

On Wednesday lunchtime came a brief newsflash. The Jury had reached a verdict. It was to be delivered when the Court reconvened. Shots of Press and television crews massing outside the Old Bailey. I longed to be with Michael, supporting and comforting him. My place was by his side – I on one side, his wife on the other. I left the television on and sat in front of it, shredding tissues and allowing them to drop unheeded on to the carpet.

At two forty seven came news from the Court. The programme was interrupted as cameras cut to the outside of the Old Bailey. A lawyer was standing on the steps. No sign of Michael!

'My client is very disappointed at the verdict. We shall, of course, appeal.'

I gasped, stuffed my fist into my mouth to stop my scream. Guilty? No! No! No!

Cameras popped. Lights flashed. The lawyer turned away to return to the Courthouse. My God! They had found him guilty. They couldn't have! How could they have found him guilty?

My mind jumped to the impassive figures I had seen sitting in the jury box. The two black men, one black woman, the youngsters, the elderly. They hated politicians. Michael was guilty in their minds before the trial even began.

'Do you find the Defendant Guilty or Not Guilty?'

'Guilty!'

No! No! No! How could they? Hadn't they listened to any of the evidence? They were all cretins.

The cameras shifted to another angle. A police van exited at speed, scattering the mobbing Media. I imagined Michael, his head high, being led from the Court. He was ashen, stricken. He would be strip-searched, given prison garb. His innocence and arrogance would carry him so far, but what then?

A reporter was speaking direct to camera. 'The mandatory twelve years' imprisonment...' he was saying. 'He will serve at least eight years.'

Michael! My darling Michael!

'His lawyers are to instigate an immediate appeal. This is a surprise result. It was generally considered that a Not Guilty verdict was the most likely outcome.'

Reporters were running down the street, no doubt to begin filing their stories. The shot panned back to the studio at Westminster. Two Members of Parliament and an eminent lawyer sat with the interviewer.

'Well!' exclaimed the interviewer. 'Michael Rutter is on his way to prison. Are you surprised at this verdict, John Dunn?' he addressed the lawyer.

'Not really! The evidence appeared more-or-less straightforward.'

What the hell kind of an answer was that? I didn't want to hear any more. I went to the kitchen and put my hands on the sink. Before me was the window from where I had so often watched for Michael's appearance. If it hadn't been for Emily and Specs and Mrs Margoloys and myself, none of this would have happened. I felt empty, as though my innards had been sucked out, as though I were a shell beached by the tide. I knew this state would change as the freeze, whatever it was, set in and freed my body. I was going to know what divers suffering from the bends endured.

How would he, how could he, deal with it? The smell of urine, the squalor and ugliness, the daily round of humiliations! Prison life would kill him. He hated nastiness of any nature, he needed luxury for his survival. And he had always had someone to protect him. Initially, I supposed, his parents. For the first time I wondered if his parents were alive. If they rang him and offered encouragement and if they had attended the Court hearings? Then his friends and family. His wife would have been constantly by his side, charming the constituents. Would she be there now for him? Whatever she was like, she didn't deserve this! Would she divorce him? What about his agent and his secretary, who would lose her job? Somebody had always smoothed his path and done his dirty work for him. Now he was no longer a Member of Parliament – no one with a criminal record is allowed to sit in the House of Commons.

I crumpled to a heap on the kitchen floor. All those people, rooting for him! And what had I done, except serve his lust!

I had to get away. I had to get out of this accursed building. Before I could change my mind, I went to the telephone and dialled a number. After some time, the 'phone was picked up and a low, slightly languid voice came across the miles.

'Mum! How are you?' My tongue was thick, my mouth dry as the Sahara. Was I intelligible?

'Frances! Hello, darling! How are you?'

My mother didn't watch the news. Did she know anything at all about what had been happening to me?

'Well, look, Mum! Is it all right if I come and stay with you for a bit?'

'Of course, darling! Love to see you. I thought you were so busy with your important London job. Have you a holiday?'

'Yes, Mum! I'll come tomorrow and we can have a good talk then.'

I replaced the receiver. In my mind's eye I saw the menacing breakers of the North Norfolk coast and the wide expanse of wet sand extending as far as the horizon. I have never returned to live there after university. I would have been bored out of my mind. But now I craved nothing more than to walk in the face of a biting North Easter for endless miles along that indifferent shore. 'Freeze, freeze, thou bitter wind!' To walk, with only the screaming gulls for company and my mother's yellow Labrador galloping by my side, until I was exhausted. My mother would pamper and cosset me without asking awkward questions. Either she knew about Michael's trial or she didn't – it would be no great matter, as far as she was concerned. It was an imperfect solution to my dilemma, but it appeared to be the only one open to me.

I packed two bags and ordered a taxi for 10.30 the following morning. I would be in Norfolk and at my mother's cottage by mid afternoon. In less than twenty four hours I could be losing myself between the sea and the sky.

CHAPTER ELEVEN

My mother coped with life largely by ignoring it. She was a very restful person to have around. She appeared to have no inkling of the wider world. She had many acquaintances but no close friends.

Her sturdy cottage was one of a dozen in a small settlement within half a mile of the sea. After my father died and my sister and I grew up and left home, she sold the family house and moved to a remote area of the Norfolk coast. She began to paint, showing a modest talent, and would take her colours and easel on to the dunes and sit, well-wrapped up in an old tweed cape, sketching and painting sea and clouds for hours on end. Homer would be ecstatic as he chased seagulls into the waves, before panting and flopping at her side.

She was also a keen gardener, even in the difficult conditions encountered on this wilful coast. She appeared to my sister, Clare, and me to be totally self-contained – satisfied with her life, not desperate for grandchildren or our company. She had reared her children to the best of her ability. Now they were adults, liberty was her gift to them. She was an undemanding parent, uncurious, uncensorious. In my present state, it was what I needed.

I had hired a car at Norwich and driven the remainder of the journey to Selmet. My mother came to the door as I parked on the strip of gravel outside. She was wearing a bleached canvas, painting smock and had a smudge of charcoal on her nose.

'Hello, darling,' she greeted me as we gave each other an affectionate hug. 'How nice to see you again!'

At one time, aeons ago, I had been ashamed of her unworld-liness, reluctant to ask my school friends to stay with us in case they made fun of her vagueness. Then, I had expected more involvement. Perhaps hers was the deepest kind of love.

My eyes filled with involuntary tears as we held each other close and Homer pressed against me, thumping his tail.

'Come in and we'll have a cup of tea. I've made some scones.'

I shivered as I bent my head beneath the low portal. My mother rubbed her hand down my arm. 'I hope you've brought some warm clothes. Can get a bit nippy here sometimes.'

I took my suitcases to the room I always used on my infre-quent visits. The views from its windows were superb. On the left, tussocky dunes stretched for miles along the side of the gently undulating, pewter-coloured sea, touched at this time of day by the red gold of the sinking sun. To the back, the garden showed evergreen shrubs bearing red and white berries, while a late-flowering honeysuckle in a sheltered spot still flaunted yellow blooms.

The continuous ache inside me had travelled from my throat to my midriff, but maybe long walks in this stark and demanding region would cauterise the pain.

My mother produced gooseberry jam and deep yellow butter for the scones. I wondered if there was a farm shop nearby as I remembered the endless shelves of low cholesterol margarines I had packed in the supermarket. Any other mother would have said, 'What's wrong, Frances? Why have you turned up out of the blue after scarcely a word for months?' Not mine! She was glad to see me, of course, but my arrival would change her routine hardly at all. I flexed my toes and sighed with gratitude. This Enid Blyton living was about as far as one could journey from the vicissitudes of twentieth century London.

'I was tired of London,' I said, as I bit into a scone. God! It was good to be looked after! I tried to imagine Michael here.

It was impossible. I refused to contemplate his life in prison. I relaxed into the chair with the saggy bottom and looked at the vases of fresh, late autumn flowers around the room: pink and purple dahlias and tiny, tight roses, no doubt from the garden. The furniture had been polished to a pleasant gleam. The room was tidy, the linen laundered. My mother must have worked hard after yesterday's 'phone call. I hadn't given her much notice. I seemed to remember my home as untidy. Homely was the kindest adjective you could use. But that style suited the house. Modern minimalism would be ridiculous in this setting.

'I've given up my job,' I said.

'Well, you can stay here as long as you like,' said my mother. No questions, no exclamations of surprise. 'But I am very quiet, you know. The isolation may get on your nerves after a time.' She smiled at me.

'It's lovely,' I said over the lump in my throat. I closed my eyes.

'Well, we'll see,' said my mother. She went into the kitchen to refill the teapot with hot water.

It's a good thing, I thought, that she hasn't a live-in lover, or my sudden appearance could be a great inconvenience for her. I felt inclined to giggle. The notion was preposterous.

'Why did you decide to leave your position?' she asked when she returned. 'I always thought you were settled there.'

'Well, I hoped I was, as well. But things change,' I replied, deliberately ambiguous. 'Yes, darling! I am sure they do. You are very welcome to stay here as long as you like,' she repeated. 'Have a good rest before you go back.'

After a time I roused myself. My mother refused my offer of help with the clearing up and preparation for the evening meal.

'No, Frances! Why don't you go and unpack your bags? I have a surprise for you this evening.'

'Good! I like surprises. I think I'll go for a short walk on the beach if you don't mind. Stretch my legs. I have been sitting down all day.'

'You won't mind if I don't come? I am just at an interesting point in my latest attempt.'

I remembered belatedly that I had not enquired about my mother's progress with her painting. 'No, of course not,' I answered her. It was a relief. Thank the Lord that my mother and I understood each other. I desperately wanted to be alone.

I donned anorak and scarf and stepped outside into the keenness of the wind. Michael would be almost at the end of his first day of imprisonment. I would commune with him in solitude.

I passed the two end houses and turned into the sandy track that led to the beach. A little girl was bouncing a ball just beyond the last house. I smiled at her but she only stared back with the incurious gaze of the solitary child. Homer dashed ahead, joyous to be out, then ran around me in rapturous delight. Mewling gulls circled overhead, diving towards the shore. I breathed deeply, sea smells and the sour tang of rotting vegetation.

Almost at once I became aware of the immensity of the landscape. It was all sky and bleached marsh grass. A bird scuttled away from under my feet and rose into the air, squawking with indignation. I pushed my hands deep into my pockets and plodded on. Homer trotted at my side. A sting-ing wind came off the sea, lifting Homer's fur and whipping my scarf round my head and chasing it into my eyes. I ran along the sands, trying by my acceleration to diminish my pain. It didn't work, and after a while I collapsed on to the wet sand near the breakers' edge, pulling myself into a tight ball, unsure whether the moisture on my cheeks was tears or sea spray.

Homer had loved the running game. He had skidded and barked round me. Now he pushed his soft muzzle into my arm, trying to rouse me to more action. I clasped him to me, burying my face in his soft fur, turning him into Michael. How long would I have to stay here before I was able to face any sort of life again? I was so tired, I could sleep for ever.

I wondered whether my mother had picked up my name from the infrequent newspapers she read. If she knew of my involvement in the whole sorry affair, she wouldn't mention it. She would wait for me to speak first. She was sensitive to the point of indifference.

In this immensity of sky and sea, did it matter? Did any of it matter? I would never heal. I knew that. I would carry the stigmata to my grave. This had been the defining experience of my life, no matter whom or what I encountered in the future. The future? What future did I have?

After a time, I got up and retraced my steps. My trousers were uncomfortably damp from sitting on the wet sand. I would not think about my lost employment or Mrs Margoloys and the murder premises. I would think about Michael since I could not help it. I would live my life in seconds and minutes until I could rejoin the human race.

Now, if this were a novel, there would be a personable young man staying in one of the adjoining houses. He would be visiting his elderly relatives, just as I was doing. In a different age he would be a fisherman, braving the ferocious elements with gusto and abandon. But in real life such things do not happen. There would be no young people, personable or otherwise, residing in this out of the way hamlet. The population would be either old or young – children whose harassed mothers hated the remote and stark landscape. Only truly integrated souls, like my mother, would find peace or any kind of tranquillity here.

For me, it was a step outside my life. It was so unlike the way I would propose to live. It was only the seismic shock of Michael's trial and imprisonment that had moved my normal boundaries to the sad indifference of this endless sea and sky.

Every day I walked till I was exhausted, then sat on the beach until I was stupid. Incessant rain did not deter me. My mother asked no questions. When I returned she gave me hot drinks and put my wet clothes in the washing machine. Somewhere at the back of my mind was a grain of gratitude that I had this bolthole. But I knew another life awaited me out there. Before long I would have to retrieve it.

There were books in the cottage. I devoured them without registering the contents. One day a bird knocked itself unconscious by flying into an upstairs window. It lay stunned on the patio for some minutes before it perked up and hopped a few unsteady steps. Then it remained still, quivering with fear, before eventually finding the will to fly away.

If I had been alone, I would no doubt have stayed in bed all day. I was exhausted and at the same time pumped full of adrenalin, restless, manic and carrying the burdens of the world.

What did I expect? I didn't know. I was merely dragging myself through my existence. Occasionally I would take a trip to the nearest town for groceries. Wisely, my mother did not seek to accompany me. Instead she painted glowing canvases in iridescent colours of rose madder, chrome yellow and ultramarine. She had become surprisingly good. Why do we take so little account of our parents' talents?

The days passed. I had been in Norfolk for two weeks. Nobody called. We were quiet and companionable together. No questions. No recriminations. I deliberately did not buy newspapers on my trips to town. We seldom switched on the television. In the evenings my mother stitched tapestry – another hobby I had not suspected. Pictures grew under her nimble fingers as I sat with my head buried in a book, aware of nothing but Michael's face.

How was he coping with imprisonment? Badly, I had no doubt. He could have committed suicide in prison for all I knew. Not him! Not Michael! He would be too busy planning his appeal, his revenge on society for its treatment of him.

What did I expect as I sat on the windy beach, digging my fingers into the sand and trickling it between them? What did I hope for while mindlessly watching minute marine creatures glistening in the shallow pools, as they scurried across their grainy hollows with no instinct except for their next meal?

Perhaps I expected Jason or Archie to walk along the beach towards me. Darling, come to my next photo-shoot! Come to the flicks with me! Or Specs bundled into his anorak as Emily trotted by his side waving concert tickets over her head.

However, what did happen one day as I sat with Homer pressed to my side was quite different. Homer gave a low wuff, then exploded into the distance, barking wildly. Two figures were approaching across the hard sand on which I sat. I scrambled to my feet. Two late season trippers, no doubt! 'Homer! Homer! Come here, you silly dog!' I screamed into the wind. 'What's the matter with you? Come back!'

Then I saw it was my mother, dressed in a long, dark raincoat and holding the arm of an unknown man. Homer bounced round them in excitement, then dashed back to me before taking off again. I walked toward them.

'So here you are, darling! What a long way you have come!' She turned to her companion. 'This is my younger daughter, Frances. I told you she is staying with me for a while.'

I stared stupidly at the unknown man. My hand was clasped firmly. Two keen and friendly eyes appraised me.

'I am delighted to meet you at last,' he said. 'You are nearly as beautiful as your mother.'

Who the hell was he?

'This is Harry! Harry Matthews,' my mother introduced us. 'He lives at Number 3 in our row.'

So was he merely a neighbour, a good friend, or something more? I felt a surge of irritation. Why hadn't my mother mentioned him? Why was she so secretive? Was she carrying on her own affair up here in this bleak landscape? Tit for tat! No intrusive questions about your emotional entanglements, darling, but I expect the same sensitivity regarding mine. For the first time, I resented the miles my sister had put between us. This was something we should discuss together.

'Harry is coming for lunch,' said my mother, looking up at him in what I construed as an adoring way. For Christ's sake! She was nearly sixty!

'So we came to tell you we plan to eat at about half past one. Drinks first! And Harry's brought us a lovely bottle of wine.'

'I've just come back from a business trip to France,' said Harry. 'And I don't like drinking alone. So I was really glad to find out that Susan doesn't have any teetotal hang-ups.' He smiled down at her. So when had he found that out? How long had this been going on?

'That will be nice,' I said lamely. I felt gutted. Why had I imagined that my mother spent all her time in solitary confinement? From the way they looked at each other, it seemed they found each other's company most congenial. In this remote spot they had discovered each other, whilst amongst the teeming hordes of the metropolis I had only found Michael.

Again, that conspiratorial look between them.

'If you can manage to get back by one, darling, we can have a Sherry before I serve lunch.'

They turned and went away. Homer ran a short distance with them before they sent him back to me. As they walked, they laughed together at something that was said. I walked in the opposite direction, savagely kicking the sand. Why was I so upset? Neither of them would care two figs about my reaction. I was sure of that.

The next day I drove the hired car to Norwich station.

'There are one or two things I want to do in London,' I informed my mother. 'Do you want to come with me and have a look at the shops?'

'No, darling! My London days are long behind me. You go and do whatever you have to do.'

Perhaps she thought I was going to the capital in connection with other employment.

'Have a good time!'

'Well, I expect to catch the early evening train. I shan't be too late back.'

'Whatever is convenient for you, darling. Take a key.'

There was a spare key in the drawer of the hall table. I had always considered my mother foolish to leave it there. I picked it up and put it in my handbag. I thought of Mrs Margoloys secure behind a heavy door with no spare keys available and an intercom system for her protection. I thought of a houseful of people who were all absent when she needed them.

'I expect to be back well before you are in bed,' I said, 'but just in case there is a hold up on the trains, I will take it.'

I kissed my mother and drove out of Selmet down the road with its single row of houses facing the sea. Harry lived three doors away from my mother, but this morning there was no sign of him as I accelerated away. What a time-warp this place was! No wonder all the young people left!

I had no clear purpose in mind for my journey. I only knew that if I were not closer to Michael I should go mad. I knew I was living a dream – or a nightmare, on the North Norfolk coast. I would have to call at Job Centres and scan the Appointments Vacant columns before too long. Now I had no monthly salary, I had to be economical. But I felt too weak to do anything positive today.

I would also have to give notice at the flat. I realised I could not return to live there. But I had nowhere else to go in London and for today, at least, I had a base if I became tired of walking the streets. In my troubled dreams, it was always Specs who appeared around corners and from behind shop doorways as I searched fruitlessly for I didn't know what. Shocked and anxious, I was always losing important items, such as my money or passport. And always it was Specs who appeared to watch my discomfort.

As I sat in the train to Liverpool Street, staring aimlessly out of the window at the soaked green fields, I told myself that I would do something useful during my time in the capital. When I left the train with the few other travellers, my feet took me to the Underground and the Central Line. At Holborn I changed to the Northern Line where I boarded the South bound train.

South of the river, the landscape became waste ground, soiled and ravaged. As the train ran above ground, I noted wrecked vehicles and evil-looking children playing with tyres, everywhere a general air of dereliction and neglect. Had Michael seen all this from his prison van?

Balham and then Tooting Beck rumbled by. The train stopped. I alighted and walked for a long time. My misery appeared to isolate me from the rest of humanity. Nobody approached me. It seemed I gave off an aura of dejection and despair that was too great for any kind of intercourse. Eventually I came within sight of a boundary fence. This was the nearest I could get to Michael's incarceration. This was as far as I could go.

I stood there, perhaps for five minutes, perhaps for half an hour, before I retraced my steps to the station. I had seen nothing and no one behind the barrier. Either it was lunchtime or lock-up time. The scanty grass stretching towards the square brick buildings was neatly cut. But the prison could have been full of dead souls, invisible spectres, for all I saw of the inmates. I thought of nothing I can now recall on that forced march back.

I found myself at the Underground and boarded the next train. I changed at Charing Cross and took the Bakerloo line to Baker Street. I was too exhausted to further walk the streets. At least I could make an inventory of the things in my flat and decide what to do with them when I moved.

For move I must. But where to and what for, at that time I had no clear picture. I was living like an automaton, doing the minimum required for my survival. Passengers banged into me and hustled me as I embarked at the familiar station. Life would surely go on!

Back in my flat, I found a message on my answer phone from Margot.

'Hi! I've tried a number of times, but you must be away. The thing is, your old job is yours, if you want it. Do hope so! Seems they can't manage without you! Seriously, they will hold it another fortnight. 'Bye.'

The message clicked off. The call had been made at the beginning of the week. So I had ten days in which to make up my mind.

* * *

Of course, I moved back to London. For one thing, it was as near as I could get to Michael. I had to give spiritual support. But I drew the line at finding rooms in South East London. I continued for the time being to use Nottingham Place as my base and looked around North and West London. Eventually I found a pleasant bed-sitter with French windows opening to a patio and flowery garden about half a mile from Ealing Broadway.

I rang Margot from Norwich. She was not in, but I left a message thanking her for the call and saying I would make up my mind within a week.

Obviously, I took the job. Much as it stuck in my craw to return after the way I had been treated, it had many advantages. I knew the work and was not unduly hassled. Margot and I were always busy, but it was largely under our own control. And Margot was the best of office mates: supportive and kind without intrusive curiosity into my private life. Not that I had any, at that time!

Also, it was a convenient location, with Marble Arch and Bond Street Underground five minutes' walk away. If I felt the urge, I could take another trip to the environs of the prison. I didn't do so. My pain gradually eased. It did appear that the cauterizing wind of the East Coast had stripped away much of my excessive anguish. The underlying ache took a great deal longer to subside.

Michael made an appeal against the Guilty verdict a few months after his trial. It was unsuccessful. He faded from the headlines. Other news, more scandalous and shocking, replaced him.

I gave in my notice at Nottingham Place and was out less than a month after returning to London. I saw nobody in the house before I moved, with one exception.

One morning, a white van appeared on the road outside. As I peered down the stairwell, the cold draught informed me that the front door was propped open. Then Sammy came into view carrying square cardboard boxes from his room at the back. I ran down to the first flight of stairs.

'Are you leaving us, Sammy?'

He put the boxes down with relief. I noticed the thick doormat was holding the door open.

'Never have used the place much,' he said. 'I'm moving in with Patsy.'

'I'm sorry!' I said. 'About you going, I mean.' And I was. Sammy was the only uncomplicated individual amongst us. I walked down the rest of the stairs. He held out his arms and gave me a great bear hug.

'Aw!' he said. 'After what happened to poor old Mrs M., I didn't fancy it here any more, to tell you the truth.'

'I'm going as well!' I said. 'I'm looking around for somewhere else, and I shan't be here long after you.'

'Don't blame you,' he said. He looked around the hall as though for the first time, at its black and white chequered tiles and the umbrella stand with its array of sticks.

'The old place isn't the same now. Pity! It was convenient for most things.'

'Yes!' I said.

'Well, life goes on!' He hugged me again. 'Take care of yourself, Fran! Rotten luck, what happened.'

I didn't know whether he was referring to the murder of Mrs Margoloys or my own predicament.

'Yes!' I repeated. 'Well, all the best, Sammy! My regards to Patsy!'

Three weeks later, I was out of the place myself. The history of the house was just that: history!

I moved into a cheap hotel until my new home was available. And that, for some time, was the end of my acquaintance with the residents of 19A Nottingham Place.

EPILOGUE

As I have said, that, for a couple of years, was that. After some months in my flat in Ealing, I upped sticks and went to join my sister in Canada. I asked my mother if she wanted to come with me, but she said she was contented with her Norfolk idyll. She didn't explain, but I knew she didn't wish to leave Harry.

They still lived in their separate cottages, which was probably why they got on so well.

'Are there going to be wedding bells?' I asked slyly before I left, breaking our habit of no questions and no lies.

'Don't be silly, darling,' she said. But she looked very happy and I had no qualms about leaving her.

'Well, I'll come back and see you, of course.'

'Go and have a good time, darling. You are still young. Enjoy yourself.'

So, my plans were made. After being drawn constantly to the magnetic pole of Michael's presence, I was now putting a great deal of space between us. It was apocalypse now, but London had grown stale as a worn sock to me. Perhaps the vibrancy of a new country would brush the cobwebs from the closet of my mind.

And it worked, at least for a time. It was good to be with Clare again and she eased me into the pleasures and vagaries of Canadian life which were not, after all, so different from our own. I found a congenial situation, moved into a larger flat with my sister and we kept up a flourishing social life.

But that is another story. This one merely concerns my relationship with an arrogant, beguiling man. There is just one more encounter with the past before I am finished.

One Saturday morning I was alone in downtown Toronto. Clare was off with her latest conquest and I was relishing my solo time by wandering around the shops and relaxing into the easy ambiance of Canadian life.

I went into a sandwich bar for a cake and a coffee, then carried my choices outside and sat down at a table without paying much attention to the other customers.

'Fran! Fran!'

I swivelled in my seat. A handsome, fair man was waving at me from the other side of the sidewalk. I stared. He had definitely used my name.

'Jason! Jason!' I exclaimed in delight.

He had filled out from the scrawny youth I had known at Nottingham Place. His angular cheek bones had softened and his hair was short and springy rather than sleeked back. He came over to me and gave me a great bear hug.

'By all that's wonderful,' he said. 'What are you doing here, Fran? Are you on holiday?'

He stood beaming above me. For my part, I was inordinately pleased to see him.

'Wait! I'll get some coffee. Then I want to know all about you.'

He sat down opposite me.

'I live here,' I told him. The smile seemed to be nailed to my face. 'I came to Toronto to join my sister. She has been here for years.'

We started talking in great rushes of words, then just sat and smiled at each other.

'I'm in a production at the Royal,' he told me. I realised he was holding my hand. 'This must be the first time I have seen you since all that nasty business at Nottingham Place.'

I bit my lip. Was it malign fate that had brought Jason to me as a harbinger of memory of that dreadful period?

'I owe you an apology,' said Jason, looking directly into my eyes.

Now what? My stomach lurched. Could I stand any more revelations just as I had put it all behind me? Did he know that Michael had not committed the crime and had withheld information? How much had Jason known about my involvement with Michael? Had he followed the Court case closely? He may well have done, of course!

'What for?' I asked quietly. My heart began pounding in a way it had not done for years.

Jason stroked my hand as he held it between his two large ones.

'I left you by yourself without support at those shitty times,' he said.

'But I didn't expect your support, Jason. What could you have done?'

I wondered if he was being melodramatic. After all, acting was his profession.

'I chickened out,' he said. 'I didn't go near the place for weeks.'

'You and everybody else,' I said. 'It was deserted.' I was perplexed. Why berate him for a normal reaction? 'I don't blame you. It wasn't very cheerful with the thought of Mrs Margoloys ...' I trailed off. Perhaps I wasn't the only sufferer at that time. 'I would have gone myself if I had had anywhere to go.'

That wasn't strictly true. Margot had offered hospitality. I could have gone to stay with my mother sooner than I had. But I had wanted to be near Michael in his hours of trial. And, to be honest, I had no desire to leave the scene of my trysts with him.

'Sweetheart!' said Jason. 'I withheld evidence.'

The gleaming surfaces of the counter reflected the bright sunlight.

'What?' I felt faint. Jason could have cleared Michael and he had not done so? In order to cover his own back, he had not divulged what he knew? I pulled my hand from his grasp.

'What are you telling me, Jason?' My voice was cool, all the earlier friendliness dispersed. Why, why, why had dastardly fate brought us together again just as I was getting my life in order and learning to live again? What had I done to deserve such treatment?

'It didn't make any difference to the verdict.' Jason was staring over my head into the dark recesses at the back of the building. 'They convicted the right person. If it had gone another way, I might have come forward.'

I pressed the back of my hand to my forehead. The café with its bright neon lighting, the display cases of sandwiches, the hiss of the cappuccino machine coalesced into a kaleidoscope of distorted images.

'Are you saying that Michael Rutter was guilty?'

The handsome face before me turned devilish, sprouted horns. Jason had committed the crime and now he was trying to convince me otherwise.

'Oh, yes! He was guilty as hell!' said Jason cheerfully. 'For once, they got the right man.'

'How can you know?' I tasted blood in my mouth as my teeth dug into my lower lip. 'The evidence seemed very flimsy.' The agonizing lump in my throat with which I had lived for so long grew again in an instant. 'He appealed against the verdict,' I finished lamely.

'Well, of course he did. They all do.'

Jason produced a small flask and poured some of its contents into my coffee.

'You have gone very pale,' he said. 'I shouldn't have brought it up. I know it is upsetting for you.'

'For Christ's sake, Jason, tell me what you mean,' I implored. My voice was high and hysterical. One or two customers glanced in my direction. Again Jason put his hand over mine.

'Gently!' he murmured. 'Gently!' Then, 'I saw him.'

I took a deep breath. He must be lying.

'You saw him commit the crime?' Now my voice was low with disbelief.

'Not exactly! But I saw him in the hall. He went up the stairs. I assumed he was one of Francesca's paramours. Then, a while later, I saw him leave.'

Of course! Jason and Archie's flat had a window with a view of the street, just the same as that of the woman opposite. And they could see the hall and staircase from outside their own door.

'He was carrying a long, thin object in a black dustbin bag, just as that old biddy said.'

Icy fingers stroked my spine. 'Why didn't you tell the police what you saw?'

'I was into a dodgy drugs scam at the time. I didn't want undue delving into my activities.'

'So are you saying that Mrs Margoloys was attacked while you were in the house?'

'I heard a bump and a thud. I waited a bit. I thought maybe Francesca and her buddy were having a frolic. I looked out the window and saw this guy. Then I went upstairs.'

This was a nightmare come back to haunt me. Jason's eyes were unfocussed.

'There was a smear of blood on the floor. Mrs Margoloys' door was ajar. I tapped and called. Then I pushed the door open. She was lying there.'

'You didn't telephone for a doctor? Or the police?'

'I did. From down the road. Eventually.' Jason continued speaking. 'But she was dead. Quite dead! I knew that. I was quite sure. And I was scared. Shit scared! With my history, I could see them pinning the crime on me. Archie and I gave each other alibis. I didn't tell him what I had done. Keep the water clear! After all,' he went on, 'I hadn't done it. I knew Archie hadn't done it. So where was the harm?'

He looked at me intently. 'You are white as a ghost. I shouldn't have told you. I'm a bastard! Why bring it all up again? I shouldn't have mentioned it.'

I knew, without knowing how I knew, that Jason was telling the truth. And somewhere inside me, a persistent stinging insect lay down and died.

ABOUT THE AUTHOR

"Golden Lads and Girls" author MAVIS FROST MBE

Mavis was brought up in Nottinghamshire. After various secretarial jobs she worked as a secretary for Labour MPs. Her talents soon noticed when Labour got into government and she worked in Harold Wilson's office in No 10 Downing Street. In 1976 Mavis was awarded an MBE in Harold Wilson's retirement honours list.

In October 1982 Mavis married Squadron Leader Donald Frost. It was both their second marriage and since 1988 lived in Ingatestone Essex. They travelled widely and enjoyed their social life both within the RAF as an officer and wife and with friends and interest groups.

After retirement Mavis studied for and achieved a First Class Honours degree with the Open University degree. Mavis enjoyed her family, writing, piano, garden and books and has left a big library.

Mavis was born in June 1936 and passed away after a short illness in September 2017.